GIDEON DRAKE

Inherited Burden

Brittain
PUBLISHING HOUSE

For my family,
who have seen every version of me
and stayed.
For the ones who carry quietly.

The boundary does not hold because it is
strong. It holds because someone remains

Preface

There are stories about houses that are possessed.

This is not one of them.

There are stories about darkness that invades, corrupts, and devours.

This is not one of those either.

This is a story about proportion.

About the quiet spaces between breaths.

About the way silence can feel like threat until it becomes structure.

About what it means to stand in relation to something older than you and choose not to dominate it, not to flee from it, but to remain.

We inherit more than names and walls.

We inherit rhythm.

We inherit drift.

We inherit the subtle tightening of patterns that no one notices until they fracture.

Some burdens are loud.

Others are precise.

The work in this story is not to banish what lives beneath the floorboards. It is to understand it well enough to keep it from tipping.

Balance is not the absence of darkness.

It is the refusal to let it distort.

If you are reading this, you may already know the feeling of standing at the top of your own stairwell. Listening. Measuring. Deciding whether to descend.

This book is not about triumph.

It is about steadiness.

And the quiet, generational courage of those who hold the line without spectacle.

Welcome.

Acknowledgments

This book did not come into the world alone. Stories never do. They are shaped, sharpened, and sometimes rescued by the people who stand just outside the page, holding the light steady while the writer finds the way through the dark.

First, to my wife—my editor, my first reader, and the one who tells me the truth even when it would be easier not to. Thank you for reading every draft, for catching the things I missed, for reminding me when something didn't ring true, and for believing in these stories even when they were only fragments and late-night ideas. This book is better because of you. Every book is.

To my daughter, D.D. Phoenix, thank you for bringing this story into the world visually. The cover illustration is the first doorway a reader walks through, and you created something that feels exactly like the story inside—quiet, unsettling, and full of questions. Seeing your artwork become the face of this book is something I will always be proud of.

And finally, to my readers—thank you for taking a chance on my stories, for stepping into strange houses and walking dark roads with the characters I create. Writing is a solitary act, but storytelling is not. A story only becomes real when someone else reads it, imagines it, and carries it with them after the last page.

Thank you for being part of this journey, and for allowing these stories a place on your shelf and in your time.

— Gideon Drake

Prologue

1891

The night was wrong for summer.

No crickets. No frogs. The stillness that didn't feel peaceful so much as watchful, like the world had leaned back and folded its arms. Even the wind had decided it had nothing to say.

A single lantern burned on the ground near the south fence, its flame low and amber, casting a shallow circle over weeds that clawed up through warped slats. Beyond that light, the ridge rose dark and close; the trees pressed shoulder to shoulder. They had the posture of witnesses. The patient kind.

A woman knelt in the dirt.

She moved slowly, not out of care for her knees, but out of instinct. The kind you develop when you believe something is listening, even if you'd never say it out loud. Her gloves were thick canvas, stiff with age and use, the palms darkened by a rust-colored stain that had never fully washed out. She had dug a shallow hole. Nothing ambitious. Just enough to hide a small mercy. Or a minor sin.

The pouch beside her knee rustled softly as she opened it.

First came the tooth.

A child's tooth, milky and smooth, its root curved like a question that hadn't yet learned how to be polite. She rolled it between her fingers, feeling its weight, or lack of it, before laying it gently into the hole. Then the braid of hair, bound with red thread. Dull. Brittle. In the lantern's weak light, it refused to declare its color. Brown, maybe.

Black, maybe. It didn't matter anymore.

Last came the bones.

Three of them. Small, bird-like. Lashed together with twine. They rattled softly when she lifted them, a dry, accidental sound that reminded her of dice shaken in a gambler's palm. She hesitated here. Longer than she had with the others. Her lips moved, shaping something she didn't quite allow herself to hear. A word, perhaps. Or a name she no longer used.

When the bones touched the soil, the air changed.

It wasn't dramatic. No wind, no flash. Just pressure, subtle but unmistakable, as if the earth had drawn in a careful breath. The lantern guttered once, dimmed, then found its nerve again. She looked toward the fence-line, where weeds gave way to the downward slope and the black spine of the woods beyond.

For a moment, she thought she saw something move.

Tall. Thin. Sliding between the trunks with the grace of something that had learned patience a long time ago.

She blinked.

Nothing there.

"Keep what's given," she whispered.

The words came out cracked, older than her voice. The wind shifted then, not toward the woods, but back toward her, carrying the phrase with it. The echo returned wrong. Not louder. Not softer. Just... altered. As if something had repeated it without fully understanding the meaning.

Her hands trembled as she brushed soil over the offering. The smell rising from the hole wasn't just dirt. There was sweetness to it. Faint, cloying. Like flowers left too long in water, their stems rotting while the petals pretended everything was fine.

She paused, head tilted, listening.

The silence on the ridge was absolute. Not empty. Expectant.

She pressed the soil down, firm and slow. When the last of the lantern light skimmed the buried twine, the tooth caught it, a brief wink of white, before disappearing for good. The woman rocked back on her heels, exhaled sharply, and wiped her forehead with the back of her glove.

Behind her, something drifted through the trees.

Not a whisper. Not quite a sound at all. More like a lullaby half-remembered and half-hummed, the kind sung by mothers who never stopped mourning, even after they learned how to smile again.

She froze.

Her pulse climbed into her throat, cold and fluttering. For one terrible second, she was certain that if she turned around, she would see who—or what—had been waiting for her to finish.

Then the night closed over the sound.

The woods fell silent.

She was alone again.

For now.

She did not stand up right away.

That was the first rule. Never rush the ending. The ground needed time. So did she.

She remained kneeling, hands resting uselessly in her lap, eyes fixed on the small mound of disturbed earth. It looked harmless enough now. Just another patch of poor soil along a fence that had been leaning south longer than she'd been alive. Anyone passing by tomorrow, if anyone ever did, would see nothing but weeds and rot and neglect.

That was the idea.

Her breathing slowed. The tightness in her chest eased, though it didn't disappear. It never did anymore. The ridge remained quiet, but the silence had changed. It no longer felt held. It felt released.

She reached for the lantern.

The moment her fingers closed around its handle, the flame flared higher than it should have, licking up the glass chimney in a sudden, eager rush. She hissed and nearly dropped it. The light settled again, but her heart didn't.

"All right," she muttered. "All right."

She told herself it was done. She had buried what needed burying. That the land had accepted the trade the way it always had before.

That was the lie she needed to carry back with her.

As she stood, her knee popped softly. The sound felt too loud in the open night. She glanced once more toward the trees. They stared back, dark and close and utterly unconcerned.

The lullaby did not return.

That, more than anything, troubled her.

She turned from the fence and started toward the house; the lantern swinging low at her side. With each step, the light pulled away from the south line, shrinking the circle until the disturbed soil slipped back into darkness.

Behind her, the ridge held its breath.

And somewhere beneath the fence, the earth remembered the gift it had received.

Chapter 1

I woke before the house did, as I usually did. There's a thin slice of time before dawn when the world hasn't chosen its shape yet. Night still clings to the corners, but morning hasn't gathered the nerve to push it out. I lay there watching the ceiling, tracing the long crack that ran from vent to light fixture. In the half-light, it looked like roots spreading outward.

I blinked.

Just a crack.

I listened.

The house normally announced itself: pipes ticking, beams shifting, floorboards easing into place. I knew the sounds. Which meant the weather. Which meant age. Which meant nothing.

This morning, there was nothing.

Not even the east wall pipe. It always popped once before sunrise.

I waited.

It didn't come.

The silence didn't feel empty. It felt arranged. As if something had pressed a finger to the house's lips during the night and told it to hold still.

I didn't move right away. My fingers tightened on the sheets. I had the strange sense that if I got up too quickly, something would react.

Eventually, I swung my legs out of bed. The floor was colder than it should have been. A draft skimmed across my ankles.

Coffee came first. It always did.

Two level scoops. Scraped flat with the back of a knife. The metal rasped louder than usual against the container, sharp enough to make me pause. A few grains spilled across the counter. They landed wrong, scattered instead of neat.

I wiped them away. Wiped the counter. Set the pot down. Wiped it again.

Ritual is a kind of armor. Small, repeatable magic. If you do things the same way long enough, the world learns the pattern. It behaves.

The kitchen window went up six inches. No more. No less.

The latch stuck.

My pulse ticked once, hard.

I reset it and pressed again. This time it snapped shut with a clean click. I trusted that sound more than I trusted most people.

Cool air slid inside, damp and loamy. Too thick for a dry morning. I leaned toward the screen and looked out.

The yard appeared almost polite in the early light. Dew softened the weeds. The shallow dip near the south fence held a darker patch of earth, shadowed longer than the rest.

For a minute, everything felt manageable.

I poured the coffee and picked up my notebook. Bent corners. Soft spine. Pages filled in straight lines. Paper made sense. It stayed where you put it.

Outside, the grass soaked through the thin soles of my shoes as I walked the property the way you read a page, slow, deliberate.

The dip near the south fence pulled my attention again. Bloodroot would take to that spot. Shade-loving. Stubborn. Red sap hidden underground.

Contained.

I crouched and pressed my fingers into the soil. It gave too easily.

Not mud. Not dry. Just soft.

Order calms things.

Order keeps them where they belong.

I drew rows in my notebook: straight lines, even spacing. Practical. Roots would hold the soil after storms. That was true.

But there was something beneath that explanation I didn't write.

Things behave better when they have borders.

A bird landed on the fence post behind me. I turned slowly. It stared back, black eyes reflecting me, small, warped. It didn't blink.

"Go on," I murmured.

My voice sounded too loud in the quiet. The bird tilted its head, considering.

When it finally launched into the air, the fence post wobbled slightly. The motion traveled down the boards toward the dip in the earth. I followed the movement with my eyes.

The soil there looked darker now.

I stepped back toward the house.

My heel sank half an inch into the dip.

I froze.

The ground there was warm.

Wrongness doesn't announce itself. It waits. Then something ancient inside you freezes and says, No. That doesn't belong.

My pulse jumped before I saw it.

The sapling stood a few feet in from the fence, leaning as if it had reconsidered its place in the world. The trunk curved unnaturally. Bark puckered and dark.

I set my coffee down and crouched, pushing weeds aside. My knees sank into the cold earth.

Wire.

Old, rusted the color of dried blood. It looped around the sapling like a lazy noose, half-buried, half-forgotten.

Someone had put it there.

The tree had grown anyway. Swelled around the metal. Bark stretched, split, tried to accommodate the pain the way living things do when they don't believe relief is coming.

"Well," I said quietly, "that won't do."

The wire resisted when I tried to move it. Rust flaked beneath my fingers. At one point it snagged tight, digging deeper into the bark.

Don't yank.

Yanking makes it worse.

I adjusted my grip. The metal bit into my palm. A shallow slice opened, bright red against the rust.

"Fine," I whispered.

When the wire finally gave, it came free with a low, ugly sound, metal tearing loose from living wood.

The sapling shuddered. Leaves trembling.

I pressed soil gently around its base. The exposed wood beneath the torn bark was green.

Alive. Still trying.

"You should've asked for help," I whispered. "You don't have to carry it forever."

I packed the earth firm, not tight. Just enough. The trunk straightened slightly under my hands.

I picked up the wire and carried it to the bucket by the fence. Dropped it inside.

Metal hit metal.

I frowned and looked in.

Another length of wire lay coiled at the bottom.

I didn't remember putting it there.

The yard was very still.

Slowly, I turned toward the house.

One of the upstairs curtains shifted. Just slightly.

The air hadn't moved.

My phone buzzed in my pocket, and I flinched hard enough to feel it in my teeth. For half a second, I thought the sound had come from the house.

I pulled the phone out.

Are you up early again?

Ellie

I exhaled slowly.

Ellie had always checked in without asking questions. Small tethers tossed across the distance.

Always. Trying to outpace the sun.

Three dots appeared. Vanished. Appeared again.

Insomnia's winning again? What're you up to?

For a moment, I considered telling the truth. Wire in bark. Rust like dried blood.

Instead, I took a picture. Cropped out the darker patch of soil. Framed the sapling so the scar disappeared in shadow.

On the screen, everything looked manageable.

Saving the local ecosystem, one tree at a time.

You're ridiculous. Coffee later? Ten-ish? I'm in town anyway.

Town meant people. Intersections. Someone who knew my face well enough to notice when it changed.

Maybe. Let me see how the morning goes.

Don't work too hard. You don't have to earn rest, you know.

I looked at that message longer than I should have.

Then the phone buzzed again.

A new message.

No name. No number.

Just one word.

Watching.

The yard did not feel cooperative anymore.

Back inside, the house smelled of old coffee and wood. Morning light cut through the windows in pale bands, straight and measured across the table.

I turned on the faucet. Water struck porcelain too loudly. It spiraled toward the drain in a tight silver coil.

The drain gurgled once.

I turned the tap off.

Silence expanded into the space it left behind. Then the pipes ticked in the walls. Slow. Deliberate.

I laid seed packets on the table. Bloodroot. Trillium. Shade mix. I aligned them by height and bloom time. One packet refused to sit flat. Its corner kept lifting.

I pressed it down. It lifted again.

I picked up the bloodroot packet and read the instructions slowly. *Slow to establish.*

I underlined the word slow harder than necessary. The pen tore slightly through the paper.

Outside the window, the sapling leaned a fraction to the left. Not fallen. Just wrong enough to notice.

Then something hummed.

Not loud. Barely sound at all. More vibration than tone. It rose through the floorboards and settled behind my teeth.

"The refrigerator," I said.

The hum deepened.

In the sink, the thin layer of water trembled. Ripples widened across the surface.

"Stop," I said.

The hum cut off instantly.

The silence that replaced it felt held. Contained.

I stacked the papers into a neat pile. Too neat. Adjusted the seed packets again.

The bloodroot packet had moved.

Half an inch from the others.

A visible gap where there had been none.

I was certain I had not left it that way.

Chapter 2

I woke with the strong sense that the day had already passed without me.

Sleep should have reset things. Whatever had unsettled me the night before should have dissolved in the dark and returned as something manageable. Instead, my limbs felt heavy and used, as if I had worked through the night without permission from my mind.

The air in the room was still and faintly stale. My mouth carried a metallic taste. I swallowed and turned toward the window, waiting for the pale light to steady the room into something recognizable.

It didn't.

The house was quiet, but not empty. The silence had presence. It seemed to settle when I noticed it, patient and deliberate. I lay still and tried to catch the last fragments of whatever had pulled me from sleep.

Roots.

That part remained.

Pale strands pushing through dark soil. Weight from above. Dirt packed down, shovel by shovel. My arms straining. My hands gripping something I could not see. I knew I could not let go. If I loosened my hold, something would surface. Or sink. Something irreversible.

The image collapsed when I reached for it, leaving only the sensation of having failed to keep something contained.

I pushed myself upright.

That was when I noticed my hand.

A red stain marked the center of my palm. Faint but unmistakable. Not smeared. Not wet. The color rested neatly in the creases of my skin, as if it had settled there deliberately.

Not blood, I told myself. Blood darkens. Cracks. This was too even. Too composed.

I washed it under cold water. Rubbed slowly at first, then harder. The drain swallowed diluted ribbons of red. On the third wash, the stain faded to a pale shadow that would escape notice unless someone were looking for it.

In the mirror, I looked like myself. Tired, but intact. No scratches. No dirt beneath my nails.

Dreams leave impressions sometimes, I told myself. You clench your hands. You press your palm into something and don't remember it.

The explanation sounded reasonable. It also sounded rehearsed.

Back in the bedroom, the sheets were smooth. No soil. No marks. I sat on the edge of the bed and pressed my feet flat against the floor.

Roots, my mind whispered again.

I stood and reached for the door.

That was when I saw it.

Beneath the nail of my ring finger, pressed into the crescent of skin, was a thin line of dark soil.

Not dust.

Soil.

I did not remember touching the earth.

I sat at the kitchen table with my journal open in front of me, exactly as I had every morning for months. Same chair. Same position. Facing the window.

I wrote the date first. Always the date. Then the time. Then the weather.

Order separated observation from drift.

Below that, I wrote one word.

Dream.

The pen hovered. I forced the fragments into lines.

Roots.

Weight.

Holding something down.

I added the iron taste in my mouth. The heaviness in my limbs. The faint red stain on my palm. I kept the tone flat. Clinical. Facts without interpretation.

Meaning could wait.

When I finished, I turned back through earlier entries. Not curiosity. Verification.

A week ago: *Roots again. Wrapped tight. Hard to breathe.*

Two weeks before: *Hands dirty. Soil under nails.*

Further back, three entries ended with the same sentence:

Do not let go.

The handwriting was mine. The pressure familiar. But the tone felt wrong.

This was not reflection.

It was instruction.

I flipped another page. The margins were crowded with spirals—tight, dense, nearly black at the center. The grooves pressed deep enough to feel through the paper.

Soil remembers.

Keep it sealed.

It is safer this way.

I closed the journal. Then opened it again.

If something was happening, I needed to see it before it reached me. Writing was containment. If I documented it, it couldn't surprise me.

I turned to a fresh page and began again. The sapling. The wire. The stain on my palm. I wrote smaller now. Tighter. As if compressing the words would keep them from spreading.

I didn't notice how much time had passed until the coffee went cold and the light shifted across the floor.

The house creaked behind me and I flinched.

Documentation was not fear.

It was preparation.

I closed the journal and rested my hand on the cover.

Proof I was paying attention.

Proof I was still ahead.

My gaze drifted to the bottom corner of the page.

In the margin, beneath the last line I had written, a sentence curved in smaller script.

Do not let go.

The ink was still wet.

Ellie called just after noon.

I was rinsing dirt from the trowel when the phone buzzed. I flinched and pinned it between my shoulder and ear.

"Hey," I said. "You caught me doing yard work."

"Of course I did," Ellie said, laughing. Her voice filled the kitchen in a way nothing else ever managed.

"Occupational hazard of owning land," I said. "Dirt finds you eventually."

"Careful," she replied. "That place is older than it looks."

"Everything's older than it looks," I said. "That's just time."

"My dad used to say land remembers," she said. "You dig long enough, it gives things back."

I snorted. "Your dad also believed aluminum foil cured headaches."

"That doesn't mean he was wrong about everything."

I turned off the tap and looked out the window. The yard lay pale and still. The sapling stood upright, cooperative and narrow.

"It's just a tree," I said. "I'm planting flowers, not unearthing secrets."

"Roots are the problem," Ellie said quietly. "You cut them back, they grow again. Split foundations. Push through concrete. You can't really get rid of them."

"I'm not worried," I said too quickly. "I've got it under control."

Silence stretched.

"Some roots don't let go," she said softly.

I laughed, louder than necessary. "Are you trying to scare me out of my yard?"

"Just saying, don't fight the place. Let it be what it is."

"I am," I said. "Everything's fine."

We talked about coffee plans. Schedules. Ordinary things. When we hung up, the quiet returned immediately.

Some roots don't let go.

I repeated the phrase under my breath.

Outside, the soil around the flower bed looked darker than before. I stepped into the yard and knelt beside the sapling. The scar in its bark looked deeper up close, a thin metallic memory beneath the surface.

I dug carefully around the base.

The trowel struck something.

Metal.

I brushed soil aside slowly.

The wire I had removed yesterday lay coiled there again, half buried, as if it had never left.

That night, I wrote the phrase down.

Some roots don't let go.

I stared at the words, then drew a hard line through them.

Metaphor, I wrote in the margin. *Common phrase.*

Below that: *Invasive plants. Kudzu. Bindweed.*

I made a list:

Root barriers.

Pruning.

Herbicide.

Time.

Control lived in inches. In margins. In patience.

Outside, darkness pressed against the windows. The south fence had vanished into black.

I closed the journal and turned off the light.

Halfway up the stairs, the board near the landing creaked beneath my foot. It hadn't done that in weeks.

I paused.

Nothing followed.

In bed, I told myself tomorrow would be better. Tomorrow I would dig test holes. Check drainage. Follow the plan.

Sleep came slowly.

Just before it took me, a thought surfaced, calm and complete:

Some things stay buried.

I didn't argue with it.

Sometime in the night, I woke.

The room was dark, but not silent. A faint rustle came from the nightstand.

I turned my head.

The journal lay open.

I did not remember opening it.

Moonlight caught the page. At the bottom, beneath my notes about root barriers and spacing, a final sentence curved across the margin:

Some things are meant to stay buried.

The ink was still drying.

Chapter 3

Morning crept in thin and colorless, as though it had arrived by accident and was waiting to be told to leave. The sky was clear in a way that felt rehearsed. A sharp, brittle blue that flattened shadows and stripped depth from everything it touched. Sound carried differently under a sky like that. Even the scrape of metal against soil seemed louder than it should have been.

I did not trust mornings like this.

Still, I preferred them. Calm light meant fewer surprises.

I hauled my tools down to the south fence and laid them out carefully. The trowel went first, blade facing away. Then the shovel, aligned parallel to the fence boards. Gloves folded with the fingers tucked neatly inside, each thumb pressed flat. The notebook rested against a fence post, squared with the grain as if I had measured the angle.

One glove refused to lie flat. The cuff curled slightly upward.

I pressed it flat.

It curled again.

I pressed harder until the fabric yielded.

Seeing everything in order quieted the hum beneath my thoughts. This was work. Defined. Predictable. Not me wandering the yard chasing half-formed fears that dissolved when examined too closely.

The fence line was a mess. Water collected here after every rain, sitting too long and souring the soil. Weeds had taken hold with thick, defiant stems. They grew as if they had rights.

Bloodroot required boundaries. Shade. Structure.

So did I.

I knelt and pressed my palm into the dirt. The soil felt cooler than the air. Dense. Unwelcoming. It resisted pressure as if offended by the intrusion. When I lifted my hand, the imprint lingered longer than it should have.

Compaction. Poor drainage. Neglect.

I cataloged the problems in my mind with clinical precision. Naming them made them smaller. Manageable.

This was not digging.

This was a correction.

I drove the trowel into the ground. The blade met resistance before giving way with a muted crack. The earth split cleanly again and again. Push. Pry. Lift. Shake the clods loose and cast the weeds aside.

The rhythm steadied me.

For a while, nothing existed beyond the pattern.

Ellie's voice drifted at the edge of my thoughts. Some roots do not let go.

I dismissed it before the sentence had finished forming. Just a phrase. A comfort people offered when they had no solution.

It did not apply here.

I worked deeper. Broke apart clumps with the edge of the blade. Cleared small stones. Bits of debris surfaced. I did not remember burying them. A rusted nail. A fragment of glass smoothed by time. The yard had layers. That was normal.

My gloves darkened with soil. Sweat gathered along my spine despite the cool air. The physical effort felt clean. Grounded. It left no room for speculation.

I was not afraid. There was no tightening at the base of my skull. No instinct urging retreat. The house behind me remained still, its windows blank.

I drove the trowel in again.

This time, the resistance felt different.

Not dense.

Hollow.

The blade struck something that rang faintly beneath the soil. A dull vibration traveled up the handle and into my wrist.

I paused.

The sky above remained painfully blue.

I shifted my grip and cleared more dirt from the spot. The soil here was darker. Slightly looser, as though someone had disturbed it before.

The trowel struck again.

Metal.

A piece of scrap.

My pulse slowed instead of quickening, which unsettled me more than fear would have. I brushed the dirt away with my gloved hands.

A length of something curved lay just beneath the surface. Not root. Too smooth. Too deliberate.

Wire.

Not rusted like the one from the sapling.

Newer.

I sat back on my heels and studied the exposed arc. The surrounding soil did not look decades old. It looked recent.

Behind me, the house creaked once. A small, almost approving sound.

I stared at the ground.

Nothing bad ever came from taking care of your own yard.

The trowel slipped slightly in my grip as the wire shifted on its own, settling deeper into the loosened earth.

The trowel struck something it should not have.

Not a clang. Not a crack. Just a dull, hollow thump that traveled up the handle and into my wrist. The vibration lingered longer than the sound itself. It felt as though the ground had not resisted the blade but yielded around it.

I froze with the handle half-twisted in my grip. My knuckles tightened. I waited for an echo, for a shift in the earth, for some rational follow-up that would explain what I had felt.

Nothing came.

The air thinned.

Not dramatically. Not in a way I could measure. The warmth along my forearms retreated as if an unseen hand had pulled it back. Sweat cooled too quickly. Goosebumps rose in its place. I lifted my face toward the sky, squinting, half-expecting a cloud to have slipped over the sun.

The sky remained sharp and indifferent.

Then I noticed what was missing.

The insects.

A moment earlier in the yard had been threaded with sound. A low, unfocused hum of wings and friction and life. Now there was nothing. No cicadas. No flies. No distant bird calls. The quiet did not feel natural. It felt selective.

It felt centered.

My gaze dropped slowly back to the hole.

The silence pressed inward, heavy enough to distort my hearing. My breath sounded amplified, pulled too close to my ears. The fence leaned where it always had. The sapling stood near the corner, leaves suspended in a movement that did not finish. Behind me, the house remained still.

The attention was not coming from behind me.

It was below.

I crouched again, slower this time. The soil around the blade looked darker now. More compact. As though someone had handled it recently. I placed my bare hand beside the hole.

Cold.

Not the cool of morning shade. This was deeper. The chill rose into my palm and settled there, dense and deliberate. The dampness beneath the surface did not match the dryness of the surrounding yard.

My fingers pressed lightly and met resistance that felt wrong. Not rock. Not root. A curved firmness beneath the soil, too smooth to be natural.

I pulled my hand back and stared at it. My skin remained pink and ordinary. No frost. No mark.

"You are fine," I said, the words heavier this time. "It is just dirt."

The silence did not argue. It simply stayed.

I returned to the trowel and began brushing soil away instead of digging. The blade skimmed through the earth with unsettling ease. Each stroke exposed a fraction more of something beneath, though I could not yet define its shape. My pulse hammered hard enough to make my vision flicker at the edges.

Then I felt it again.

A tremor.

Faint. Brief. More suggestion than force.

The loose soil at the rim of the hole shifted inward. Not collapsing. Not dramatically. Just settling in a way that did not correspond to my movement.

I stopped breathing.

Nothing else moved.

The insects did not resume.

I stood halfway and wiped my gloves against my jeans, smearing dark soil across the denim. A strained laugh escaped before I could stop it. The sound fractured midway and fell flat.

"Get it together," I whispered. "You are projecting."

The yard remained stripped of sound.

I could have stepped away. Walked back to the house. Closed the door. Rewritten the morning as an overreaction.

Instead, I knelt again.

This time I pressed the trowel deeper without hesitation.

The blade slid down farther than it should have, as though it had found a hollow space waiting for it.

The soil at the bottom of the hole dipped slightly inward.

And from somewhere beneath the surface, a thin ribbon of air escaped, rising through the dirt in a slow, deliberate line before vanishing into the morning light.

I slowed down after that.

Not because I was afraid. That was the version I gave myself, tidy and reasonable. I slowed because the ground resisted first, in a way I could not name. The trowel did not strike rock or root. It met pressure. A dense cohesion that felt deliberate. When I pressed harder, the vibration traveled up the handle and settled into my wrist like a warning.

The soil felt as though it remembered being pressed together and resented being disturbed.

I worked the weeds free one at a time, careful now. Deliberate. Each clump set aside in a neat pile, roots aligned as if cataloged. The more earth I cleared, the more the silence thickened. No insects returned. No breeze tested the leaves. The quiet did not feel natural. It felt contained.

That was when I saw it.

At first it was only a shift in tone. The dirt ahead of me seemed darker along a faint curve. Light slid across the surface and then stopped, interrupted by a change in texture. I leaned closer. The edge was subtle but undeniable. The soil there was packed tight, almost polished. Not by erosion. Not by weather.

By pressure.

I brushed at it with my glove. The dirt did not crumble the way the rest had. I used the flat of the trowel and scraped lightly. The blade made a soft dragging sound, different from the surrounding ground.

A circle revealed itself slowly.

It was not precise or decorative. It was roughly three feet across, uneven at the edges but intentional in its shape. The outer ring was darker and more compacted, as though fingers had pressed and smoothed it repeatedly over time. The center was smoother still. Compressed. Quiet.

My stomach tightened. Not sharply. Just enough to register.

I told myself a story. An old fence post. A shallow pit filled in years ago. Animal disturbance. Settled soil. Ground does strange things when left alone.

Normal explanations.

The shape did not blur.

I lowered myself fully to my knees and extended one finger toward the center. The soil there was cool and faintly damp. When I pressed lightly, the surface yielded with a subtle springiness, making my breath catch. Dirt should not respond like that. It should crumble or compact.

This held.

I jerked my hand back.

"Enough," I said, though the word did not carry conviction.

The notebook was in my hand before I consciously reached for it. I sketched quickly. Fence line. Sapling. Slope of the yard. The circle marked in rough outline. My pen pressed harder than necessary. The word anomaly appeared heavier than the rest of the notes.

I underlined it once.

My hand hovered, considering a second line.

I stopped myself.

Writing it down shrank it. That was the rule. If it lived on paper, it did not have to occupy the rest of me.

The air remained unnaturally cool around the circle even as sweat gathered at my spine. The rest of the yard looked unchanged. Sunlit. Ordinary. But the ground beneath my knees felt detached from the morning.

I stood and closed the notebook against my ribs.

Animal burrow, I decided. Old work. Settled soil.

I tested the surface with the toe of my boot.

The circle did not sink.

It did not crumble.

It held with a firmness that felt reinforced.

That was when the thought arrived, clear and unwelcome.

Someone made this.

The idea lingered longer this time. It carried an implication. Intention requires purpose. Purpose requires presence.

I shook my head as though I could dislodge the notion physically.

People do not press circles into the earth and walk away without reason.

I picked up the trowel again. The bed still needed clearing. The planting still needed doing. Bloodroot required timing. Structure. Discipline.

I stepped carefully around the circle, making sure not to disturb the edge, and resumed working.

I told myself it was caution.

Behind me, something shifted.

Not in the house.

In the ground.

When I looked back, the center of the circle had sunk inward by the width of a fingertip.

The cold did not leave in a rush. It receded slowly, sensation returning to my fingers in a prickling burn that made me flex them inside the gloves. Warmth followed in increments. The sun pressed lightly against the back of my neck. Air moved again, gentle and familiar, carrying the faint scent of dry grass.

A single cicada buzzed.

The sound startled me more than the silence had. It droned for a second on its own, uncertain. Then another answered from farther down the yard. A third joined in. The layered hum rebuilt itself cautiously, as though testing the air before committing to it. Birds resumed their small territorial arguments in the trees. Something shifted in the brush near the fence.

I exhaled.

"See?" I said, forcing a lightness into my voice. "Nothing."

The word echoed flatter than I intended. I waited for the pressure to return, for the sense of attention pressing upward from beneath me. It did not. The soil under my knees felt cool in a way that made sense. Damp where shade lingered. Firm without resistance.

Relief came quickly, almost humiliating in its clarity. I had startled myself. Too much quiet. Too much imagination layered over ordinary ground.

I picked up the trowel and resumed digging.

The soil broke apart more easily now. Roots snapped with small, dry pops. The rhythm settled into something mechanical and reliable. Dig. Lift. Clear. The circle remained just behind me, intact and undisturbed. I did not look at it directly. I did not need to.

That felt prudent.

The insect's hum stabilized into its steady drone. The yard sounded alive again. Predictable.

I laughed once, short and thin. "Jesus, Clara," I muttered. "Get a grip."

I leaned into the work. The blade cut through the loosened soil with less resistance than before. The ground seemed to open ahead of the trowel, as if preemptively yielding. I told myself that was because I had already broken the surface layer. That was how soil worked.

I pictured the bloodroot in place, roots stretching downward with patient certainty. Settling because they belonged there. I liked the idea of belonging as something that could be engineered.

The trowel struck something firmer beneath the loosened earth. Not rock. A different density. I pressed harder.

The blade broke through with a muted crack.

The sound did not carry.

It vanished into the ground as though padded from below. No vibration traveled up the handle this time. The absence of resistance unsettled me more than resistance would have.

I paused and listened.

The insects continued. The breeze brushed lightly against the fence boards. Everything sounded correct.

I continued digging.

The layer beneath gave way in a wide patch, soil collapsing inward in a soft spill that should have required more effort. A faint scent rose from the disturbed earth. Not unpleasant. Just older. Damp leaves left too long in the shadow. For a second, something metallic, thin, and sharp, threaded through it. I breathed in again to confirm it.

The smell faded.

I worked until my shoulders burned and sweat slicked the inside of my gloves. When I finally straightened up, the cleared space looked clean and open. Ready.

A breeze crossed the yard, carrying the smell of turned soil past me. The cicadas maintained their steady hum. Birds shifted in the trees. The house stood quiet behind me, its windows reflecting the sky.

I wiped my forehead with my sleeve and turned back toward the fence.

The circle was gone.

Not erased. Not filled.

The surface where it had been was level with the rest of the ground, smoothed as if no boundary had ever existed.

For a long moment, I stared at the spot where the darker ring had been pressed into place.

The soil there began to sink inward, slowly and evenly, as though something beneath it had exhaled.

Chapter 4

I spent the morning at the kitchen table because it was the only place in the house that didn't argue with me. The light came in pale and flat across the wood grain. The table was scarred—knife marks, a burn ring I didn't remember making—but it was solid. It stayed where it was. That mattered.

I spread my papers out carefully. Planting schedules on the left. Soil notes stacked by pH and type. Yard maps in the center on graph paper with faint blue lines that kept everything honest. I uncapped my pen and started working.

The scratch of ink settled me. Each line stayed where I put it. No shifting. No second guessing.

I redrew the south fence line. The measurement hadn't changed, but I tightened the angle where the fence met the tree line and rewrote the note, poor drainage here, cleaner this time.

Precision mattered. Small mistakes spread if you let them.

Outside, the yard sat quiet. I didn't look at it long.

I flipped to a fresh page and started a new list. Tools. Amendments. Timeline. My handwriting tightened as I went, margins respected. I liked margins. They told you where to stop.

That was when I saw the page.

It sat between two filled sections, blank except for one word at the top, written in my own hand.

Dreams.

I turned the page and kept working.

I reorganized the soil notes instead. Rewrote a paragraph from the night before. Added seed trays to the supply list, then added a second note so I wouldn't forget why I needed them.

The pen never hesitated. My hand didn't shake. Everything behaved.

Somewhere in the house, a pipe clicked. I paused, listened, then kept writing. Houses made noises. That didn't mean anything.

I flipped another page. The word *Dreams* flashed past again before I could stop it. I frowned and drew a neat box around a heading that didn't need one.

I told myself I'd get to it later. You didn't start with the messiest part. You built toward it.

The stack of papers grew orderly under my hands. Aligned. Accounted for. I leaned back and looked at what I'd done, a small swell of satisfaction moving through me.

This is how you handle things.

I closed the notebook and rested my palm on the cover, feeling the weight of it. Solid. Contained.

I didn't open it again.

I didn't notice the faint smudge my finger left on the front cover, right where the word *Dreams* pressed through from the page beneath.

That night, I stood at the kitchen window long after the light should've been turned off.

The yard lay pale under the moon, smooth from a distance. The fence ran straight. The ground looked calm. Even the south corner—where I'd dug—had settled back into itself, neat as a tucked sheet.

I imagined it finished. The bloodroot bed full and balanced. The sapling taller. No weeds. No bare patches. Just quiet, predictable growth. A yard that made sense.

If I could get the land right, the rest would follow. The house would breathe easier. I would too.

Peace through order.

The kitchen clock ticked behind me. My reflection surfaced faint in the glass, layered over the yard. For a moment, I didn't look like part of the house at all. Just a shape hovering between inside and out.

I pressed my hand against the cool pane. The glass held. Solid. Real.

Then the thought came, slow and unwelcome.

It wasn't the yard I needed to fix.

The idea rose like pressure behind my eyes. I pushed it down, but it didn't leave. It waited. Patient.

What I needed wasn't silence. Silence just gave things room to speak louder.

What I needed were answers.

The word sat heavy in my chest. Answers meant digging where I didn't want to dig. Standing still long enough to feel what I'd been stepping around. Grief. Fear. The truth I kept organizing my way out of.

I tightened my grip on the window frame until my knuckles ached.

"No," I said softly.

I turned away before the thought could finish forming. The room behind me felt safer. Smaller. Manageable.

I went back to the table and opened the notebook. The familiar pages waited. I added a few notes. Revised a schedule. Drew a clean line where one hadn't been before.

The pen moved easily. The ink stayed where I put it.

Outside, the yard didn't move at all.

I told myself that was proof enough.

And as I went over my lists, chasing quiet, chasing balance, I didn't see how the ground beyond the window held its shape a little too well.

Or how what had already taken root didn't need my permission to grow.

Chapter 5

The house went quiet the way a room does when conversation stops because you have entered it.

I did not recognize it at first. The refrigerator clicked off and did not resume. The pipes, which usually sighed in irregular intervals, settled into stillness. Even the wind that teased the eaves every evening seemed to withdraw without announcement.

The quiet accumulated.

I stood in the hallway and listened carefully, cataloging the absence of sound. Old houses had rhythms. You learned them. You adjusted your own breathing to them without thinking. This felt different. Not the absence of noise, but the removal of it.

I took a step forward.

The floorboard answered with a sharp creak, but the sound did not seem to originate exactly beneath my foot. It carried from somewhere slightly to the left, as though the house had anticipated my movement and responded before I completed it.

I froze.

The creak ceased. The silence returned immediately, filling the space like water rushing into a hollow.

My shoulders tightened.

"Get a grip," I said softly, and the words felt intrusive. Too loud for the space.

I waited for the house to counter with something ordinary. A settling beam. A faint pipe knock. Any confirmation of routine.

Nothing followed.

I moved again, slower, distributing my weight deliberately. Each step produced a single clean sound and nothing more. No echo. No trailing resonance. Just action and response, stripped of the comforting clutter that usually softened it.

The hallway lights were on, but the rooms seemed dimmer at their edges. Shadows pooled more deeply in corners that had never concerned me before. As I passed the staircase, my gaze lifted without permission.

The upper landing held no movement.

Still, I felt the certainty of being observed from that direction.

Not seen.

Measured.

The thought irritated me immediately. Houses did not observe. They contained. They aged. They decayed. They did not watch.

I turned into the kitchen and braced my palms against the counter. The surface was cool and solid beneath my skin. The clock on the wall ticked once.

Then it stopped.

I stared at the second hand. It hovered between numbers. One second passed. Then another. I counted to five silently before the hand jerked forward and resumed its rhythm, louder than before.

My pulse jumped in answer.

"You are tired," I muttered. "That is all."

The refrigerator remained silent.

The quiet did not thicken. It drew closer.

I became acutely aware of my own breathing, the way the air moved in and out of my lungs. The swallow in my throat sounded amplified in my ears. I shifted my weight, and the faint rustle of fabric against fabric seemed exaggerated.

This was how it began, I told myself. This was how people assigned intention to coincidence. A few aligned absences and suddenly everything felt staged.

I turned on the faucet.

The rush of water filled the room with immediate relief. It splashed against the basin with reassuring force. I let it run longer than necessary, listening to the uncomplicated roar of it.

When I shut it off, the silence that followed felt sharper for the contrast.

One drop fell.

Another.

Then nothing.

I waited for the refrigerator motor to engage.

It did not.

I stood there longer than I meant to, palms flat on the counter, listening to the house breathe around me in a way that felt almost synchronized with my own pulse.

Old houses did this, I reminded myself. They paused. They shifted. They withheld sound without meaning anything by it.

I turned off the kitchen light.

The room fell into shadow, lit only by faint spill from the hallway.

As I stepped toward the doorway, something moved above me.

Not loudly.

Not dramatically.

A single, measured step from the upper floor.

The floorboard overhead responded with the same clean creak I had heard beneath my own foot.

Only this time, I was not moving.

I was folding laundry when I heard it again.

There was no clear beginning. No rise in volume or sudden intrusion.

Just a thin strand of melody weaving itself through the quiet, so faint that for a moment I mistook it for the rhythm of my own breath. I paused with a towel half-folded between my hands and listened.

The tune did not come from a single direction. It seemed to hover just beyond the edges of the room, brushing against the walls without settling on them. It faded, then returned in fragments. Three notes. A pause. Two more, spaced carefully apart.

The dryer hummed behind me, steady and low. The overhead light flickered once and steadied again. I focused on the cotton beneath my fingers, on the clean detergent scent, on the symmetry of folding corners into alignment.

As the light steadied, the melody slipped through again. This time it aligned perfectly with the flicker, the brief dimming coinciding with a higher note.

I stilled.

It was memory, I told myself. That was the simplest explanation. The mind was capable of filling quiet with whatever it pleased.

The lullaby retreated.

I exhaled slowly and resumed folding. Silence invited invention. The brain disliked gaps and patched them with whatever it found nearby.

When the last shirt was stacked neatly, I carried the folded clothes down the hallway. Each step triggered a familiar creak. The house responded in the same stripped-down way it had earlier. Action. Response. Nothing more.

In the bathroom, I switched on the light and leaned over the sink. My reflection surfaced in the mirror, pale and sharper than I remembered. For a moment, the image felt deeper than the room allowed, as if there were an extra inch of space behind the glass.

I turned on the faucet and began brushing my teeth, listening to the scrape of bristles and the rush of water. Routine sounds. Human sounds.

The lullaby returned.

Not louder.

Closer.

It threaded itself between the water and the pulse in my ears, settling somewhere behind my eyes. My grip tightened on the toothbrush. Foam gathered at the corner of my mouth as I froze.

"Stop it," I said through the bristles.

The word came out smaller than I intended. The bathroom swallowed it.

The melody shifted. A new note slid into place, one I did not recognize but felt immediately. My stomach dropped.

I shut off the water.

The sudden silence rang.

The tune lingered for a second longer, then thinned until it vanished entirely. I stood there, breathing shallowly, waiting for it to resume.

It did not.

My hands trembled as I set the toothbrush on the counter. I forced myself to look at my reflection again. My eyes moved too quickly, scanning the edges of the mirror as though expecting something to enter from just beyond the frame.

Without deciding to, I began to hum.

The sound was barely there at first. A faint vibration in my throat. I wanted to test it. To see whether I could reconstruct the pattern.

The first notes emerged easily.

Too easily.

My voice moved to the next phrase without hesitation. The interval was exact. Clean. Certain. As if I had practiced it.

I did not remember ever hearing this song before.

I continued humming.

Not because I chose to.

Because I had not realized I was mid-phrase until the melody was already unfolding.

A second line of harmony slid in beneath my own voice.

Soft.

Almost indistinguishable.

But not mine.

I stopped abruptly. The silence that followed was thick and immediate.

"How did you," I began, and the question dissolved in my throat.

The mirror reflected only me. My lips parted. My breathing shallow.

The dryer in the other room stopped mid-cycle.

No slowing.

No winding down.

Just silence.

I did not move.

Somewhere in the house, very faintly, the lullaby resumed.

Not in the air.

In the walls.

I woke the next morning to sunlight pooling across the kitchen table and my phone buzzing insistently on the counter.

I reached for it expecting a weather alert or a spam call. Instead, Ellie's name filled the screen. Three messages stacked tightly together.

You okay?

Call me when you wake up.

Clara?

There was a missed call.

I had been brushing my teeth around then. I remembered the mirror. The humming.

I did not remember the phone ringing.

A hollow space opened where that memory should have been.

I typed, sorry. Fell asleep early and hit send before the words could rearrange themselves into something truer.

As I set the phone down, something else pressed at me. I could not remember turning off the bathroom light. I could not remember getting into bed. I did not remember dreaming.

The refrigerator hummed steadily behind me, a reassuring mechanical sound. I stood still and waited for panic.

It did not arrive in a rush. It seeped in slowly, more like doubt than fear.

The days after that lost their edges.

I meant to write dates in my journal and then found blank pages where entries should have been. I prepared food I did not recall cooking. One morning I discovered a plate in the sink with dried sauce along its rim. I could not remember eating it.

I moved through the house without switching on lights, trusting the dimness to map itself around me. Shadows seemed less resistant than they once had. They accepted me easily.

Mirrors became inconveniences. In the hallway, in the bathroom, in the bedroom, I learned the angles that let me pass without meeting my own eyes. It was not fear. It was efficiency. There were schedules to revise. Soil to amend.

Once, carrying a stack of folded laundry, I caught my reflection anyway.

For a second, the figure in the glass did not move when I did. My shoulder dipped, but the image held still for half a beat too long.

Then it corrected.

Just me.

The house began to respond differently.

Floorboards did not protest under my steps. They anticipated them. A door I reached for opened as my hand approached, as though it had already decided to comply. The rooms felt accustomed to me in a way that unsettled me more than resistance ever had.

It was as if my presence required less acknowledgment.

That thought lingered.

One afternoon, I stood in the doorway and watched dust drift through a narrow beam of light. I could not remember when I had opened the curtains. I could not remember closing them the night before. Time slid forward without friction.

It was easier not to question it.

The realization came quietly.

If I continued like this, keeping my head lowered and my movements efficient, I would not be living in the house at all.

I would be passing through it.

A shape without weight.

The word ghost resisted me at first. It felt theatrical. Too convenient. But the idea pressed closer.

Ghosts did not slam doors. They did not howl. They adjusted to rooms. They learned how to move without disturbing the air.

I looked down at my hands and tried to remember the last time someone had held them.

The memory would not surface.

Outside, the yard lay still beneath the afternoon light. Inside, the house felt composed.

I stepped forward into the hallway and glanced once more at the mirror.

The dust in the beam of sunlight continued drifting.

It did not shift when I passed through it.

That night, I lay in bed with the light off.

The day had worn me down in small ways. Not exhaustion, something quieter. I felt like I'd been spread too far across too many hours without anchoring myself anywhere. The mattress dipped beneath my weight. The ceiling above me held its shape.

I reached for the notebook on the nightstand and pulled it closer. The pen rested on top where I'd left it, aligned with the spine. That small order gave me comfort. I flipped to a blank page and waited for the words to come.

They didn't arrive as sentences. They arrived as understanding.

Denial had a cost.

The thought didn't scare me at first. It landed in my body before it reached my head—a tightening in my chest, a weight settling behind my ribs. I understood, suddenly and completely, that nothing needed to chase me. Nothing needed to touch me at all.

I swallowed and stared at the page. My hand hovered over it, pen poised. Writing made things manageable. If I put the truth on paper, I could box it in. Label it. Return to it later.

But the truth resisted that. It didn't want to be documented. It wanted to be acknowledged.

I thought of the rooms I'd stopped entering. The messages I'd answered late, or not at all. The way I moved through the house now, careful not to disturb anything, like I was borrowing space instead of owning it.

The warning wasn't loud. It didn't threaten. It didn't beg.

It simply existed.

If I kept choosing quiet over honesty, control over understanding, the house would do nothing at all. It would wait. It had time.

My pen touched the page, then lifted again. I closed the notebook without writing a word and slid it back onto the nightstand. My hand lingered there longer than necessary.

That was the choice.

Silence.

I turned onto my side and pulled the blanket up to my shoulder. The fabric smelled like detergent and something older beneath it, a trace I couldn't place. The room felt close, but not oppressive. Watchful.

The lullaby drifted in then. Soft. Incomplete. Just enough to remind me it existed. It didn't come from anywhere I could name. It settled into the space between my thoughts, gentle and persistent.

I didn't hum along this time.

I closed my eyes and let the sound pass through me without answering it. My breathing slowed. My body did what it had always done when faced with something it didn't want to face.

It went still.

As sleep crept in, I had the clearest thought I'd had all day.

This wasn't the end. It was the warning.

And I was choosing not to listen..

Chapter 6

I went back to the south fence the way you return to a chore you have already half-finished, without giving it enough thought to let doubt take hold.

I wore the same gloves. Carried the same trowel. The shallow trench lay where I had left it, the soil loosened and compliant. Morning had settled into something neutral. Not warm. Not cold. The kind of air that made work feel possible.

I knelt and set my weight carefully, letting my hands fall into the rhythm they already knew.

Dig. Lift. Shake the soil free. Set it aside.

The ground behaved at first. It broke where I asked it to. It shifted without resistance. That steadiness steadied me in return.

Routine was the point. Repeat something long enough and it stops questioning you.

Then the trowel struck something.

The impact was not heavy. The sound followed a fraction of a second later. A clean click. Too sharp to be stone. Too hollow to be root.

I stopped.

The air felt the same. The fence above me did not move. I pressed the blade lightly against the spot again.

Click.

It carried just enough resistance to register and then give, as though whatever lay beneath the soil had shifted to accommodate the strike.

"Great," I muttered. "More junk."

Old land surfaced debris all the time. Nails. Glass. Bits of wire that had lost their purpose decades ago. That was all this was. Something forgotten.

I angled the trowel and scraped carefully along the surface. Dirt fell away in thin sheets. The blade tapped against it once more, and irritation edged ahead of curiosity.

I disliked surprises in the soil. They complicated spacing. They required adjustment.

I worked around the object instead of directly at it, widening the hole. My glove brushed against something smooth.

Not slick.

Not rough.

Smooth in a way that suggested density.

I pulled my hand back and stared at the exposed patch. A pale curve emerged through the brown. Not bright white. Dull. Weathered. A color that had absorbed the earth around it.

"Debris," I said again, more firmly.

I cleared another inch. The curve lengthened. The surface was not flat like plastic. It bowed gently outward. There were faint irregularities along it, tiny pits that caught the light differently than stone would have.

My pulse quickened without permission.

Plastic pipe, I told myself. A fragment of irrigation line. Anything with a rounded edge could look like this when half-buried.

I slid the trowel beneath the object and levered upward carefully. It shifted too easily. Too lightly.

The soil released it with almost no resistance.

The piece rolled once in the loose dirt and settled with its concave side angled toward me.

I did not reach for it.

At first, it was only shape. A curve. A hollow. A suggestion.

Then my eyes adjusted.

The hollow was too symmetrical.

Too deliberate.

There was a ridge along one edge, delicate and thin. A faint seam where something had once joined to something else.

My breath shortened. The glove around my hand felt suddenly too tight.

"This is still fine," I said aloud, my voice measured.

The words hovered uselessly between me and the ground.

I brushed more soil away with the back of my fingers. Dirt fell from the interior of the hollow, revealing a darker pocket within. The curve extended farther than I had first seen. Beneath it, the soil dipped slightly inward, as though shaped around it.

The object was not alone.

I swallowed.

The pale surface beneath my hand ended in a narrow ridge that bent at an angle no pipe would bend. The texture shifted from smooth to faintly porous.

I did not need to pick it up to understand that it had once belonged to something structured.

Something that had held shape on its own.

The ground had not changed.

Only what it was holding had decided to show itself.

I told myself to finish clearing around it. Just enough to see what I was dealing with.

The soil slid away in thin layers, whispering against the blade of the trowel. The top crust crumbled easily. Beneath it, the earth darkened and grew compact. Each pass widened the opening. The pale surface beneath it lengthened, revealing more of its shape. A curve. A narrowing. A subtle change in thickness along its span.

My chest tightened before my mind supplied the reason. The trowel felt heavier in my hand, as though the handle had absorbed the weight of what it had uncovered.

"No," I said quietly. The word felt insufficient.

Animal. It had to be animal. The woods pressed close beyond the fence line. Foxes. Deer. Strays. Things died. The ground held them. That was ordinary. That was nature.

I worked more carefully now. My hands did not feel steady. They trembled, then steadied, then trembled again. Dirt smeared across the back of my glove, but the pale surface beneath it stayed clean, almost resistant to the soil that clung to everything else.

I cleared the end of it.

The shape resolved itself without asking permission.

There was a rounded edge at one end that curved inward slightly. A shallow hollow where something had once connected. A subtle ridge that mirrored the structure of my own wrist when I flexed it.

My mouth went dry.

The air felt thinner. I had the sudden, irrational urge to look over my shoulder, as though someone might be watching me reach the same conclusion they already knew. The yard remained empty. The fence did not move. The sapling stood still.

Animal, I repeated in my head.

But I knew bones. Not academically. Not clinically. I knew the weight of my own skeleton. I knew where joints bent and where they did not. This curve carried intention. It carried proportion. It carried familiarity.

Recognition came from somewhere lower than thought, closer to the spine.

I crouched there longer than I realized, staring. The soil around the bone seemed different now. Not disturbed. Not recently dug. It held its edges too cleanly, as though it had been shaped around what it concealed and then left undisturbed for years.

My breathing grew loud in my ears. I forced it to slow. In. Out. Control returned in narrow pieces.

"It's still nothing," I said, though my voice had thinned.

I reached out and touched it with the tip of my finger.

The surface was cold.

Not damp. Not cool from shade.

Cold in a way that felt independent of the air around it. The contact sent a sharp line of awareness from my fingertip through my wrist and into my chest. It did not shock me. It clarified me.

I pulled my hand back and stood abruptly, heart racing. The yard offered no ordinary sound in return. No insect buzz. No shifting leaves. Only the open space and the shallow pit I had created.

The animal explanation did not explode.

It simply ceased to function.

I stared down at the bone and felt something inside me shift. The point where denial thins and something harder moves into its place.

Then my gaze drifted slightly to the right.

The soil there dipped in a second, smaller curve. Subtle. Barely visible. A contour that mirrored the first at a slight angle.

I had not uncovered a stray fragment.

I had interrupted a pattern.

And the ground was not finished giving it back.

I did not move.

That was the second decision, and it felt heavier than the first.

The bone rested where it lay, half held by dirt, half exposed to air. My hands stayed close to my body, fingers curled into my palms as if restraint alone could keep the situation contained. My heart pounded hard enough that I felt it in the hollow of my throat.

Think.

Old land surfaced things. That was a fact. Fence posts collapsed. Tree roots dragged debris sideways. Animals carried remains from one place to another and abandoned them without ceremony. Water shifted soil in ways that made order impossible.

Bones moved.

That explanation assembled itself neatly. Logical. Manageable. I nodded once, deliberate and controlled.

"That's all this is," I said quietly. "Old ground doing what old ground does."

The words sounded stable.

The bone did not.

I crouched again, keeping a careful distance. I studied it the way I would study a structural flaw, searching for evidence that it belonged to something ordinary. Too small for livestock. Too clean to be recent. Too proportioned to dismiss.

My breathing came shallow at first, then steadier as I forced it into rhythm. Panic would not help. Panic rushed you into errors. Calm allowed correction.

The right way.

The phrase struck harder than it should have.

Because beneath the rational explanation, another word had already surfaced.

Rules.

It did not arrive as an option. It arrived as instruction. Clear. Fixed. Bones meant reporting. Not interpreting. Not deciding privately what they were worth. Not covering them and promising to revisit the question when it felt safer.

Consequences followed choices, not feelings.

I shook my head sharply, as if I could dislodge the thought. "You don't know that," I said under my breath. "You don't know what this is."

The yard remained silent.

I did know.

Not officially. Not conclusively. But enough that pretending otherwise felt like a lie spoken directly to my own reflection.

I pictured the call. The voice on the other end shifting from polite to attentive. The questions. The pause. I saw bright tape strung along the fence line, fluttering against the sapling I had straightened days ago. I saw boots pressing into my soil, strangers bending to examine what I had uncovered.

The house filled with voices that were not mine.

Loss of control tightened around my ribs.

"This doesn't have to be that," I said more quietly. "Not yet."

But even as I spoke, the space around the decision narrowed. Fear could be postponed. Fear could be reasoned with. Obligation could not.

Once you saw something like this, truly saw it, you could not unsee it. You could not bury it again and expect it to remain patient. Recognition altered the ground it stood on.

I stared at the exposed bone and felt the shift settle in.

The earth had not merely revealed something.

It had assigned it.

A faint sound broke the silence. Not from the house. Not from the trees.

From the pit.

A small crumble of soil gave way along the edge I had cleared. I watched as the dirt fell inward, exposing a second pale curve beneath the first. Thinner. Angled differently. Close enough that it could not belong to chance.

I did not breathe.

The ground had not finished.

And neither had the choice.

I covered it.

Not carefully. Not with the deliberate calm I had forced myself into moments earlier. My hands moved before I could reconsider, scooping loose soil back into the hollow. The first handful fell unevenly, scattering across the pale curve. I hesitated for half a second, staring at the white still visible through the dirt.

Then I pressed harder.

Soil slid over it in slow sheets. Grain by grain, the curve disappeared. Brown replaced white. The hollow filled. My palms flattened against the earth, pushing down until the pressure traveled into my wrists.

My fingers trembled.

I hated that more than anything.

"This is temporary," I said aloud, my voice rough and thin. "Just until I figure out what to do."

The yard did not respond.

I packed the dirt tighter than necessary, leaning my weight into it. The soil accepted the force without resistance. It compressed smoothly, almost eagerly, as if it had expected this outcome. I smoothed the surface with the flat of my glove and brushed stray crumbs aside. I erased the edges of disturbance as best I could.

When I sat back on my heels, the patch looked ordinary.

That was what unsettled me.

The fence stood as it had. The sapling caught the light. The shallow trench blended seamlessly back into the line of earth. Anyone passing by would have seen nothing unusual. Nothing out of place.

My stomach twisted.

The act felt wrong in a way that did not fade once it was complete. Not wrong like breaking a rule you could justify later. Wrong like stepping onto ice you knew was thin and pretending not to hear it crack beneath you.

I wiped my hands against my jeans, grinding soil into the seams. Dirt lodged beneath my nails. I could feel it there, stubborn and granular, no matter how hard I rubbed.

I stood slowly.

The yard remained silent. Not the casual quiet of morning, but something closer. The stillness had shifted from neutral to attentive.

I had crossed something.

Covering it had not undone what I had seen. It had not reduced it. The bone was still beneath the surface. The second curve was still beneath the first. The obligation had not dissolved. It had been delayed.

I glanced toward the house.

It stood solid and familiar, its windows reflecting light as if nothing in the yard had changed. Inside, floors creaked when stepped on. Clocks ticked in steady increments. Rules applied.

I wanted that version of the world back. The one where this was a garden problem. A drainage issue. A misplaced fragment of debris.

But that day had already slipped out from under me.

Nothing dramatic had happened. No sound. No rupture. No spectacle that marked a clear dividing line.

Instead, something finer had given way.

A hairline fracture beneath the surface.

Invisible unless you knew exactly where to look.

I stepped back from the fence. Then another step. Each one felt deliberate, as if retreating from a line I had drawn and then stepped across.

The yard did not move.

But as I turned toward the house, the soil behind me shifted with a faint settling sound.

Not a collapse.

Not a slide.

Just enough to suggest that what I had pressed down had not accepted the pressure.

I stopped.

The surface remained smooth.

But at the center of the patch, the earth had sunk a fraction of an inch, forming the faintest hollow.

As if something beneath it had exhaled.

Chapter 7

I did not sleep. I lay with my eyes closed and the house arranged around me, listening to the quiet settle into its corners. Every time I drifted, the same awareness rose back up. Not sharp. Not urgent. Just present. The yard waited beyond the glass. The fence held its line. The ground kept what I had pressed back into it.

Morning arrived without ceremony. Light slid across the floor, pale and indifferent. It did not soften anything. It did not undo the memory of my hands flattening soil over bone.

Yesterday had not ended. It had paused.

I made coffee. I rinsed a cup. I stood at the sink and watched water spiral down the drain. Outside, the yard looked calm. Untouched. The south fence cut its clean line through the grass.

The spot beneath it pulled at me anyway.

Time had moved forward. The problem had not.

I made the call standing up, phone pressed too tightly against my ear. I watched the yard through the kitchen window while it rang.

"County Sheriff's Office."

"Yes," I said, and my throat closed. I swallowed and tried again. "I think I found bones in my yard."

There was a pause. Not long. Just long enough to register.

"Animal bones?"

"That's what I thought," I replied. "But I am not sure anymore."

Keys tapped faintly on her end.

"Where are you located, ma'am?"

I gave the address carefully. Each number felt heavier than the last. The house seemed to recede a fraction with every digit.

She asked how deep. How many. Whether I had touched them.

"Yes," I admitted to the last. "I covered them back up."

Another pause.

"We will send someone out. Please do not disturb the area any further."

"I won't," I said.

When I hung up, the house felt different. Not the oppressive stillness of the night before. This was anticipatory. Waiting for something external to arrive.

The cruiser pulled into the driveway forty minutes later. The tires crunched over gravel with deliberate slowness. The engine idled, then cut. The door opened and shut with a firm, contained sound.

The sheriff stood beside the vehicle for a moment, scanning the yard.

He did not wave. He did not call out.

He waited.

I understood immediately. This was not something he came to hear about. It was something he came to see.

"It's back here," I said, stepping off the porch.

My voice felt smaller in the open air.

He followed at an even pace, boots steady behind me. A faint crackle of radio static lingered at his shoulder. The closer we moved to the south fence, the tighter my chest became. The air there felt flat again. Still. As if holding itself in place.

I stopped where I had smoothed the soil.

"There."

My hand shook when I pointed.

He crouched without hurry. He studied the ground for a long moment before touching it. His eyes tracked the slight depression at the center of the patch.

"You covered it," he said.

Not a question.

"Yes. Just temporarily."

He nodded once and pulled on gloves. He brushed soil aside with careful, practiced movements. The white curve emerged again, patient and unchanged.

He did not flinch.

He leaned closer.

Then he exhaled through his nose.

"They're human."

The word settled between us.

"Old," he added after another moment. "Very old. Mid-nineteenth century, if I had to guess. Not recent. Not something active."

Relief moved through me in a thin wave. Not recent meant no sirens. No headlines. No immediate violence.

He continued brushing soil back.

Another pale curve appeared beside the first. Then a third. Angled. Deliberate. Not scattered.

"These were placed," he said quietly.

My stomach dropped.

"Placed?"

He did not look at me when he answered. "Not dumped. Not dragged in. Arranged."

The yard shifted shape around us. What had been a single fragment was now part of something structured. Intentional.

The notebook came out. The pen uncapped. His radio crackled softly as he spoke into it.

What I had uncovered was no longer private.

As he cleared a wider arc, the soil along the edge gave way more than expected. The ground slumped inward slightly, revealing the curve of something larger beneath the surface.

Not a fragment.

A formation.

I stared at the widening hollow, feeling the weight of it settle in.

This had not come out of the earth by accident.

And it was not finished surfacing.

The tape went up fast.

Not in a rush. In pieces. One wooden stake at a time, driven into the soil with the heel of a boot. The yellow strip unspooled in long, measured lengths, pulled tight until it hummed faintly in the air. The plastic caught the sunlight and flared bright against the green of the yard, almost aggressive in its color.

I stood a few steps back with my hands clenched at my sides and watched my fence line disappear behind it.

"There's procedure," the sheriff said.

He did not look at me. His attention stayed on the tape as he tied it off, checking its tension, making sure the line ran clean and straight. "We document. We secure. Then we wait for the right people."

"How long?" I asked.

He paused before answering. Just long enough to remind me he did not owe me urgency.

"Depends."

The word settled heavy in my chest.

Another stake went in near the south fence. The boot pressed down. The wood sank deep. The tape stretched again, dissecting the yard in a bright, unnatural line.

"What about my plans?" I asked before I could stop myself. "I was working there."

"I understand."

He said it the same way he had said it before. Neutral. Even. A phrase designed to absorb reaction without altering course.

He explained timelines. Specialists. Documentation. How remains required care. How these things moved slowly because they had to.

Temporary, he said. More than once.

Each time it sounded less temporary.

Heat crept up my neck. Not panic. Not grief. Anger. Clean and focused. I watched his boots press into soil I had leveled with my own hands. The shallow impressions stayed there, dark against the surface I had smoothed only yesterday.

"This was supposed to be quiet," I said. "I moved here for that."

He looked at me then.

Not long. Not searching. Just a brief assessment.

"Quiet's a hope," he said. "Not a guarantee."

The sentence cut deeper than it should have.

I turned away before I answered him. The tape fluttered once in a stray breeze and then settled, taut and bright. The yard looked smaller now. Managed. Claimed by something procedural and patient.

I imagined more vehicles pulling in. More boots crossing the grass. Hands digging where mine had been. Neighbors slowing their cars just enough to stare. The house becoming something observed instead of lived in.

Problems were supposed to be handled. Identified. Solved. Closed.

That was the rule.

Now the rule had changed without asking me.

The sheriff tied off the final section and stepped back, scanning the perimeter. Satisfied. He made a note in his book and snapped it shut.

"We'll keep you informed," he said. "Try not to disturb anything else."

Anything else.

I nodded because arguing would not move the line of tape an inch.

The boundary was already there, bright and absolute.

As he walked back toward his cruiser, a second vehicle turned slowly into the drive behind him. Then another.

Engines idled. Doors opened.

The yellow line trembled in the breeze and stretched a little farther than it had a moment before.

The sheriff did not leave right away.

He stood near the edge of the yellow tape with his hands resting on his belt, weight settled evenly, looking out over the yard as if he expected it to volunteer something if given enough time. The engines from the other vehicles had gone quiet. The tape shifted once in the breeze and then stilled.

I stayed where I was, arms folded tight across my chest, watching him watch my property. The anger from earlier had not burned away. It had cooled into something steadier.

"There are records on this area," he said at last.

The words came without emphasis, but they interrupted the quiet like a dropped stone.

"Old ones."

I did not answer. The yard felt like it was listening.

"Land like this," he continued, eyes still forward, "doesn't always line up with what's written down. Families buried their own. Midwives handled things quietly. Not everything made it to church ground."

He did not look at me when he said midwives. He did not need to.

The word brushed something inside me that did not belong to the present moment. A flicker. A resistance that rose before I could attach it to anything specific. My jaw tightened. I told myself it was irritation at the implication, at the way history was being laid across my fence line like it had always been there.

"I just moved here," I said. "I didn't know any of that."

"I'm sure," he replied.

There was no accusation in his voice. Just closure. The kind that did not require agreement.

He spoke about old parcel maps. About deeds that changed hands without changing understanding. About stretches of land where paperwork thinned out and memory filled the gaps. The word midwife surfaced again, softer this time, and I felt that same brief flare under my skin. Not fear. Not recognition. Something closer to intrusion.

I glanced toward the house.

It stood solid and unremarkable, its windows catching light without comment. It did not look like a place carrying anything. It looked like wood and glass and angles. Mine.

"I didn't come here for history," I said. "I came for quiet."

The sheriff nodded once. It was the kind of nod that meant he had heard that before.

"Land doesn't always care why folks arrive," he said. "Just that they do."

The sentence settled into the space between us and did not move.

I opened my mouth to respond, to say something about ownership, about names on deeds and survey lines and what belonged to whom. Nothing came. The yard felt different suddenly. Not hostile. Not dramatic. Just deeper than it had a moment before.

A bird lifted from the tree line without warning, wings beating hard against the still air before disappearing beyond the fence. The sound carried longer than it should have.

The sheriff shifted his weight and finally turned toward his cruiser.

I remained where I was, eyes drawn back to the taped-off section of earth. The grass inside the boundary moved once in the breeze and then stopped.

Something in the ground had been quiet for a long time.

Now it had been noticed.

The sheriff's car rolled down the drive and disappeared behind the trees. The engine noise thinned out slowly, stretched by distance, until it dissolved into nothing. When it was gone, the quiet that followed did not settle the way it had before.

It stayed alert.

I remained near the fence long after there was no reason to stand there. My hands were clenched so tight my knuckles burned. The yellow tape cut across the yard in a clean, merciless line. Sunlight caught on it and turned it bright enough to hurt my eyes. It trembled once in the breeze and then stilled, dividing what had been mine from what was now evidence.

The grass on the other side looked unchanged. The soil showed no sign of disturbance from this distance. The sapling leaned where it always had. Nothing appeared different.

Knowing had changed it anyway.

"This is temporary," I said under my breath.

The word felt brittle. I heard it echo back at me with no weight behind it. Temporary meant weeks. Maybe months. It meant strangers with tools and measured voices. It meant my routines rearranged around someone else's timetable. It meant the careful shape of my days bending to accommodate a past I had not asked for.

I tried to picture the end of it. The tape removed. The earth smoothed back into a quiet garden bed. My plans resumed as if nothing had interrupted them.

The image slipped apart before it finished forming.

The fence stood steady, gray boards catching the light. Beneath it, the ground seemed heavier than it had been yesterday. Not visibly altered. Just deeper. I felt it through the soles of my boots, a subtle pressure that climbed into my calves and settled there. The land had been waiting for something. I understood that now. The waiting had ended.

I had not invited this. I had followed the rule. I had called. I had stepped aside and let authority take over.

None of that returned control to me.

This was not a problem that could be scheduled between errands. It was not something that would resolve itself if I stood still long enough. The yard had opened a seam I had not known existed, and whatever lay beneath it had not forced its way through. It had surfaced with patience, as if it had expected me.

I leaned back against the fence and closed my eyes. For a moment I imagined letting the process handle everything. Letting specialists measure and catalog and carry away what they found. Letting the tape come down. Letting the yard revert to something harmless.

But underneath that thought, something steadier took shape.

This was not optional.

I did not have to welcome it. I did not have to understand it. But I could not pretend I had not seen what the ground chose to reveal. The call had been made. The boundary had been drawn. The land had answered.

A breeze moved through the yard and the tape snapped once, sharp and sudden.

I opened my eyes.

Nothing else had changed.

That was what unsettled me most.

Chapter 8

I was standing at the sink with my sleeves rolled up, hands buried in warm water. Soap bubbles clung to my wrists and slid down in thin, iridescent threads. In the other room, the radio murmured. A talk show. Overlapping voices. Polite disagreement about something trivial. The refrigerator hummed behind me. The house felt functional. Ordinary. Predictable.

Then it shifted.

The radio did not click off. It quietened, as if someone were turning the volume down with careful fingers. One voice blurred into another. Words lost edges. The refrigerator's hum faltered, dipped, and flattened into silence. Even the water changed. It no longer splashed against ceramic. It slid over my skin without sound, as if the room had absorbed it.

The light above the sink did not flicker. It simply dulled. Not dimmer. Just drained.

I knew before I reached for the faucet that something had rearranged itself.

My shoulders locked. My breath stalled halfway in. I kept my hands in the water because pulling them out felt like stepping into something unseen. The counter pressed firm against my thighs. The cabinet edge dug into my hip. I focused on those points of contact. Hard surfaces. Defined edges.

You are here, I told myself. You are awake.

The scream came without warning.

It did not travel from the hallway. It did not echo down the stairs. It erupted fully formed, already inside the house. Already inside the air around me. A sound torn raw, dragged from a throat that had been forced past endurance.

It was loud.

It was strained.

That was worse.

The sound scraped across my chest and tightened there, squeezing until it hurt to breathe. My hands slipped on the plate and ceramic knocked sharply against the sink before I caught it.

"No," I said, and the word felt misplaced, like it belonged to someone else.

Stress, I thought. Exhaustion. The brain misfires. Lack of sleep does this. Memory does this.

The scream came again.

Closer. Louder.

It carried rhythm now. A broken inhale. A jagged release. A wet, desperate edge that made my stomach lurch. I leaned forward and gripped the counter so hard my knuckles blanched. My pulse stuttered in my throat. My legs felt unsteady, as if the floor had shifted half an inch out of alignment.

I waited for it to crest and collapse.

It did not.

It fractured into sobbing gasps, then rose again with a deeper, more focused terror. There was no face attached to it. No body. Just the sound of someone young and cornered, someone whose fear had stretched so long it had worn thin.

I closed my eyes and held my breath.

The scream thinned.

I inhaled.

It surged.

I froze.

It did not move through the house. It moved with me. When I straightened, it rose. When I bent, it dipped. When my pulse accelerated, it trembled in sync.

It was not in the walls.

It was not under the floor.

It was inside the space my body occupied.

The realization did not arrive as a thought. It landed as certainty.

This was not something I was hearing.

This was something I was holding.

My knees buckled. I leaned forward until my forehead pressed against the cabinet door. The wood was cool. Solid. I clung to that temperature, to the grain beneath my skin, as if it could anchor me in place.

"Stop," I whispered, though I did not know who I was speaking to.

The scream faltered.

For a single breath, there was nothing.

Then it returned.

Clearer.

And closer than before.

The sound gathered itself.

What had been fractured and directionless began to align. The scream stopped breaking apart and held its shape. The air in my kitchen thickened, as if it had weight now, pressing against my skin. The edges of the cabinets softened. The light above the sink dulled further, not fading but narrowing, as though something closer had taken precedence.

I did not move.

The room did.

Heat closed in first. Not the mild warmth of summer or running water. This heat pressed from every side, humid and breath-stealing. The air tasted metallic. Sweat and iron and something older, something soaked into fabric and dried too slowly. Candle smoke clung low, heavy in the lungs.

The kitchen did not disappear. It receded. It became thin.

She was on the floor.

A girl. Younger than I had imagined. Her hair clung to her temples in dark ropes. Her skin shone slick and fever-bright. She lay on her back on wide wooden planks worn smooth by generations of feet. Her knees were drawn high. Her heels dug into the boards, scraping uselessly for leverage.

Hands surrounded her.

Too many to count without meaning to. They entered the edge of my vision without faces attached. One pressed her shoulder down. Another clamped around her wrist. Two more forced her knees apart. None of them touched her cheek. None brushed the hair from her eyes. They held her like a task.

She screamed again.

The sound ripped through my chest and landed low in my abdomen. A sharp, twisting pain bloomed inside me, foreign and immediate. My back arched without command. My breath shortened to shallow pulls. I gasped and felt my pulse stutter wildly against my throat.

This was not observation.

This was invasion.

She cried for her mother. The word tore loose in pieces, swallowed by the thickness of the room. Someone leaned close to her ear and told her to breathe. Another voice said push, firm and practiced, stripped of comfort. The girl shook her head violently, eyes wide and unfocused, searching for something that was not there.

She was not dying.

That was the horror.

She was enduring.

The pain rolled through her and through me in identical waves. My stomach cramped. My thighs tightened. I felt the effort in muscles I was not using. I could not tell where her body ended and mine began.

The lullaby moved beneath it all.

Low. Steady. Almost tender in tone, but not in intent. A woman's voice, roughened by repetition, carried syllables I did not recognize. The melody did not rise or fall with the girl's agony. It kept time. It marked the labor. It endured.

The rhythm settled into my ribs.

Details sharpened with impossible clarity.

This is when I saw the woman in the red dress again. The dress was thick and dark, sleeves rolled and damp at the cuffs. Her bare feet were dirty, nails rimmed in earth. Candlelight flickered against her cheekbone, catching the tremor in her jaw. She could not have been more than sixteen. Perhaps younger.

Her breathing fractured.

Push, someone said again.

The word struck like command, not encouragement.

The pressure built inside me until I cried out with her. The sound tore from my throat before I understood I was making it. My fingers curled hard enough that my nails bit skin. My vision blurred at the edges. The room lurched.

For one suspended second, the wooden floor and my kitchen tiles overlapped. Candle smoke mingled with dish soap. The sink water roared like breath dragged through clenched teeth.

Then it collapsed.

The heat vanished. The metallic taste receded. The air thinned back into something breathable. I was standing at my sink again, the faucet still running.

My legs buckled.

I caught the counter and held on. My chest heaved as if I had been running. Cold prickled across my skin. The scream was gone.

The lullaby lingered.

Not in the air.

In my bones.

It held for one final measure, soft and deliberate, then unraveled into silence.

I stood there shaking, every muscle aching as if I had labored through something my body had not chosen. My abdomen throbbed. My spine felt bruised. My throat burned from a cry I had not meant to give.

I knew things now.

Not names. Not dates. Not facts.

But I knew the shape of what had happened in that room. I knew the fear of it. The isolation. The inevitability.

The girl had not come to frighten me.

She had come because I was listening.

And the next time she called, I understood with terrible clarity that she would not be asking.

I did not sit down.

The idea of lowering myself into a chair felt like surrender. Stillness had weight now. If I let my body rest, whatever had passed through me might settle too deeply, might root itself in muscle and bone. So I moved. I shut off the water. The silence that followed pressed hard against my ears. I wiped my hands on the dish towel and crossed the kitchen quickly, deliberately, as if momentum itself could outrun what had just happened.

The journal lay open on the table beneath the window. Waiting.

I picked it up and flipped to a clean page. My hands trembled, but the pen felt solid between my fingers. Reliable. I pressed the tip down harder than necessary and began writing before my thoughts could soften the edges.

Late afternoon. House quiet beforehand. Sudden onset. Female voice. Young.

The letters came tight and precise, each stroke measured. I described the scream first. Its strain. Its location inside the room and inside my body. I wrote about the heat and the metallic air. The floorboards. The hands. I drew the shape of the room as I remembered it, dark lines marking the boards, small circles for candles. I sketched the outline of her red dress, the way it clung to her shoulders, the weight of it.

My breathing began to match the rhythm of the pen.

Lullaby present. Low. Repetitive. Not soothing. Endurance-based.

I underlined that twice. The pressure of the pen cut a faint groove into the page beneath.

This is how you stay safe.

You name it.

You measure it.

You reduce it.

My heart slowed. The ache in my abdomen dulled. Panic drained away in careful increments. The page accepted everything I gave it.

I kept going.

Estimated age sixteen. Possibly younger. Verbalization included calling for mother. Commands from surrounding individuals. Push. Breathe.

I framed it clinically. Detached. Documented my own physical response as if I were observing someone else. Abdominal pain. Muscular contraction. Shortness of breath. Dissociation likely.

The words steadied me.

When I finally paused, the house was quiet again. Not empty. Quiet. The refrigerator hummed faintly. The light above the sink glowed as it should. The world had resumed its proper outline.

That should have reassured me.

Instead, something cold slipped beneath the relief.

I looked down at the page.

It was orderly. Structured. Boxed neatly within margins. Evidence rather than experience. I felt a brief flicker of satisfaction at the containment.

Then I noticed the final line.

Under the last note, beneath the clinical language and the neat bullet points, another sentence sat in darker ink.

I did not recall writing it.

She was not alone.

The handwriting was mine.

The letters were heavier, pressed so hard they embossed the page below.

My breath thinned.

I flipped back through earlier entries. Dreams. Patterns. Notes I had written late at night and forgotten by morning. Every page bore the same tight script, the same need to anchor what would not hold still.

I turned back to the present page.

She was not alone.

The ink looked slightly wetter than the rest.

I had not written that.

The quiet in the house felt different now. Not cooperative. Observant.

I capped the pen carefully and set it aside. My fingers hovered over the page before lowering slowly. I closed the journal and pressed my palm flat against the cover as if sealing something inside.

Beneath my hand, I could feel the indentation of the words pushing back.

The silence that followed did not relax.

It held.

The room felt intact, yet tighter somehow, as if the walls had drawn in a fraction of an inch. I sat back in the chair and waited for my pulse to settle into something ordinary. It did not. It hovered just beneath my throat, alert and unwilling to drop its guard.

The girl had not asked me for anything.

The realization came clean and uninvited. She had not reached toward me. Had not pleaded. Had not searched my face. She had existed in her own terrible gravity, and I had been pulled into orbit.

Witness, not rescuer.

The distinction settled heavily in my chest. It meant I had not been chosen for comfort. I had been chosen for clarity.

I flipped back through the pages I had written, scanning for places where I might have imposed meaning. I found none. Every line was observation. Every detail restrained. I had been careful not to assume intention.

That did not calm me.

The lullaby returned.

Not fully. Just a thin strand of it, barely audible, slipping through the quiet like breath across glass. It did not echo from a corner or drift from the hallway. It threaded itself through the room, steady and patient.

The clock ticked.

For one second, the melody aligned perfectly with it.

My shoulders tightened. I held my breath.

The lullaby stopped.

The clock continued.

The air felt suddenly thinner.

I waited for the scream to follow. For the heat to rise. For the room to tilt again. Nothing came. The refrigerator hummed. The house remained upright and composed.

That was when the certainty settled in.

This was not an accident.

The vision had shape. Sequence. Detail too specific to dismiss. It had structure, like something rehearsed. It had intent, even if I did not yet understand whose.

It would happen again.

Not because I wanted it to. Not because I invited it. Because something had already crossed a threshold and found no resistance.

I closed the journal and rested my hand on the cover. The warmth from my palm lingered against the cardboard. I told myself I was prepared now. I had notes. Observations. A framework.

Understanding leads to control.

Control leads to safety.

The logic felt clean.

I clung to it.

The house did not respond.

It did not creak. It did not sigh. It did not hum the lullaby again. It did not offer reassurance or threat. It remained exactly as it was, walls steady, floors solid, quiet unbroken.

That steadiness felt rehearsed.

I turned off the light and stood there in the dark, listening to my own breathing expand and contract. The house held its silence with precision.

The door had not been opened for me.

It had been opened through me.

And somewhere beyond what I could see, something had already stepped across.

Chapter 9

I woke with a plan.

Plans created structure, and structure kept days from sliding sideways without warning. I lay still and took inventory before opening my eyes. Headache, mild. Dry mouth. A dull pressure behind my eyes from too little sleep. All reasonable. All explainable.

There was also a faint ache low in my abdomen.

I ignored that.

I sat up slowly and swung my legs over the side of the bed. The room remained steady. No distortion. No lingering heat. Just pale morning light pressing softly against the walls.

Lack of sleep, I told myself. Anyone deprived long enough knew the mind reached into places it should not. Add stress. The sheriff. The tape. The quiet being fractured. Adrenaline lingered longer than people admitted. It seeped into dreams. It colored waking moments that had not fully separated from night.

An episode.

I said it out loud as I dressed.

"An episode."

The word sounded clean in the air. Clinical. Contained.

I said it again, softer, as if repetition could fix its edges.

The house did not respond.

No scream. No lullaby. The floorboards creaked in their usual places.

The air felt cool and neutral. Morning light slid through the windows without distortion. The kind of light that belonged to running small errands.

I moved through the kitchen in measured steps and made coffee the way I always did. Two level scoops. Water filled to the line. The machine hissed and gurgled and behaved exactly as it should.

I carried the mug to the table but did not open the journal. Not yet. I watched the yard instead.

In daylight, the tape by the fence looked less aggressive. A strip of yellow marking a temporary inconvenience. The word settled easily in my mind.

Temporary.

Another useful word.

I took a sip. The coffee was bitter and hot. For a fraction of a second, I tasted metal. Then it was gone.

Stress plus exhaustion equals hallucination.

The equation felt solid when I repeated it. Sensible. Predictable. I nodded once, as if I had concluded a professional consultation with myself.

Outside, a bird landed on the fence. It stayed longer than usual, head tilted, watching the house. Then it lifted off and disappeared beyond the trees.

Confirmation, I thought.

The house offered nothing to contradict me. The clock ticked evenly. The refrigerator hummed. The air did not thicken.

I finished my coffee and rinsed the mug. Water ran clear over my fingers. My hands trembled slightly, but that could be caffeine. That could be anything.

I did not think about the pain that had seized my body the night before. I did not think about the way the lullaby had threaded itself through my breathing. I did not think about the certainty that had followed the vision, the sense that something had begun rather than ended.

Those were impressions.

Impressions could be dismantled.

I dried my hands and stood at the sink a moment longer than necessary, appreciating the absence of interruption. Logic had stepped in to do its job. To close doors that did not need to remain open.

For now, the house remained ordinary.

Behind me, the clock ticked once.

Then skipped.

Then resumed as if nothing had happened.

I leaned into routine the way some people leaned into prayer.

Coffee first. Same mug. Same measured grounds leveled flat with the back of a knife. I watched the clock as it brewed and poured at the exact minute I always did, as if time itself might slip if I did not keep my hand pressed firmly against it. I wiped the counter once for cleanliness and a second time for certainty. The surface shone beneath the light, obedient and reflective.

I held my breath until the reflection stopped wavering.

I cleaned the house in strict order. Sink before stove. Stove before counters. Counters before floor. I did not skip ahead. I did not improvise. Each task completed unlocked the next. That was the rule. Rules kept things contained.

A drop of water clung to the faucet after I dried it.

I wiped it away.

Another gathered in its place.

I wiped again, harder this time, until the metal squeaked beneath the cloth.

When I finished inside, I stepped onto the porch with my notebook and a sharpened pencil. The morning air felt thin and watchful. I mapped the work ahead down to the minute. Mulch along the east border. Weed the north bed. Trim along the west side. Anything that did not require stepping near the south fence.

I did not look at the tape.

I did not need to. I felt its presence the way you feel a bruise before touching it. A defined absence in the yard. I treated that section of ground as if it had been erased from the map. This was not avoidance. This was strategy.

The pencil moved faster as I wrote. My handwriting tightened into narrow lines and squared boxes. Each finished task earned a check mark. The small click of graphite against paper gave me a fleeting rush of satisfaction.

It faded almost immediately.

I added another task.

Then another.

I moved through the yard without pause. If I slowed, even slightly, my thoughts drifted toward the fence. So I did not slow. Hands busy. Mind occupied. Breath measured. The rhythm settled into my muscles and smoothed the edges of the morning until it felt almost manageable.

Almost safe.

I checked the clock again, not for time, but for proof. The second hand moved. Forward. Predictable. I shaved three minutes from one task and redistributed them elsewhere. The adjustment was unnecessary. The change itself was the point.

My phone buzzed in my pocket.

I ignored it.

Interruptions fractured structure. Structure was the only thing keeping the day upright.

The longer I stayed inside the routine, the more normal it felt. Relief depended on constant motion. My jaw tightened. My shoulders crept upward without permission. I scrubbed dirt from beneath my nails long after it had already come clean, skin reddening under the brush.

I lined the tools up before putting them away. Handles straight. Edges parallel. I adjusted one half an inch to the left, then another to match.

Control, I told myself. This is control.

But the word did not settle.

It trembled.

I finally stopped moving to stretch my back.

Just for a second.

The yard went quiet.

Not the ordinary quiet of morning. A pause. Clean and exact.

I felt it reach for me.

The second hand on the clock inside the house hesitated.

Then held.

I went back to the journal because it was there.

Because it waited in the exact spot where I had left it, angled slightly toward the window, light settling along its spine. The cover looked ordinary. Harmless. Patient.

I sat at the table and opened it. The pen balanced between my fingers, cool and familiar. For a brief second, a thought rose clean and sharp at the edge of my mind. I pressed the pen to the page before it could fully form.

Date. Time. Weather.

Those came easily. Safe details. Anchors.

I wrote about the morning in controlled, narrow lines. Sleep inadequate but improving. Routine adjustments increased. Idle time reduced. Effective. The words arranged themselves neatly, clinical, and detached.

When I reached the vision, my handwriting tightened.

The episode occurred while awake. Auditory disturbance followed by visual intrusion. Duration unknown. Physical response elevated but transient.

I paused.

My pen hovered over the page.

Screa—

I stopped.

I crossed the half-formed word out so hard the paper nearly tore.

I did not use the word scream.

I did not use the word girl.

I described the experience the way you describe a headache to a doctor who does not know your history. Neutral. Technical. Distant. I did not mention the heat. The hands. The way my body had arched without consent. I did not mention that the sound had felt less like noise and more like arrival.

The pen slowed when I reached the lullaby.

The blank space beneath the previous sentence widened, waiting.

My fingers tightened around the barrel. The tune pressed faintly at the edge of my awareness. Not loud. Not insistent. Present.

I could have written it all again.

I did not.

My hand cramped, a sharp, manageable pain that grounded me. I welcomed it. The ache was clean. Immediate. Easier to face than the melody threatening to rise.

Instead, I wrote: Secondary auditory pattern noted. Likely residual stress response.

The words filled the space, heavy and empty at once.

As the page grew crowded, I flipped back through earlier entries. The shift was obvious. The first pages had questions in the margins. Underlined doubts. Words written too quickly. These newer ones were narrower. More contained. The ink pressed harder into the paper, but the language pulled further away.

I was no longer trying to understand what had happened.

I was trying to box it in.

The realization arrived without drama. The journal had become a shield. I held it up between myself and anything that demanded more than observation.

I closed the book and pressed my palm flat against the cover. The texture steadied me. The weight of it felt reliable.

That steadiness frightened me.

I stood and placed the journal back on the table, aligning it carefully with the edge. Spine parallel. Corners squared.

It looked responsible there. Sensible. Documented.

I did not notice that I had stopped writing questions entirely.

I did not notice that the deepest indentations in the page were where I had nearly written something true.

The house remained quiet. It did not interrupt. It did not challenge the narrative I had constructed. It allowed the language to stand.

For now, documentation felt like listening.

As I stepped away from the table, the page beneath the one I had just filled bore a faint impression where my pen had pressed hardest.

The indentation curved into the beginning of a word I had refused to finish.

I was standing in the hallway with the journal tucked under my arm, trying to decide what to do next.

The house was still. Not empty. Not quiet in the way buildings are quiet. It felt paused, as if the air itself had drawn in and held. The hallway seemed narrower than usual, the light from the bedroom cutting a thin line across the floorboards. My bare feet pressed against the wood, cool and solid. Real.

Then the sound came.

Not the scream. Not the lullaby.

A breath.

Low. Measured. Close enough that the fine hairs along my arms lifted before I understood why. It did not echo. It did not travel down the hall. It seemed to exist beside me, almost against my ear, a careful intake and release as if someone were testing the air.

It lasted no more than a second.

It was enough.

My pulse jumped hard and fast. My fingers tightened around the spine of the journal until the cover bent slightly under my grip. I did not turn my head. I did not speak.

I knew what it was.

Not who. Not how. Not even where.

I knew it was the edge.

The place where if I stopped and let the silence deepen, something would take shape. The questions I had trimmed down into tidy lines would expand. The blank spaces in the journal would demand to be filled.

I could almost feel it forming.

Not now, I thought.

The words arrived quickly, polished and familiar. I told myself I was exhausted. That clarity required distance. That any serious reckoning demanded rest and steadiness and proper light. I told myself I would return to it when I was stronger.

Later.

The word settled over everything like a blanket. Later meant control. Later meant this moment was not in charge. Later meant I still had authority over when and how things unfolded.

I shifted my weight and took a step toward the bedroom.

The breath did not return.

The house did not correct me. It did not press. It did not insist. The silence lengthened, smooth and uninterrupted.

That felt like permission.

I set the journal on the nightstand without opening it. The cover landed with a soft thud against the wood, louder than it should have been. I sat on the edge of the bed and let the mattress dip beneath me. The familiar sag steadied me. I kicked off my shoes and lay back, staring at the ceiling where faint shadows gathered in the corners.

The moment passed.

Not dissolved.

Set aside.

I felt the weight of that choice settle into my chest, heavier than it had any right to be. I had done nothing wrong. I had not denied anything outright. I had simply postponed engagement.

That was reasonable.

The house remained quiet. No reprimand. No reminder. No sound of shifting boards or distant song. It allowed the narrative to stand.

As I reached over and turned off the light, darkness folded over the room in a clean sweep. I lay there, listening to my breathing.

It sounded too loud.

For a brief second, I wondered if it was the only breath in the room.

I closed my eyes and told myself sleep would restore balance.

The house did not argue.

It waited.

And this time, the waiting felt measured.

Chapter 10

I was standing at the stove with a pot heating, oil beginning to shimmer at the bottom, onions softening in the pan beside it. The smell rose slow and sweet, familiar enough to quiet the edges of my thoughts. The burner clicked steadily. Steam curled upward and faded into the ceiling light.

My hand hovered over the knob to lower the heat.

That was when the room shifted.

Not a spin. Not dizziness. The counters did not move. The walls did not sway. But something inside the space leaned a fraction of an inch to the left, and my body adjusted before I understood why. The air thickened. The rhythm broke.

Pain struck low and fast.

It tore through me without warning, sharp and deep, stealing the breath from my lungs. I folded forward instinctively, fingers digging into the edge of the counter hard enough to whiten at the knuckles. A sound escaped me that did not feel like mine.

Voices layered over it.

Not one. Several. Close enough that I could feel the shape of them. Urgent. Controlled. The tone of people accustomed to crisis. Words tangled over each other.

"Hold her."

"Keep her still."

"Breathe."

I squeezed my eyes shut.

It did not help.

The tile beneath my feet dissolved into rough wood. Not visually. Not cleanly. But in sensation. I felt splinters where there should have been grout. I smelled sweat thick in the air, smoke from candles burning too low, fabric that had been soaked and dried and soaked again. Something sour pressed at the back of my throat.

A hand brushed my arm.

Not contact exactly. Close enough that my skin recoiled as if touched.

"Breathe," someone said again.

Another voice spoke my name.

The sound of it scraped against me. Wrong shape. Wrong history. It landed in my chest like something misplaced.

Time slipped.

Not a blackout. Not a clean absence. More like a section of tape pulled loose and flapping wildly, catching and releasing in uneven bursts. When the world snapped back into alignment, the pot on the stove was boiling over. Foam hissed against the burner. The smell of scorched starch filled the room.

I lunged forward and twisted the knob off. The burner clicked down into silence. My heart pounded so hard I felt it in my jaw. Sweat slicked my spine beneath my shirt.

Under the ticking metal and cooling glass, the lullaby threaded itself through the room.

Not inside my head.

It moved with the house. Through the settling pipes. Along the refrigerator's low hum. Between the clock's mechanical tick. A few restrained notes, patient and steady, barely distinct from the architecture that carried them.

"No," I said.

The word thinned as soon as it left my mouth.

I grabbed the journal from the table and flipped it open, pen already between my fingers. The pages rustled louder than they should have. My hand trembled as I tried to write the time.

I stared at the clock. The numbers blurred, then snapped back into place. I wrote them down. They looked wrong. I crossed them out and wrote them again, harder this time. The ink tore slightly into the paper. My handwriting did not look like mine. The loops were too tight. The angles unfamiliar.

The pen slipped and dragged a dark line across the page.

Before I could steady myself, the pain returned.

Pressure clamped around my ribs. A cry split the air. Not from the stove. Not from the hall. From everywhere at once. The smell surged back, thicker now, crawling up my throat until I gagged. The journal slid from my grip. The pen clattered across the table and dropped to the floor.

I doubled over, arms wrapped around myself as if that could contain it. The room stretched at the edges. The light flattened. The ceiling seemed too high and too close at the same time.

There was no space this time to observe.

No clinical distance.

The voices overlapped in frantic commands. A scream broke into sobbing gasps. Someone said push. Someone else said again. The word mother fractured mid-syllable.

And then it cut off.

Mid-breath.

Mid-command.

Gone.

I was left gasping, body still braced for impact that had already passed. I sank into the chair, legs unsteady, hands empty.

The journal lay open in front of me, the ink still wet where I had pressed too hard.

The lullaby lingered beneath the quiet. Faint. Persistent. Not loud enough to isolate, not soft enough to ignore. It wove itself into the bones of the house as if it had always belonged there.

I pressed my palms over my ears.

It did not stop.

Seconds passed. Or minutes. Time no longer felt reliable.

The shift came slowly.

This was no longer something that happened and then allowed me to document it. It was not an event that waited politely for interpretation. It did not care about my structure, my methods, my need to frame and contain.

It was interrupting me.

Cutting through routine. Through logic. Through narrative.

I sat there breathing hard, the house close around me, and understood with a clarity that chilled more than the pain had.

Denial depends on timing.

And whatever this was had chosen to move first.

After the last vision, I stayed inside longer than I meant to. I sat at the kitchen table with my hands wrapped around a mug that had long since cooled, staring at the faint ring it left against the wood. The lullaby had faded, but something of it clung to me. Not sound. Pressure. A weight behind the ribs that did not ease when I shifted in my chair.

I told myself fresh air would help. Noise. Ordinary life moving at its usual pace.

I told myself I needed groceries.

The drive into town was steady and uneventful. Trees lined the road exactly as they had yesterday. Mailboxes leaned at familiar angles. The bend in the road came and went without incident. The sky did not darken. The pavement did not split open. Nothing announced that anything had changed.

That almost made it worse.

When I pulled into the gravel lot outside the general store, the building sat as it always had. White paint weathered but intact. A flag hanging slack near the door. A pickup already parked crooked near the entrance.

The bell over the door rang when I stepped inside.

It sounded sharper than usual.

Conversations did not stop outright. They thinned. A chair scraped lightly across the floor. The register beep cut short. Someone cleared their throat. The shift was subtle enough to deny, obvious enough to feel.

I took a basket and moved down the first aisle without looking at anyone directly. The store smelled like old wood and lemon cleaner, the sharp artificial scent barely masking something older underneath. I focused on simple things. Milk. Bread. Canned soup. Items that did not require decisions.

As I reached for a jar, voices drifted toward me.

"That place out past the bend," one woman said.

A pause.

"Yeah," another replied. "Ground's always been heavy there."

My hand stayed on the shelf a moment too long.

"Sheriff don't come out for nothing," the first voice added quietly.

I turned, careful not to make the motion abrupt. The two women near the cooler were looking at me now, their expressions composed into something that passed for polite interest. One of them gave a small smile that stopped short of her eyes.

"Morning, Clara," she said.

"Morning."

The word felt stiff in my mouth.

"Sheriff was out your way yesterday," she continued, tone light, conversational. "Everything all right?"

It sounded harmless. It was not.

"Yes," I said. "Just some old bones. Nothing serious."

Her eyebrows lifted slightly, just enough to register.

"Old ground holds on," the other woman said. "Doesn't let go easy."

Neither of them elaborated.

They did not need to.

I moved toward the counter with my basket, aware of the space behind me filling and shifting as I passed. The man ringing up my items avoided my eyes at first. Then he met them directly and held the look a fraction too long, as if measuring something.

"That all?" he asked.

"Yes."

The register drawer slid open with a mechanical snap that made me flinch harder than it should have.

Outside, the air felt thicker. A truck idled across the lot, engine vibrating low and steady. The driver watched me without pretense. When our eyes met, he nodded once.

It was not greeting.

It was acknowledgment.

I loaded the groceries into the back seat and closed the door with more force than necessary. As I drove away, the town unfolded in neat rows. Lawns trimmed. Curtains drawn back. Flags hanging motionless in the heat.

Everything looked the same.

But I could feel the difference in how I moved through it. The glances that followed. The conversations that would resume once I was out of earshot.

Nothing had been said outright. No accusation. No warning.

Just fragments.

That place. Heavy ground. Sheriff don't come for nothing.

By the time I reached the edge of town, my chest felt tight enough that I had to consciously draw in air. I had not realized I had been holding it.

This was no longer about bones.

The land had a name here. Not written. Not official. Spoken softly and passed between hands like something fragile and dangerous. Stories traveled faster than reports. Faster than explanations.

And whether I intended it or not, I was now part of that story.

I drove home with the radio off, the quiet pressing in from all sides.

What had begun in my kitchen had stepped beyond the fence.

And the town was not waiting to see if it was true.

It was waiting to see what it would cost.

By the time I got back, the house had already been noticed.

I felt it before I saw anything different. A tightening beneath the skin. A faint prickle along the back of my neck, as if something had shifted direction and settled on me. I turned into the drive and paused, engine idling, eyes scanning the road without knowing what I expected to find.

Nothing was out of place.

That was the problem.

A truck rolled past slower than necessary. The driver had his elbow propped in the open window, sunglasses catching the light. His head turned as he passed, gaze steady and unembarrassed. He did not wave. He did not pretend to be looking at the trees or the sky. He looked at the house.

As if reading it.

I shut off the engine and stepped out. Gravel crunched under my boots, too loud in the open air. The house stood solid and unchanged, but it no longer felt enclosed. The windows reflected the afternoon light in flat panes of brightness that looked almost watchful. The yard lay wide and unprotected, every inch of it visible from the road.

Someone had come closer.

Footprints marked the edge of the drive. Fresh. The gravel disturbed and pressed inward toward the yard before veering off. The tread was clear enough to see the pattern, a clean sole with a narrow heel. The tracks stopped just short of the tape near the south fence, hovered there, then turned and retreated.

Curious. Careful.

I carried the groceries inside and left them on the counter. I did not unpack them. I went straight to the window and stood there, watching the road through the glass. My reflection layered faintly over the yard. Ten minutes passed. Maybe less. Time felt thinner now.

Another car approached.

It slowed. Then stopped.

A woman I did not recognize stepped out. She closed the door quietly, as if noise might break something fragile. Her phone was already in her hand. She walked toward the fence with measured steps, eyes fixed on the tape.

She did not cross it.

She crouched near the boundary, leaning in just enough to peer beneath the line of yellow. Her head tilted slightly, studying the ground. I could not hear the shutter from where I stood, but I saw the motion of her thumb. Once. Twice. A pause. Then another.

She stood, glanced briefly at the house without really seeing it, and returned to her car. The engine started. She drove off without hesitation.

The moment she disappeared from view, the yard felt altered.

Not physically. But defined.

I stepped outside and walked the perimeter, my pace deliberate. The fence line pulled at my attention, not only because of the tape, but because it had become the center of gravity. The point where curiosity converged. The place the story now lived.

I tried to reclaim the afternoon. I put away the groceries. I made a list I did not need. Each task felt provisional, like it existed only until the next car slowed.

The house did not feel enclosed anymore.

It felt displayed.

Shadows shifted across the ceiling when vehicles passed. The low hum of the refrigerator seemed louder, exposed. When tires crunched on the road beyond the yard, my shoulders tightened automatically.

Standing in the kitchen, listening to another engine idle just a little too long outside, I understood what I had lost.

Invisibility.

The house had once blended into the background of other lives. It had been a place people passed without thought. Now it held narrative weight. It had been named, quietly, in other rooms. It had been pointed at. Photographed.

Interpreted.

A car door shut somewhere beyond the trees. I heard footsteps on gravel.

I did not move toward the window this time.

I stood very still, listening, aware of how easily a private life could become a public curiosity.

And knowing that once something is watched long enough, it rarely stays only a story.

I saw her through the front window while I was still pretending the afternoon could be salvaged.

She parked crooked, one tire angled too close to the ditch. The engine stayed running a moment longer than necessary. She sat behind the wheel, hands locked at ten and two, staring at the house like it might look back. Then she cut the ignition and stepped out slowly, smoothing her shirt.

I knew her by sight if not by name. That was how it worked here.

You did not need introductions to recognize someone.

I did not open the door right away.

She climbed the porch steps and knocked once. Waited. Knocked again. Not aggressive. Measured. The kind of knock that assumed it would be answered.

When I opened the door, she smiled with a softness that did not reach her eyes.

"I won't take long," she said, already leaning closer, lowering her voice before I had invited her to. "I just thought you should know."

I said nothing. The space between us tightened.

"My grandmother used to talk about this land," she continued. "The Wren place, she called it."

The word struck somewhere beneath my ribs. The hallway behind me seemed to narrow. For a second the porch light hummed louder than it should have.

"The Wren place?" I asked, keeping my voice even.

The air felt thinner.

"She said there was a girl," the woman went on, her tone softening into something that pretended to be sympathy. "Young. Didn't make it through childbirth. Middle of the nineteenth century, I think. No church burial. Family handled it quiet."

The boards beneath my feet felt unfamiliar. Too solid. I held onto the doorframe without meaning to.

"What was her name?" I heard myself ask.

She hesitated. Just a fraction. Enough to show the choice being made.

"Temperance," she said. "Temperance Wren."

The name moved through me slowly.

Tem-per-ance.

Each syllable settled into place with cold precision. I saw dark fabric pulled tight over a trembling body. Candlelight catching sweat. A face too young for the fear it held. I heard breathing that did not belong to me and yet moved in my chest.

"You probably didn't know," the woman added quickly. "I just figured with everything going on..."

She let the sentence trail off, generous enough to let me complete it myself.

"How old was she?" I asked.

"Sixteen," she said. "Maybe younger."

The number aligned too cleanly. No distortion. No uncertainty. Sixteen.

Behind her, a car slowed on the road, lingered, then moved on. I could feel the town listening even when it was not present.

"Well," she said, forcing a small laugh that fell flat between us. "People talk. You know how it is."

I did.

She stepped back first. I had not realized how close she had come. When she reached the drive, she turned once more toward the yard, as if confirming something for herself, then returned to her car and left.

I stood in the doorway long after the engine noise faded.

The late light stretched across the floor inside, reaching toward the hallway. The house felt open in a way it had not that morning. Not violated. Revealed.

Temperance.

The name echoed with the same rhythm as the lullaby. The same patient endurance.

This was no longer rumor brushing up against coincidence. The dates aligned. The age aligned. The vision had not been shapeless. It had been specific.

I could deny it. I could tell myself stories changed over time. That grief rearranged facts. That towns embroidered their past to make it more interesting than it had been.

But denial had weight now.

Silence would not quiet this. Silence would amplify it. Every step I refused to take would be taken for me by someone else, shaped into something I did not control.

I closed the door slowly and leaned my forehead against the wood. It felt cool. Steady. The house pressed in around me, not hostile, not protective. Expectant.

The option to wait had dissolved without ceremony.

Temperance Wren had a name.

And once something is named, it does not return easily to the dark.

Chapter 11

The world was bright before I understood where I was. My eyes stung. My mouth tasted stale and metallic. Something hard pressed against my spine. When I tried to shift, pain answered from my neck and shoulders, slow and resentful.

The porch boards were cold under my bare legs. Damp had seeped through the thin fabric of my shirt and into my skin. I felt it now, creeping upward, claiming me inch by inch. The railing dug into my back. The house loomed behind me, door closed, windows pale and unreadable in the early light.

The yard stretched out in front, flattened by dawn. Every shadow thin. Every corner exposed.

For a moment, I thought I was still inside it. Another intrusion. Another rearranged room stitched together by whatever had been taking liberties with my mind.

Then the cold settled in properly.

I was barefoot. My toes were numb, pressed against wood that still held the night's chill. When I pushed myself upright, my hands trembled. My muscles protested with the dull ache of someone who had been held in one position too long without consent.

I did not remember coming outside.

I reached for my phone. It lay beside me on the boards, screen dark. My fingers felt distant as I picked it up. The brightness flared when it lit, forcing me to squint.

The numbers took a second to settle.

6:12 a.m.

I stared at them without understanding.

The last thing I remembered was standing in the hallway. The journal under my arm. The decision to sleep. That was 3:04 a.m.

Three hours.

Gone.

No calls. No messages. No notifications that might suggest an interruption. Just the steady, indifferent record of time passing without me.

I waited for memory to rise and meet the gap. For some blurred fragment of movement or intention to float to the surface.

Nothing came.

There was no fog to push through. No dream residue clinging to the edges.

Just absence.

Clean. Complete.

That was when I saw the journal.

It lay open on the porch beside me, spine bent back, pages damp at the corners from the morning air. A pen rested neatly across the margin as if it had been placed there with care.

I knew I had not brought it outside.

The certainty hit before I allowed the thought to finish forming.

I reached for it slowly.

The paper felt cool and swollen from the moisture. I lifted the pen first. It left a faint imprint where it had pressed into the page.

Then I began to read.

The handwriting was mine. There was no arguing that. The same slant to the right. The same heavy downstrokes where my grip tightened. I could see where the ink had darkened at the edges of certain words.

The lines marched across the page in tight, deliberate script.

Confident.

Uninterrupted.

I did not write any of it.

Names appeared first. Dates. References to land records. Parcel numbers. A sketched outline in the margin caught my eye. Long sleeves. Dark fabric. A body bent forward under strain.

Below it, written twice in darker ink.

Temperance Wren.

My breath left me without warning.

I flipped the page. More notes. Connections drawn in clean lines between the past and the present. Arrows linking the south fence to burial practices. Observations about midwives. Quiet births. Quiet burials.

There were no hesitations in the writing. No qualifiers. No careful language.

Whoever had written this had not been afraid.

They had not been uncertain.

They had known exactly what they were doing.

I looked up at the house.

The door remained shut. The windows held the morning light without reflection. I tried to imagine myself stepping out into the dark. Sitting here. Writing for hours while the night passed unnoticed.

The image would not come.

Because there was nothing there to remember.

The yard remained motionless. No birds yet. No wind. Just the light climbing higher, revealing to me where I sat as if I had been placed there deliberately.

This was not a vision.

This was not an intrusion.

This was time taken.

I closed the journal and pressed it against my chest. The weight of it felt heavier than paper should. Proof of hours that had belonged to me and no longer did.

The cold seeped deeper into my skin.

For the first time since this began, I understood the shift.

It was no longer about what I saw.

It was about what I did when I was not the one in control.

I stayed on the porch longer than I meant to, not moving, letting the light climb higher around me. It felt like the quiet was waiting to see what I would do next. I took stock the way you do after a fall, slow and careful, bracing for the discovery of something broken.

There was dirt under my nails.

Not a surface smear. It was packed in deep, dark and stubborn, wedged into the crescents like I had clawed at something with intention. When I flexed my fingers, the skin around the cuticles pulled tight. My palms were scraped in thin, raw lines. The tenderness flared when I pressed my thumbs into the bruised spots.

My knees ached. My calves felt used. Not stiff from the cold. Worked. The soreness ran through me in a way that suggested repetition. Movement with purpose. The kind that comes from kneeling, standing, kneeling again.

I had not drifted out here in my sleep.

I stood slowly and tested my balance. The porch tilted for half a second, then steadied. My bare toes curled against the boards. I would not have chosen that. I hated being barefoot outside. Splinters. Rusted nails. Sharp things hidden in the shadows.

Risk.

Inside, the house felt sealed, as if it had held its breath through the night. I stepped in and locked the door behind me automatically. My hand froze on the knob.

I did not realize I had unlocked it.

The kitchen looked almost right.

A chair was angled slightly away from the table, not knocked over, not misplaced. Just moved. The sink was empty, but the dish towel that always lay folded across the divider hung limp and damp, wrinkled like it had been twisted in restless hands. My keys were not in the bowl by the door. They sat on the counter instead, aligned neatly beside the journal I had found on the porch.

I walked through the house slowly, cataloging shifts the way you inventory a scene. A lamp that I always left on overnight was turned off. A window cracked open an inch in the spare room, letting in a thread of morning air. The faint smell of earth lingering where it did not belong, subtle but persistent, woven into the air as if it had been invited.

Nothing broken. Nothing overturned. Nothing missing.

Nothing accidental.

I went back to the sink and turned on the water. It ran clear at first, then turned faintly brown as the dirt loosened and slipped away. I scrubbed harder than was necessary. The grime resisted. It clung beneath my nails as if it had decided to stay.

When my hands were finally clean, they did not look right. Too pink. Too exposed. As if something protective had been stripped away.

I dried them slowly.

That was when I heard it.

Not fully. Not boldly. Just the faintest suggestion at the edge of hearing. A few notes that carried weight without words. The lullaby slipped through the house and then withdrew, leaving a pressure behind, as if it had leaned in to confirm something and found what it was looking for.

I stood there, listening to the quiet that followed.

Sleepwalking came with confusion. With the shock of waking mid-motion. With bruises that bloomed without context and rooms that felt unfamiliar.

This felt different.

This felt arranged.

I picked up the journal again and turned the pages more carefully this time. The handwriting did not waver. The lines did not trail off. One thought moved cleanly into the next, building toward conclusions I would not have allowed myself in daylight.

Whoever had written this had been steady.

Focused.

Present.

My stomach tightened.

I had not lost time.

Time had been taken from me and used.

The distinction settled in with a cold clarity. Used implied intention. Direction. A goal.

I pressed my thumb into the page where the ink lay darkest, grounding myself in its physical reality. The indentation was deep enough to feel. The pressure had been deliberate.

Something had moved me through the night. Something had decided where I went, what I touched, and what I recorded.

I had not chosen any of it.

And the most terrifying part was not what had happened.

It was the quiet certainty that it had known exactly what it was doing.

"Visions," I said out loud. My voice sounded scraped thin. "Names. Missing time."

The word kitchen felt almost wrong. The room stood around me in its usual arrangement: cabinets square, clock steady, light flat against the floor. Nothing shifted. Nothing acknowledged me. That refusal to react made the air feel tighter.

The journal lay open in front of me. I braced my hands on either side of it and bent closer, following the lines with my finger as if they might rearrange themselves under scrutiny. I forced myself to read slowly this time. No skimming. No flinching.

First the dreams. No scattered fragments. Always the same strain in the body. The same pressure low in the spine. The same breath torn loose.

Then the lullaby. Not random. No intrusive noise. It threaded itself through sleep and waking both, steady and deliberate.

Then the names.

They had surfaced without hesitation. Written in my hand with a certainty I had not earned.

And now, the missing hours.

I exhaled slowly and felt something inside me click into place.

"This is a pattern," I said.

The words did not echo. They did not falter. They settled into the room like a stone dropped into water, heavy and final.

Patterns meant repetition. Repetition meant intention. Intention meant direction.

I turned back to the page where Temperance Wren was written across the margin in darker ink. My stomach tightened. Not fear. Not exactly. Resistance. The kind that rises when you stand too close to something you have trained yourself not to name.

Family.

I had kept that word sealed. Used it sparingly. Filed it away with legal documents and distant obligations. I had told myself I came here to escape it. To start clean. To lighten the weight on my shoulders.

That had been convenient.

The truth sat in front of me now, patient and unblinking. The house had not reached for a stranger. It had not chosen randomly. It had not waited this long for coincidence.

It had waited for blood.

The realization did not arrive with spectacle. It arrived like recognition. Like a face you have seen before, and only now understand.

I straightened and looked around the room with new attention. The table scarred with old cuts. The cabinets were older than they appeared at first glance. The floor worn thin in subtle paths where feet had crossed and crossed again. The house did not feel haunted.

It felt layered.

"I didn't imagine this," I said quietly. "I didn't make it up."

The house offered no reassurance. It did not need to.

I thought of the writing in the journal. The steadiness of it. The way the thoughts had moved forward without doubt or qualification. That certainty had not been forced. It had not been manic or fractured.

It had been familiar.

Something in me had known where to look.

That was what frightened me.

Not because it suggested something supernatural. Because it suggested something inherited. Something that had always been there, waiting for the right pressure to surface.

I pressed my palm flat against the table and felt its solid resistance beneath my skin. My breath slowed. My thoughts sharpened. Denial had been loud and frantic. This felt quieter. Heavier.

"I'm not losing my mind," I said. The statement held, but it carried a tremor at its edge. "I'm remembering."

The shift happened in that moment.

I was no longer bracing for interruption. No longer waiting to be overwhelmed. I was standing inside the pattern now, tracing it back through ink and bone and story.

Whatever had started this was not circling me from the outside.

It had been moving through my name long before I stepped into this house.

And it was no longer asking whether I was ready to see it.

I did not let the realization settle.

Stillness had become dangerous. If I sat with it too long, it would root itself deeper than I could manage. So I moved.

The hall closet door stuck for a second before giving way. I pulled down the boxes I had stacked there when I first moved in. Documents. Photos. Miscellaneous items. I had labeled them neatly, then shoved them into shadow. Order as postponement.

The cardboard scraped against the floor when I set them down. Dust lifted into the air, fine and dry, carrying the smell of paper that had been closed too long.

I opened the first box.

Envelopes breathed up at me. Deeds folded thin from repeated handling. Birth certificates written in careful ink. Death notices clipped from newspapers that had browned at the edges. I sorted without sentiment. Small piles formed on the floor around me. Dates. Names. Each one a marker. Each one a thread.

Wren.

The name surfaced again and again. On certificates. On margins. On brittle paper that felt one crease away from tearing.

I carried the stack to the table and opened my laptop. The screen lit my face in a pale wash. County records. Probate files. I typed my own name first. It felt necessary.

Results returned faster than I expected. Older than I expected.

My throat tightened as I scrolled.

Temperance Wren.

There she was again, not in ink I could blame on sleep or intrusion. Listed in a church ledger. Midwife. The entry stopped abruptly. No burial record attached. No marked date of death. Just a line where a line should have been followed by closure.

Absence, preserved officially.

I pulled another box toward me, heavier this time.

Photographs.

Stiff poses. Direct eyes. Women mostly. Hands folded in laps that looked built for work. Their expressions were not soft. They were composed. Steady.

I felt something shift in my chest as I studied them. The tilt of a chin. The set of a mouth. A resemblance that did not require imagination.

Not identical.

Aligned.

I checked the backs for notes. Some were labeled in tight script. Some left blank. I set the blank ones aside. The gaps felt deliberate.

I opened the journal to a clean page and wrote a heading.

FAMILY LINE.

Beneath it I began listing names. Arrows linked one to the next. Dates circled. Gaps marked. I was no longer documenting experience. I was constructing sequence.

This was not curiosity.

Curiosity wavered when things sharpened.

This was preparation.

The word did not frighten me. It steadied me.

The house remained quiet. Not withdrawn. Not approving. Present in the way it had always been present. Watching the table fill with proof.

At some point the sun shifted. The light moved across the surface and caught on the edges of photographs, on the metallic hinge of my laptop. Hours had passed. I noticed and did not mind.

This time I had chosen to stay.

My hand hovered over the small wooden box at the back of the closet. I had avoided it deliberately since moving in. It had belonged to my mother. I had told myself I would open it when I was ready.

I lifted the lid.

Letters, bound with string. The paper thinner than the others. Ink pressed deep enough to leave faint impressions on the pages beneath. Her handwriting was tight and controlled. Intentional.

Names appeared that I recognized. Others that did not belong to any story I had been told.

Temperance surfaced again, but not as rumor. As reference.

The past did not reach for me dramatically. It did not scream or demand.

It closed around my wrist with quiet certainty.

I did not pull away.

When I finally leaned back, the table was covered in lines and connections. Threads stretched from document to photograph to ledger entry. The gaps were still there, but they were shaped now. Defined.

There was no comfort in what I had assembled.

No neat resolution.

Only direction.

I closed the laptop slowly and looked around the kitchen. The sink. The chairs. The routines I had built to keep the days contained.

They were still present.

But they were no longer in front of me.

They were behind.

The moment I chose to dig with intention, something irreversible shifted. Whatever waited ahead carried history in its teeth and patience in its bones. Whatever safety I had known belonged to the version of me who had not looked.

I picked up the journal and added one final line beneath the web of names.

I am not stepping back.

The ink pressed hard enough to score the page.

The house did not protest.

It did not need to.

Its silence felt less like absence and more like recognition.

And that was how I knew the threshold was already behind me.

Chapter 12

I stood in the doorway longer than necessary, keys pressed into my palm hard enough to leave an imprint. I listened for the subtle tightening that had begun to pass for warning. For movement inside the walls. For the faint pressure that sometimes rose before something shifted.

Nothing came.

The rooms remained still. The table sat behind me layered with papers and arrows and names I had threaded together with deliberate hands. Temperance Wren rested at the center of it all, written once in ink and repeated endlessly in my thoughts.

I locked the door. The click carried cleanly through the frame, decisive and final.

The drive into town passed too quickly. The trees thinned. The road straightened. Air shifted from damp earth to exhaust and distant bread baking. I rolled the window down and let the wind cut across my face, trying to remember what it felt like to be anonymous. The name rode with me anyway.

Temperance.

I had not spoken it aloud since leaving the house, yet it pressed against the inside of my mouth as if waiting for permission.

I parked near the square and chose to walk. The bakery window reflected me back thinner than I recalled. The hardware store door creaked open for someone else and shut without a greeting. At the diner, a fork paused halfway to a mouth as I passed.

Not obvious.

Not friendly either.

The historical society sat at the edge of the square in a converted house trimmed in white paint that had been reapplied carefully over the years. The sign out front was neat, restrained. Curtains drawn halfway down the windows gave the impression of moderation. Enough visibility to seem open. Enough cover to control what was seen.

Inside, the air carried the scent of paper aging in confinement. Dust, paste, something faintly chemical. Preservation, deliberate and quiet. The floorboards gave a controlled creak under my steps.

A woman sat behind the desk beneath a framed photograph of the town from a century ago. Her smile arrived quickly, practiced.

"Good morning. What can I help you with?"

"I'm researching a property," I said. The words came steady. "And the family connected to it."

She nodded and reached for a clipboard. "Name?"

I hesitated just long enough to feel the weight of the pause.

"Wren," I said.

Her pen moved. "First name?"

"Temperance Wren."

The shift was subtle but immediate.

Her hand stilled. The smile did not vanish. It narrowed, edges tightening slightly as if drawn in by thread.

"That goes back a ways," she said.

"So I've found."

Her eyes flicked toward the shelving behind her, where labeled boxes lined the wall in careful rows. Orderly. Curated. A visible archive of what the town had chosen to remember.

"Records from that period can be incomplete," she said.

"I understand."

"Some names," she continued evenly, "carry more talk than documentation."

The boundary landed gently. Firm enough to hold.

"I'm not interested in talk," I said. "I'm interested in what exists."

She held my gaze for a moment longer than courtesy required, measuring something I could not see.

"There's what's written," she said. "And there's what people decided not to write down."

She returned a few minutes later.

She slid a thin folder across the desk.

It felt too light when I lifted it.

Inside were dates without context. A church ledger reference. No burial. No recorded death. Margins where something had once been and then removed.

Temperance Wren reduced to implication.

"Is there more?" I asked.

Her fingers rested lightly on the edge of the counter, still and composed.

"This is what is publicly available."

Publicly.

The word lingered.

I thanked her and stepped back into daylight, the sun brighter than it had been a moment earlier. The folder rested against my side, thin as denial.

As I crossed the square, I felt it then.

Not the house.

The town.

A quiet awareness that the question had been asked and registered. That a file had been opened not just on paper but in memory.

I glanced once over my shoulder.

The curtains in the historical society window had shifted slightly.

Just enough to suggest someone was still watching.

By the time I reached the end of the block, I could feel it settling into place.

Not hostility. Not yet. Attention.

It moved quietly, the way a draft moves through a room without disturbing anything obvious. A truck idled a second longer than necessary. A conversation thinned as I passed. A window curtain shifted and then stilled.

Coincidences, individually.

Together, they formed a pattern.

I turned into the hardware store because I needed twine and because I refused to drive straight home. Going home now felt like retreat. The bell over the door rang once, high and loud, then let the sound fall flat against the walls.

The clerk looked up from behind the counter. Recognition flickered across his face before settling into something neutral and practiced.

"Morning," he said.

"Morning."

The store smelled of oil and old wood. The shelves stood tight and orderly. No one else was inside. My footsteps sounded louder than they should have as I moved toward the back and found the spool I needed.

When I brought it forward, he rang it up without comment. The register drawer slid open and shut with a muted clack. I handed him my card.

He turned it once in his fingers.

Then again.

Checked the name. Checked the expiration. Let his eyes lift to meet mine and linger a second too long.

"You moved into that Wren place, right?" he asked, tone light enough to pass as curiosity.

"Yes."

He nodded slowly. "Old house."

"That seems to be the consensus."

He ran the card through the machine, then rested his forearms on the counter.

"Ground like that remembers things," he said.

It was not a joke. It was not advice. It was a statement.

"Does it," I replied.

His mouth tightened, almost a smile, almost not. He slid the receipt toward me.

"That'll do," he said.

Outside, the light struck sharper than before. The square appeared unchanged. Trucks parked in familiar angles. The courthouse steps held the same two men talking quietly. Flags lifted and fell in the mild breeze.

Nothing overt.

Yet the space felt narrower, as if the town had shifted its weight and I had stepped into the place it preferred remain empty.

I reached my car and paused with my hand on the door. For a moment I considered turning back, asking one more question, testing the boundary.

I did not.

I got in and shut the door. The lock clicked into place. The sound felt louder than the bell had been.

Inside the car, the air was stale and contained. I sat with the engine off, the thin folder resting on my lap. My reflection stared back at me from the dark windshield, thinner around the eyes, sharper at the edges.

Before today, I had been a newcomer with a project. A woman

renovating an old house on quiet land.

Now I carried a name the town recognized.

Temperance had been a midwife. She had stood in rooms at the worst possible hour and placed her hands where no one else would. She had borne witness to pain that belonged to other people. The town had learned to live with her, and perhaps to fear what followed her.

Now they were watching to see what followed me.

I started the engine and pulled away from the square. In the rearview mirror, the courthouse shrank. The hardware store receded. The historical society windows reflected sunlight in a way that made them unreadable.

The sense of being observed did not fade as I left town. It sharpened.

By the time I turned onto the road home, I understood something with quiet certainty.

Whatever Temperance had done, she had crossed a line this place never forgot.

And the moment I spoke her name aloud in daylight, so had I.

Chapter 13

Ellie called just after dusk, when the house was settling into its evening quiet and I was trying to convince myself that quiet meant safety.

The phone vibrated against the counter, skidding slightly before going still. I watched it ring twice before picking it up. Long enough to feel deliberate. Not long enough to invite questions.

"Hey," I said.

"Hey yourself." Her voice came through warm but measured, like she was stepping carefully across something fragile. "You alive out there?"

I glanced at the kitchen table. The folder from town lay half-hidden beneath a stack of mail. My coffee had gone cold beside it, untouched.

"Last I checked," I said. "What's up?"

There was a pause. Small. Precise. Ellie never wasted silence.

"I was just thinking about you," she said. "You've been quiet."

"I've been busy."

"With what?"

"House stuff. Yard stuff. Sheriff stuff." I gave a short laugh that sounded rehearsed even to me. "Nothing exciting."

Another pause. Longer now.

"You sound tired," she said.

"I didn't sleep much."

"Yeah," she replied softly. "That tracks."

I shifted the phone to my other hand and leaned against the counter. My legs ached in ways that felt earned and unexplained at the same time. Ellie did not rush to fill the space. She let the silence settle between us until it began to feel intentional.

"I'm fine, Ellie."

"I didn't say you weren't."

There it was. The tone. The one she used years ago when my life had fractured quietly and I insisted it had not. She was using it again.

"You're doing that thing," she said.

"What thing?"

"The thing where you turn everything into logistics so no one can touch it."

I let out a faint breath that might have been a laugh. "I like logistics."

"You like hiding inside them."

The words slid under my skin more cleanly than I expected. I pushed away from the counter and walked to the window. The yard beyond the glass had gone dark, the fence a thin line separating order from whatever waited beyond it. My reflection hovered in the pane, pale and slightly distorted.

"It's been a weird week," I said. "That's all. Anyone would be off their game."

Ellie exhaled quietly. Not impatience. Restraint.

"Clara," she said, using my name with care, "I know stress. This isn't just that."

"You don't live here."

"No," she said. "But I know you."

I crossed my arms, pressing my hands against my ribs as if that might steady something loose inside me.

"I've got it handled," I said. "Really."

"Handled how?"

"I'm dealing with it."

"You're deflecting," she said. Her voice remained gentle, but the edge was there. "You're exhausted. You're avoiding questions. And you're acting like this is an inconvenience instead of something that's actually affecting you."

The house creaked softly behind me, a small settling sound that felt almost timed.

I did not turn around.

Ellie's voice softened further. "I'm not trying to scare you. I just don't want you doing this by yourself."

"I'm not alone," I said.

The words left my mouth before I examined them.

There was a pause on the line. Heavier now.

"You are," she said gently. "You always are when you say that."

I watched my reflection again. For a moment, it did not quite match my posture. The darkness outside pressed closer to the glass.

"I appreciate the check-in," I said carefully. "I really do."

"I know you do," she said. "Just don't disappear on me, okay?"

"I won't."

The promise came out too fast. Too smooth. Like something practiced.

On the other end of the line, Ellie hesitated, as if she could hear the difference.

Behind me, the house settled again, quiet and attentive, as though it had been listening to both sides of the conversation.

Ellie did not let the conversation end where I tried to leave it. I heard the shift in her breathing, the way she settled in as if she had pulled up a chair instead of standing near the exit.

"Okay," she said. "Let's stop dancing."

"I'm not dancing."

"You always say that right before you step away."

My grip tightened around the phone. The kitchen light hummed faintly overhead. I reached up and switched it off. The room fell into shadow, leaving only the stove clock glowing green and a thin strip of dusk at the window. The sudden quiet felt intentional.

"I just don't want to make a big thing out of nothing," I said.

"That's not what you're doing," Ellie replied. "You're making a small thing out of something that's already big."

I leaned my hip against the counter and stared into the dark. The folder on the table caught a slice of fading light. Without thinking, I turned it face down, hiding the name beneath it.

"You've been alone a long time," she said. Her voice held no judgment. Only fact. "Longer than you admit."

"I like being alone."

"I know. You're good at it. That's the problem."

Something tightened low in my chest. I opened my mouth to argue and felt the words dissolve before they formed. Ellie waited. She always waited. She let silence do the work.

"You didn't call me when the sheriff came," she said.

"It wasn't necessary."

"You didn't call me after."

"I didn't want to worry you."

A quiet exhale. "You didn't want to be told to slow down."

"That's not fair."

"It's accurate."

The word settled heavily between us. Outside, something shifted in the yard. A small sound. A brush of movement.

"You're digging into your family now," she continued. "Into the land. Into things people avoid for a reason. That isn't just research, Clara. That's pressure."

"I can handle pressure."

"I know you can," she said. "You shouldn't have to."

Heat flared up my neck. "I didn't ask for this."

"No," she said softly. "But you walked into it."

The words landed cleanly. Not loud. Not dramatic. Just true enough to hurt.

She did not press harder. She rarely had to.

"Listen to me," she said. "You cannot do this alone."

There it was. The sentence I had been skirting since the phone began to ring. I stared down at the tile floor and noticed a faint crack running from one corner to the other. I had never seen it before.

"I'm not helpless," I said.

"I didn't say you were."

"I'm not falling apart."

"I didn't say that either."

Another pause. Then, quieter, "I'm saying there are things you do not get to manage the way you manage everything else."

I rubbed my thumb along the edge of the phone, feeling the slight ridge in the plastic.

"You're talking like I'm in danger."

"I'm talking like you're pretending this is a project," she said. "You cannot organize your way through it."

I almost laughed. It rose up sharp and brittle and then died in my throat.

Ellie shifted again, her voice lowering in a way that felt deliberate. "You know what my grandmother used to say about old places?"

I did not answer.

"Some roots do not let go," she said. "You do not get to tidy them up and pretend they were never there."

The word roots seemed to press into the room itself. The house gave a faint settling creak, the sound moving through the walls like a response.

"I'm not pretending," I said.

"You are," she said gently. "And you're very convincing."

I closed my eyes. The dark behind my lids felt deeper than it should have.

"I hear you," I said.

"I know you do," she replied. "I just do not think you are listening yet."

We ended the call a few minutes later. When the line went dead, I kept the phone against my ear, nodding once as if she could still see me.

The house was silent. Not relieved. Not restless. Just waiting.

"I have this under control," I said into the dim kitchen.

The stove clock ticked over to the next minute.

From somewhere deeper in the house, something shifted.

I lowered the phone and set it on the table. The wood made a dull sound when it met the glass screen. I did not sit down. Sitting would have meant settling into something. Instead, I stood with my arms folded tight across my chest and stared at the place where Ellie's voice had existed only seconds earlier.

Ellie had been unsettled. I could hear it in the careful space she put between her last words and the hang-up. She had not believed me. She had wanted to stay on longer. To press. To peel something back and hold it up to the light.

I had not let her.

That was fine, I told myself. Necessary.

I replayed the conversation, isolating the moments where I sounded steady. Where my tone did not waver. Where I had turned her concerns into logistics and come out composed. I held onto those parts and let the rest blur at the edges.

My jaw ached. I had not realized how tightly I had been holding it.

I moved through the house turning off lights as I went. The living room went dark first, then the hallway, then the kitchen overhead.

Each switch clicked softly. Each room folded into shadow without protest. The quiet gathered behind me, smooth and complete, like it had been waiting for me to choose it.

No questions. No interruption.

The floor stayed solid under my feet. The walls did not shift. The air did not thicken. Everything behaved.

At the window, I paused and looked out over the yard. Night had settled fully now. The fence cut its familiar line through the dark, precise and dependable. Beyond it, the ground was unreadable. That felt right. Things were easier when they stayed where I put them.

People complicated things. They asked for explanations. They carried concern like it was a solution. Ellie meant well. I did not doubt that. Caring did not make her correct.

I picked up the folder from the table. For a moment I considered leaving it there, visible, proof that I was not avoiding anything. Instead I slid it into the drawer with the other paperwork I preferred not to see.

The wood stuck slightly before closing. I pressed harder. The drawer shut with a firm, contained thud.

I did not lock it. I did not need to. I knew where it was.

The phone buzzed in my hand. The vibration sounded too loud in the darkened room. A text. Probably Ellie. I turned the screen over before it could light up and set it face down again.

I would read it later.

Later was safe.

The hallway felt narrower as I walked toward the bedroom. Shadows leaned closer along the walls. The air carried a faint coolness that did not match the thermostat. I noticed it and dismissed it. Old houses shifted at night. Wood contracted. Space changed shape.

In the bedroom, I sat on the edge of the bed and listened. The house breathed around me in low, patient tones. No lullaby. No voices. No borrowed pain.

Just quiet.

I lay back and stared at the ceiling. The darkness pressed close but did not threaten. It offered relief. No one asking me to share the weight. No one questioning my version of events. No one insisting I needed help.

I told myself this was safety.

I told myself isolation was a choice.

Somewhere deeper in the house, a board settled with a soft, satisfied sound.

Chapter 14

I was not looking for anything new. That was the truth of it. I was sorting, the way I always did when my thoughts grew too loud. Boxes pulled down from the closet. Contents spread across the floor in clean, manageable rows. Keep. Toss. File. The system worked because it did not ask questions. It did not linger on implication.

The cardboard scraped against the hardwood as I shifted the last box closer. House Papers. I labeled it in thick black marker, pressing hard enough to leave an indentation on the other side. Deed copies. Tax statements. Appliance warranties for things long gone. I opened it because finishing a job meant finishing it all the way.

The journal was at the bottom.

Not tucked away. Not wrapped in anything protective. Just lying there, pressed flat beneath a stack of yellowed documents that smelled faintly of dust and old ink. The leather was dark and worn smooth in places where hands had held it often. Not cracked. Not neglected. Used.

My chest tightened before I touched it.

That reaction meant nothing, I told myself. Objects did not carry weight unless you gave it to them. That had been a rule I lived by for years. Still, my fingers hovered above the cover, and I became acutely aware of my pulse. Not racing. Focused. Deliberate.

When I lifted it, the response was immediate. A sharp, inward jolt that began in my palms and traveled up my arms. Not pain. Recognition. The kind that does not explain itself.

The leather was warmer than it should have been after sitting under paper in a dark closet. My thumbs brushed over a faint indentation on the cover, as if a name had once been pressed there and worn away over time. I had the sudden, irrational sense that I knew what that missing name was.

I knelt there longer than I meant to, the box forgotten, the floor biting cold through my jeans. The room felt smaller with the journal in my hands. Not crowded. Focused. Like everything else had taken a step back.

"This wasn't here before," I said aloud.

The words sounded insufficient.

I opened it.

The handwriting crowded the pages in tight, controlled lines. No wasted space. Ink faded to brown in places, darker in others where the pen had pressed harder. Margins filled with symbols that should have been foreign and were not. My eyes skimmed without reading, catching fragments that landed too quickly.

A date I recognized.

A name written twice.

A phrase underlined three times as if emphasis could anchor it in the world.

My breathing slowed instead of quickened. That frightened me more than panic would have.

I flipped further. The paper was uneven at the edges, cut by hand. There were faint stains along one corner. Ink, I told myself. Age. Nothing more.

The certainty did not hold.

I closed the journal and pressed my palm flat against the cover. The leather yielded slightly, familiar in a way that scraped against the back of my mind. A flicker of memory rose and dissolved before I could grasp it. A room with candlelight. A table scarred by use. My hand moving in the same deliberate slant.

I looked back into the box.

Everything else remained exactly as it should. Receipts. Envelopes. Official copies with embossed seals. Order preserved.

The journal did not belong among them.

It had not been misplaced.

I stood and carried it to the table with a care I had not planned. Light from the window caught the edges of the pages, revealing the slight ripple of paper that had absorbed more than time. I told myself that was imagination.

I believed it for several seconds.

Then I pulled out a chair and sat.

This was not curiosity. It was not accident. It was not luck.

It was a move.

And the game had already begun without me.

I opened the journal expecting words to meet me halfway. Dates. Names. Something fixed enough to grip. That was how this usually worked. You began with a foothold and worked outward.

There was no foothold.

The first page stared back at me with a script so tight and disciplined it felt severe. Every letter was placed with deliberate pressure. The lines ran straight without guides, as if the margins lived inside the writer's bones. The shapes of the words were familiar, but the spellings bent just enough to fracture recognition. A vowel missing. A consonant doubled where it should not be. Meaning hovered, then withdrew.

I leaned closer, tracing one line with my finger without touching it.

The ink had sunk deep into the page. I could see faint impressions beneath the surface, grooves left by a steady hand that did not tremble. The page had memory. I did not.

I scanned for anchors. A date. A surname. Anything that would let me orient myself.

Nothing yielded.

Heat climbed into my face before I could stop it. I did not like not understanding. Paper was supposed to be honest. It accepted what you gave it and stayed still afterward. It did not resist.

This did.

I turned the page with more force than necessary. Then another. The same hand continued throughout, unwavering. Some passages stretched across the paper in long, unbroken blocks. Others broke into short lines, indented and numbered as if they were procedures. Instructions. The structure was deliberate even when the meaning remained sealed.

In the margins, symbols repeated.

Curved lines intersected by straight ones. Small marks grouped in threes. A shape like a closed eye pressed hard enough to scar the paper beneath. I ran my thumb lightly across one indentation and felt the ridge where the pen had carved itself into the page.

These were not decorative. They were emphatic. Ritualistic in their consistency.

Something in me stirred. Not fear. Engagement.

The tension in my shoulders eased. My breathing slowed. This I understood. A problem that refused to be simple was still a problem. And problems could be solved.

"Okay," I said quietly. "You're not going to make this easy."

I retrieved a notebook and placed it beside the leather-bound one. I copied a line carefully, matching the slant, the spacing, the deliberate pressure. The act steadied me. Pen on paper. Repetition. Control regained in small increments.

As I worked, patterns began to surface. Certain symbols clustered near repeated words. Some phrases ended the same way again and again. Other sections grew heavier, the handwriting darker, spacing uneven as if emotion had pressed through discipline.

I did not know what it meant yet. But I was close enough to feel the structure beneath it.

Time slipped without announcement. The light at the window shifted, stretching longer across the table. I did not notice when the room cooled. My focus narrowed to the page in front of me.

This was not fear. It was pursuit.

I flipped back to the beginning and started again, slower. The dialect had rules. I could sense them hovering just beyond articulation. The symbols were too consistent to be arbitrary. They marked emphasis, transition, warning. I began grouping them, sketching them into my own notebook, assigning provisional meanings.

Confidence settled in. Not recklessness. Competence.

I smiled despite myself.

Whatever this journal was, record or warning or confession, it had structure. Structure meant logic. Logic meant progress.

I ignored the passages where the handwriting pressed harder, where the symbols crowded too close together. I told myself those were emotional deviations. Noise. I focused instead on the lists. The repeated endings. The procedural tone.

Survival was not the problem here.

Understanding was.

And understanding was something I had always believed I could extract, piece by piece, if I stayed patient long enough.

The journal lay open beneath my hands, silent and unyielding.

I mistook that silence for permission.

The recognition came quietly.

No flash of insight. No triumphant clarity. Just a tightening behind my eyes and the faint sensation that the air had shifted closer, as if something had stepped within arm's reach without making a sound.

I was copying symbols when it happened. Slow work. Careful curves. I drew the same shape again, this time paired with a mark I had already written twice on the previous page. My pen hovered above the paper.

I had seen this before.

Not here. Not on any page.

The shape lived somewhere else. In the dark space behind sleep. In the half-remembered memory of the cellar walls, damp and breathing. In the edges of dreams I had woken from with my jaw clenched and my heart pounding hard enough to bruise my ribs.

A thin line intersected by a crescent. Three small marks grouped beneath it.

My pulse skipped.

I turned back through the leather journal and found it again. Then again. Always near the same clusters of words. Always pressed harder than the surrounding script, the ink sunk deeper as if the hand that wrote it had meant to carve rather than record.

My mouth went dry.

I copied the symbol again. Then once more. I lined them up side by side and compared the angles, the pressure, the spacing.

They matched.

"That's you," I said under my breath.

I did not know whether I meant the symbol or the part of me that recognized it.

The words on the page still refused me. I could not translate a single full sentence with certainty. The language bent away each time I tried to fix it in place. But the symbols were different. They did not reach for logic. They reached lower.

I flipped to a blank page and began sketching the cellar from memory. The rough outline of the walls. The narrow stair. The place in the corner where the air always felt wrong, heavy and waiting. My hand hesitated before marking the first symbol.

Then I placed it.

Another near the base of the stairs. One along the far wall. Not perfect. Not measured. But close enough.

They aligned.

The realization struck low in my body, a tightening that was not quite fear and not quite relief. I leaned back and stared at the page, at the way the marks fell into place as if I had always known where they belonged.

This was not understanding.

This was familiarity.

My pen moved faster after that. Pages filled with clusters and groupings. Three marks together shifted meaning from two. Certain shapes appeared only at the beginning of passages, others only at the end. Boundaries. Transitions.

Warnings.

Instructions.

The house remained still around me. No lullaby. No movement in the walls. Only the scratch of my pen and the steady weight of the journal beneath my hands. My breathing synchronized with the rhythm of copying, curve after curve, line after line.

I felt chosen.

Not in any grand or holy sense. In a narrow, practical way. These marks made sense to me because they had already been inside me. The dreams had not been random. The cellar had not been coincidence. The journal was not a relic waiting to be decoded.

It was a mirror.

The word carried a flicker of wonder. It also carried dread, settling low and patient beneath my ribs.

I traced one of the symbols lightly on the inside of my wrist, just to test the shape against skin. The curve fit too easily. My breath caught before I could stop it.

I leaned back and studied the pages I had filled. I had proof now. Evidence of connection. Something structured. Something solid enough to build on.

I told myself that meant safety.

I told myself recognition was the same thing as mastery.

The language itself remained closed, but meaning continued to seep through the margins, through repetition, through pressure. Not into my thoughts.

Into me.

I closed the journal carefully and rested my palm on the cover. The leather felt warmer than before. The last symbol I had copied lingered behind my eyes, as clear as if it had been branded there.

I had won something. I could feel the shift.

I did not yet understand what had shifted back.

By the time the light outside thinned to evening, I was convinced I had done something useful.

The sky beyond the window had faded from gold to ash without my noticing. I had been bent over the table for hours, shoulders tight, fingers stained faintly with ink. The journal no longer felt like an intrusion. It felt like work.

Pages bristled with notes in the margins, my handwriting layered over the original script in firm, assertive strokes. I had numbers now. Categories. Repetition tracked and labeled. Symbols circled, grouped, assigned provisional functions. Not translations, exactly. Functions were safer. Functions implied mechanics.

I built a system.

Index cards for recurring marks. A separate notebook for structural patterns. Dates extracted and aligned against town records. I drew arrows between names. Marked clusters. Cross-referenced margins. The pieces did not fit cleanly, but they fit well enough to suggest direction.

Progress lived in the gaps.

The passages that resisted me were easy to identify. The handwriting cramped. The spacing uneven. Ink pressed hard enough to scar the page beneath. Emotion leaked through structure in those sections. Urgency. Something close to confession.

I skimmed them.

I told myself they were unreliable data points. Noise in the signal. I marked them with a faint pencil line and moved on.

Later was a flexible word.

The lullaby notation appeared twice in the journal, reduced to a handful of repeating symbols near the spine. I traced them carefully, then copied them into my notebook and labeled the page Recurring Motif. The act of naming it steadied me.

Music could be mapped. Rhythm could be broken down into pattern and count. There was nothing mystical about repetition. There was only structure waiting to be diagrammed.

For a brief second, as I finished copying the marks, I thought I heard a faint echo of the melody in my own breathing. I paused, listened, and then dismissed it. Air moving through lungs could sound like anything if you listened too hard.

"Okay," I said quietly. "I see how this works."

The words settled comfortably in the room.

The journal was no longer a threat. It was a manual written in a difficult hand. Difficult did not mean unknowable. Rules were rules. Rules could be learned.

I turned to a clean page at the front of my notebook and wrote, in careful block letters: WORKING HYPOTHESES.

The pen hovered for a moment.

I did not write about fear.

I did not write about pain.

I did not write about the girl.

My hand almost formed the word before I stopped it. The ink left the faintest mark on the page where I had hesitated. I angled the notebook slightly so the indentation would not catch my eye and continued.

Framework first. Meaning later.

I stacked the papers neatly when I was done. Aligned the edges. Squared the corners. Closed the journal and placed it on top of the pile, centered and contained. The leather cover lay flat beneath my palm, calm and compliant.

The quiet in the house deepened around me, but it did not feel oppressive. It felt earned. The kind of silence that followed order restored.

I carried the notes to the shelf by the desk and set them within easy reach for tomorrow. Not hidden. Not avoided. Available.

Control returned in stages. Subtle. Convincing.

I moved through the house turning off lights. The floorboards answered under my weight the way they always had. The air remained even and undisturbed. No shift in pressure. No lullaby. No warning.

At the bedroom door, I paused and looked back toward the table.

The journal waited where I had left it.

I felt no pull. No urgency. Only readiness.

I had the beginnings of a map now.

I told myself that meant I knew where I was.

The house did not correct me.

It let me keep the rules I had written.

It let me believe the game had boundaries.

And while I slept, certain that the system would hold, the journal lay open by a fraction of an inch, the page I had marked for later no longer where I had left it.

Chapter 15

I was rinsing a mug at the sink, watching steam rise and dissolve into the morning air, when the phone buzzed against the counter. The sound was ordinary. Familiar. I glanced at the screen and felt a brief, foolish relief.

Ellie.

Ellie meant normal. Ellie meant continuity. Ellie meant a world that had edges and stayed where it was put.

I answered with damp fingers. "Hey."

"Hey," she said. Her voice carried warmth, but there was something under it. "I just wanted to make sure you were okay after last night."

I turned the water off.

The sudden quiet felt too clean.

"After what?" I asked.

There was a pause. Not careful. Not measured. The kind that happens when someone realizes the script has changed.

"Our talk," she said slowly. "You sounded better by the end of it. I figured you might still be sleeping, but—"

"We didn't talk last night. We talked yesterday morning."

The words left my mouth easily. Too easily.

Another silence, longer this time.

"Yes, we did," Ellie said. "Around nine. Maybe a little after."

I leaned my hip against the counter, pressing into it as if the wood could anchor me. "Ellie, I would remember that."

"You called me," she said. The warmth had thinned now. "You said you didn't want to be alone with your thoughts. You joked about the house finally teaching you manners."

My throat tightened.

"I didn't," I started, then stopped. The denial felt brittle. "What did I say?"

She shifted on the other end. I could hear fabric move. A chair creak.

"Nothing alarming," she said carefully. "Just specific."

"Specific how?"

"You asked if I remembered my grandmother's stories," she said. "About the midwife. You said you'd found something that explained the singing."

"Singing," I repeated.

"Yes." A small hesitation. "You laughed when you said it. Not scared. More like you'd solved a puzzle."

I closed my eyes. The kitchen seemed to tilt slightly, not physically, but in distance. The counter under my hand felt less solid.

"I don't remember any of this," I said.

"That's not funny."

"I'm not joking."

Silence again, but heavier now. I pictured Ellie at her kitchen table, brow furrowed, waiting for me to correct myself.

"You sounded tired," she said. "But clear. You told me not to worry. You said you'd write everything down in the morning."

My eyes opened and drifted to the table.

The journal sat exactly where I had left it. Closed. Centered. My notes stacked neatly beneath it. There was no new entry. No rushed handwriting. No evidence of a late-night call.

"What time did we hang up?" I asked.

"A little before ten," she said. "I remember because the news came on right after."

My phone felt heavier in my hand. I opened the call log and scrolled. There it was.

Outgoing call. 9:43 p.m. Duration: twelve minutes.

The numbers sat there, indifferent. Unmistakable.

For a moment, I thought I might have misread them. I blinked and looked again.

Still there.

"Clara?" Ellie's voice felt far away now. "Are you there?"

"I'm here."

"You don't sound okay."

"I'm just surprised," I said, and heard how thin it sounded. "I must've been more tired than I realized."

Ellie did not answer right away.

"You asked me not to come over," she said at last. "You said you needed to do this part yourself."

My stomach dropped.

"Did I say why?"

"No."

The mug slipped out of my hand and knocked against the side of the sink. I barely registered the splash of water against my wrist.

"Ellie," I said carefully, choosing each word as if it might move under my feet, "if I start saying things that don't line up—"

She cut me off. "Clara, this isn't about lining up. This is about you losing time."

The word stayed between us.

Losing.

I thought of the porch. The dirt under my nails. The hours that had vanished. Now this.

"I'll call you back," I said.

"Clara—"

"I need a minute."

I ended the call before she could say anything else.

The kitchen returned in fragments. The hum of the refrigerator. The faint tick of the clock. Light falling through the window onto the table.

The journal waited where I had left it, closed and orderly.

I had not imagined the call.

I had not misunderstood.

I had been awake. I had spoken. I had chosen words. I had told her not to come.

I looked at the leather cover and felt something shift.

It was not just that I was losing time.

It was that something else was using it.

I sat at the table and began the inventory.

It felt less like reviewing a night and more like counting valuables after a break-in. I folded my hands once to steady them, then reached for the phone.

Battery at sixty percent. No missed calls. One outgoing call to Ellie.

I tapped the entry and held my thumb there, waiting for some correction. A glitch. A delay. A second line to appear and contradict the first.

Nothing moved.

The call remained, indifferent and precise.

I checked messages next. Nothing sent. Nothing received. The screen looked scrubbed clean, as if the night had known better than to leave fingerprints.

I scrolled backward through the day.

Morning texts. Casual and ordinary. A grocery receipt emailed at eleven. A weather alert at three warning of wind that never came. A reminder about trash pickup. The small, steady markers of a day behaving properly.

The gap sat between them like something cut out with careful hands.

Everything else lined up too neatly around it.

I opened the photos app. No accidental pictures. No dark frames from a pocket. No blurred shots of floorboards or ceilings. Just the deliberate images I had taken earlier in the week. Fence angles. Soil patterns. Notes disguised as pictures.

Evidence of planning.

Evidence of control.

I set the phone down and rubbed my hands together. They felt colder than the room.

The house remained still. No creaks. No settling wood. No sympathetic noises to explain anything away.

"Okay," I said. My voice sounded sharp against the quiet. "Let's do this properly."

I stood and walked through the house room by room.

I did not rush. Rushing invited error.

Front door. Locked. I tested the handle twice. Windows. Latched. Glass cool beneath my fingertips. The living room lamp unplugged the way I always left it overnight. The couch cushions held their shape. The rug lay flat without a wrinkle.

The shoes by the door were lined up exactly as I had placed them, toes parallel, heels even.

There was no evidence of interruption.

The air smelled faintly of soap and old wood. Nothing else.

The house offered no memory.

Back at the table, I reached for the journal.

The leather cover settled under my palm with familiar weight. This was supposed to be the anchor. The record. The place where the gaps ended.

I flipped to the most recent entry.

The handwriting was mine. Neat. Measured. Dated correctly. I recognized the phrasing, the cautious distance in the language. Notes about symbols. Cross-references. A summary I remembered writing with deliberate restraint.

I turned the page.

Blank.

I turned another.

Blank.

The paper lay clean and unmarked, pale against the darker ink that came before it. I flipped again, slower now, as if speed might change what I saw.

Nothing.

The gap was exact. From early evening to this morning. No stray marks. No half-formed sentences. No impressions from heavy pen pressure bleeding through.

I ran my fingertips across the surface, searching for grooves. Ghost lines. Anything.

There were none.

"I didn't write," I said quietly.

The words did not feel like relief.

I closed the journal and pressed my palm flat against the cover. The leather felt cool, not warm. Not responsive.

I tried to replay the night.

Dinner. The scrape of a fork against a plate. Water running in the sink. The last stretch of light fading across the fence outside the window.

Then nothing.

Not a blur. Not a haze.

A cut.

The memory did not fade. It stopped.

Whatever came next had not belonged to me.

I scanned the room again, hunting for betrayal. A chair pulled slightly too far from the table. A glass left near the sink. A misplaced key. Anything to suggest movement, intention, choice.

There was nothing.

My routines had failed. My records had ended precisely where I would have needed them most.

The systems I trusted had not protected me.

They had simply stopped.

A slow weight settled in my chest, not panic, but recognition.

This was not forgetfulness. Not exhaustion. Not stress.

Something had moved through my life cleanly enough to leave no mess.

Something had acted in my place.

And it had not needed my permission.

The house remained still around me.

It did not deny it.

It did not confirm it.

It did not have to.

The proof was already in my hands.

Ellie called back an hour later.

I let the phone vibrate across the table. It moved in small, restless bursts, the screen lighting up and dimming again, over and over, like something trying to get my attention without daring to shout.

I watched it for three rings before picking it up.

My hand felt steady. That steadiness felt rehearsed.

"Hey," I said.

"Hey," she replied.

Her voice had changed. Not louder. Not sharper. Controlled. The kind of careful tone people use when they are choosing each word in advance.

"I didn't want to leave it like that," she said.

"I know."

There was traffic behind her. A passing engine. A car door closing somewhere nearby. Real life moving forward. I pictured her outside, walking, not sitting still.

"You scared me," she said. "This morning."

"I didn't mean to."

"I know," she said again, softer. "That's not what I mean."

I pulled out the chair and sat. The legs scraped loudly against the floor. I did not correct the sound. I let it stay.

"Can you tell me what you remember from last night?" she asked.

I closed my eyes, not because it would help, but because it felt necessary.

"Dinner," I said. "Dishes. The light fading. After that, nothing."

"Nothing at all?"

"No."

Silence expanded between us. It did not feel empty. It felt evaluative.

"You sounded different," she said.

My fingers tightened around the phone.

"Different how?"

"Focused," she replied. "Like you'd already decided something."

"Decided what?"

She hesitated long enough for me to feel it.

"You said you were done pretending it was just history."

My chest constricted. The words slid into place too easily, like they had been waiting for me to hear them.

"That doesn't sound like me," I said.

"It sounded exactly like you," she answered. "Just without the part where you hedge."

I opened my eyes and looked at the journal on the table. Closed. Harmless. Exactly where I had left it.

"What else did I say?" I asked.

"You asked if people confuse silence for peace," she said slowly. "You said the house didn't want quiet. It wanted attention."

The air in the room shifted. Not physically. Internally.

Those words were wrong.

Worse than wrong. They felt familiar in a place memory could not reach.

"That's not something I would say," I told her.

Ellie did not rush to correct me. She did not rush at all.

"You also told me not to tell anyone we talked," she said. "You said it would complicate things."

My throat tightened.

"Did I sound scared?" I asked.

"No," she said. "You sounded convinced."

The distance between who I thought I was and who she described opened slowly, like a crack spreading across glass.

"You don't think I'm lying," I said.

"I think you believe what you're saying right now," she replied. "I just don't know which version of you I was talking to last night."

The kitchen felt smaller. The ceiling lower. I pressed my fingers into my thigh, grounding myself in pressure and bone and skin.

"Ellie, I would never keep something like this from you on purpose."

"I know," she said. "That's why this bothers me."

The line stayed open. I could hear her breathing now, steady and controlled. I imagined her standing still wherever she was, no longer pacing.

"I need you to tell me something," she said. "Are you okay being alone right now?"

The question landed harder than any accusation.

It did not ask about safety. It asked about reality.

"I'm fine," I answered.

"That's not what I asked."

The correction was gentle. It cut anyway.

I opened my mouth to insist. The words formed, familiar and

automatic.

I stopped.

The truth hovered just beyond reach, shapeless and unwelcome.

"I don't know," I said.

Ellie exhaled slowly. Not relief. Not frustration. Acceptance of a problem she could not see.

"Okay," she said. "Then listen to me. If you lose time again, real time, not misplacing your keys, you call me immediately. You do not decide whether it's important. You do not write it down first. You call."

"I can handle this," I said too quickly.

"I'm not questioning your strength," she replied. "I'm questioning how much of this you're actually present for."

I looked around the room. The table. The chair. The journal. Everything exactly where it should be.

"I hear you," I said.

She waited a beat.

"I'm not going anywhere," she said. "But I need you to stop pretending this is contained."

"I'm not pretending."

"You are," she said gently. "And it's starting to feel like you're choosing it."

The call ended a few minutes later. No raised voices. No resolution. Just a quiet disconnection.

I set the phone down and remained seated, staring at the dark surface of the table.

Usually, after a hard conversation, there was relief. A sense of something settled.

There was none.

Instead, something colder moved in. Not panic. Not guilt.

Recognition.

Trust does not collapse all at once. It thins. It stretches. It begins to separate at the edges.

I could feel it widening between Ellie and me.

Worse, I could feel it widening inside me.

Chapter 16

I told myself I was fine. That all I needed was proof. Something measurable. Something that did not depend on memory or conversation or the shifting space between words.

My eyes moved to the cellar door before I consciously chose the direction.

It stood at the end of the hall, plain and square, as it always had. Nothing about it invited attention. Nothing about it warned me away. The stillness around it felt neutral.

That neutrality felt deliberate.

If the house kept answers anywhere, they would not be upstairs among windows and daylight. They would be below, where things were placed with purpose and left undisturbed.

I picked up the flashlight. My hand did not hesitate.

The cellar door opened without complaint.

The hinges gave no protest. No drag. No resistance in the frame. The wood shifted inward as though it had been waiting for the pressure of my hand.

That almost irritated me.

The steps creaked in the same familiar rhythm as always. I counted them automatically. Eight. The air cooled as I descended, dry and faintly metallic, carrying the scent of old boards and dust that never fully settled. Nothing rushed toward me. Nothing retreated.

I clicked on the flashlight.

The cellar looked exactly as it had the last time I stood here.

Storage shelves. A workbench. Exposed beams. A ceiling low enough to keep you aware of it.

Harmless.

The beam cut a narrow path through suspended dust, each particle drifting lazily in the light. At the bottom of the stairs, I planted my feet and waited.

Not searching yet. Just observing. Taking inventory.

This was not a wandering. Not a blackout. Not confusion. I had chosen this descent.

I started with the far wall.

I did not touch it. Not yet. I let my eyes move slowly along the boards, the way I would scan a ledger or a data sheet, noting repetition, variance, structure. I kept my breathing even.

The boards were old. Some darker, some lighter. A few bowed outward slightly. Others sat flush. Nails driven deep, their heads dulled to soft gray by years of air and oxidation.

At first glance, it was random.

Age disguised intention well.

I stepped closer.

The flashlight moved deliberately. One vertical seam. Then the next. I measured distance with my eyes before taking the tape measure from my pocket.

The metal hook clicked lightly against the wood.

I recorded the first measurement. Moved two boards over. Measured again.

The spacing was inconsistent.

But not careless.

I measured a third section. Then a fourth. The irregularity repeated. Not symmetrical. Not decorative. Repeated.

My pulse stayed steady.

That was the difference.

Before, I would have felt watched. Before, I would have felt the room leaning inward.

Now I felt focused. Narrowed. Contained.

I stepped back until my shoulders brushed the opposite wall. The contact grounded me. Cold wood against fabric.

From that distance, the pattern shifted.

It did not form a shape. It did not resolve into symbols. But the spacing grouped itself in ways that resisted randomness. Clusters. Gaps. Clusters again.

The wall held structure.

I felt something tighten in my chest. Not fear. Not excitement.

Recognition.

I flipped open my notebook and sketched what I saw. Straight lines. Measured intervals. Empty spaces marked carefully. There was nothing artistic about it. Just record. Just proof that I was not imagining the repetition.

The cellar remained silent.

No shifting air. No distant lullaby. No pressure at the back of my skull.

The house did not interfere.

It let me work.

Dust clung to my palms. A smear of graphite marked the side of my hand. I wiped it absently against my jeans and looked back at the wall.

"This isn't nothing," I said aloud.

The words sounded small in the enclosed space.

For the first time in days, I did not feel like I was chasing something that wanted to stay hidden. I felt like I was approaching a system that expected to be understood.

Slowly. Carefully. On its terms.

I turned back to the wall and measured again.

When I reached the final section, I paused.

The spacing shifted there.

Not dramatically. Just enough.

As if the pattern had adjusted to accommodate me standing where I was.

I worked the wall in sections, slow and methodical, the way I would approach a problem that punished impatience.

Left to right. Top to bottom. No shortcuts.

The flashlight beam moved in clean, controlled lines. It did not waver, even when my wrist began to ache. Dust drifted lazily through the light, briefly visible before disappearing again into the dim.

The boards were old, but not neglected. They carried the wear of years without the collapse of care. No water stains. No rot. No splits deep enough to suggest structural failure. Whatever had been done here had been maintained.

What unsettled me was the spacing.

The gaps between boards were not uniform, but they were not accidental either. Some boards leaned closer together. Others stood slightly apart. The variation was subtle enough to ignore at first glance. Subtle enough to pass for age.

I ran my fingers along the nail heads.

The metal was cool and faintly rough beneath my skin. They were not spaced in straight, efficient lines as you would expect from someone working quickly. Some nails stood alone. Others gathered in twos and threes. Small clusters punctuating the wood.

Intent does not fade the way surfaces do.

I stepped back.

Then farther.

My shoulders brushed the opposite wall again. The contact steadied me. I began counting without moving my lips. Gaps. Nails. Gaps again.

My pulse fell into rhythm with the numbers. I counted twice. Then a third time.

The numbers refused randomness.

My chest tightened, not in fear, but in recognition beginning to lock into place.

I had seen this rhythm before.

Not here. Not consciously. But it existed somewhere just behind my eyes, like a pattern I had nearly remembered in a dream.

I flipped open my notebook and turned to the pages where I had copied the journal symbols. The uneven spacing. The clusters of marks. The repetitions that had resisted translation.

I held the notebook up beside the wall.

Then lowered it.

Then raised it again.

The spacing aligned.

Not perfectly. Not mathematically. But closely enough that my fingers began to tremble when I tried to still them. The same pauses. The same groupings. The same refusal of clean symmetry.

This was not decoration.

This was not structural necessity.

This was language.

I moved along the wall more quickly now, not rushing, but following the pull of recognition. The pattern continued. It slipped behind the shelving, disappeared beneath a support beam, then resurfaced near the corner. It did not cover the entire cellar. Only this section. Only enough to matter.

I crouched and marked fresh measurements in my notebook. Sketched the nail clusters. Counted intervals again. Each notation felt heavier than the last, not because it frightened me, but because it stripped away doubt.

The dreams. The symbols. The pull toward this place.

They were not separate incidents stitched together by exhaustion. They were components of the same structure.

I pressed my palm flat against the wall.

The wood was cool and solid. Ordinary in every way. It did not hum. It did not shift. It did not acknowledge me.

Beneath that plain surface, though, was a decision. Someone had placed these boards with intention. Someone had embedded spacing that could be read. Someone had assumed that the right eyes would eventually stand here and see what others had missed.

I swallowed.

This was not belief.

This was evidence.

I stepped back once more and let my eyes take in the entire section.

The cellar remained silent. No sound rose to meet the realization. No pressure pushed against my ribs.

The quiet felt cooperative.

My gaze drifted past the measured section to the adjoining wall.

The spacing changed there.

Not abruptly.

Gradually.

As if the pattern did not end.

As if it turned the corner and continued behind me.

I did not trust the moment to stand on its own.

Certainty, I had learned, preferred witnesses. Left alone, it could soften. Blur at the edges. Rearrange itself into something easier to dismiss.

I took photographs.

Three angles. Then three more.

Before each shot, I braced my elbows against my ribs to steady the slight tremor in my hands. The flashlight beam cut a pale stripe across the boards, catching the nail heads where they clustered in uneven groups. I zoomed in until the metal filled the screen. Pulled back until the full stretch of wall reasserted its quiet geometry.

I photographed the notebook beside it. Measurements clearly visible. The sketched intervals. The mirrored spacing.

Not because I doubted what I was seeing.

Because this house had a way of rearranging things when you were not looking.

I stepped back from the wall and called Ellie.

She answered on the second ring.

"Hey," she said. "You okay?"

"I need you to listen," I replied. My voice sounded level. Too level. Like I had practiced the cadence in advance. "I'm in the cellar. I found something."

There was a pause. Not skepticism.

Attention.

"What kind of something?" she asked.

I described the wall. The spacing. The nail clusters. The rhythm that only revealed itself when you stopped searching for damage and started searching for intention. I used words like measurement and repetition. I avoided words like ritual. I avoided anything that would let her categorize it too quickly.

Ellie did not interrupt once.

When I finished, she said, "You're sure."

"Yes."

It was not defensive. It was not fragile.

It was fact.

I heard her shift on her end. Paper rustled. A chair creaked softly.

"Send me the pictures," she said.

I did.

While the images transferred, I stood still and listened.

The cellar offered nothing in response. No settling boards. No altered air. The house did not react to being documented. It did not bristle at explanation. It did not push back.

The lack of resistance pressed harder than any sound would have.

Ellie came back on the line.

"That's not random," she said quietly. "Someone did that."

"Yes."

"And you're saying it matches what you've been seeing. The journal. The symbols."

"Yes."

Silence again.

"I believe you," she said.

The words did not soothe.

They settled.

Belief meant this was no longer mine alone. It meant the pattern had crossed the boundary of my perception and entered the world outside my head. It meant I could not dismiss it later without dismissing her too.

"I don't know what it means yet," I said. "I'm not claiming I understand it."

"But you found it," she replied.

We ended the call soon after. There was nothing left to say that would not dilute the clarity of it.

I stood alone in the cellar again, phone warm in my palm, notebook pressed against my side. The wall remained unchanged. The pattern held its quiet logic. Patient. Exact.

I was not imagining this.

That was the victory.

Small. Verifiable.

And victories, I was beginning to understand, did not pass unnoticed.

They shifted balance.

The house remained silent.

Not approval.
Not warning.
Recognition.

Chapter 17

I went back to the cellar with tools instead of questions.

That felt like the difference.

The notebook lay open on the workbench, its pages held flat beneath a wrench. Measurements. Sketches. The neat proof I had already earned. I did not look at it again. I did not need to. The wall had already indicated where I should stand. My body returned to the same section without hesitation, the place my eyes had drifted toward even when I tried to pretend they were not.

I set the flashlight on the floor and angled it upward. The low beam distorted the boards, throwing long shadows that exaggerated every gap and nail head. The pattern did not dissolve under scrutiny. It sharpened.

I pressed my palm against the wood first.

Not searching for anything supernatural. Just pressure. Resistance. Feedback.

The board was cool and dry beneath my skin. I tapped it lightly with my knuckles. The sound came back dull and contained. No hollow echo. No obvious weakness.

I slid the flat end of the pry bar into the seam and leaned my weight into it.

Nothing.

The metal bit into old wood with a faint scrape, but the board did not yield. I adjusted my grip and pressed again. The bar groaned softly, a low complaint that traveled through my hands into my wrists. The board flexed a fraction of an inch and stopped.

That was not age.

That was resistance.

I knelt and examined the nails more closely.

Iron. Thick shafts. Square heads dulled to a matte gray but still firm in their grip. Each one had been driven deep, deeper than necessary for simple reinforcement. The spacing was uneven but deliberate. Whoever placed them here had not been careless.

They had been thorough.

A tightness gathered in my chest. Not fear. Not yet.

Intent.

I told myself I could stop. That documenting this much was enough. That evidence did not require escalation.

The thought rang hollow as soon as it formed.

I had already crossed that line the moment I came down here with tools instead of doubt.

I repositioned the pry bar and pulled harder.

The wood cracked sharply as one nail shifted within its hold. The sound snapped through the cellar, louder than it should have been. I froze, breath suspended, listening for response.

The house gave me nothing.

No shifting air. No pressure behind my eyes. No distant lullaby.

Only silence.

I pulled again.

The nail squealed as it tore free, rust dust falling in a fine reddish line to the floor. The board lifted by an inch. Then two. Darkness showed behind it.

Not shadow.

Space.

My hands trembled now. I did not try to steady them.

I set the pry bar aside and worked the board loose with my fingers, splinters grazing my skin as I pried it from the remaining nails. The wood scraped along iron as it came free, a long dragging sound that seemed to linger in the air even after it ended.

When the board finally gave, I stumbled back half a step.

I stood there holding it, heart hammering against my ribs, staring at what I had uncovered.

The wall behind it was not open.

It was layered.

More boards. Packed tighter. Nails driven deeper and closer together than before. The spacing here was compressed, almost urgent. Reinforced from within.

This was not simple reinforcement.

This was containment.

I leaned the removed board against the opposite wall and stepped back, breath shallow, pulse loud in my ears.

Whatever lay beyond this section had not been hidden out of neglect.

It had been shut away.

And by pulling that first board free, I had not discovered something.

I had announced myself.

The moment the board came free, the cellar changed its mind about me.

Nothing dramatic happened. No crash. No rush of air. The bulb overhead did not flicker. The change arrived quietly, the way a room does when someone steps inside and chooses not to announce themselves.

The air thickened.

I felt it in my lungs first. Breathing required a little more effort, as if the space had narrowed without physically shifting. Sound seemed to settle lower, closer to the floor. Even the faint hum of the house above dulled.

The opening behind the board looked darker than the rest of the cellar. Not shadowed. Not simply unlit.

Absorbed.

I angled the flashlight toward it. The beam struck the surface and flattened, as though the light had lost direction. It slid across the boards without catching properly, refusing to reflect the way it had moments before.

I stepped closer.

The second wall was not unfinished in any casual sense. It was deliberate.

Vertical boards ran tight against one another, closer than the first layer, their seams almost invisible. Iron nails held them in place, driven deeper and closer together than necessary. The heads had been struck repeatedly, the metal slightly mushroomed from force.

Between the nails, small objects had been worked into the wood.

At first I saw only shape. Pale against dark grain.

Then detail.

A fragment of bone, smoothed by handling. Not large. Not dramatic. The curve of something once functional. It had been pressed flat against the board and pinned in place by iron.

A length of knotted string, stiff with age, darkened to a dull brown. The knots were precise. Intentional.

A loop of rusted metal twisted into a crude circle and hammered partly into the seam.

Not decoration.

Placement.

I did not touch them.

I did not need to.

The meaning arrived without translation.

This was not storage.

This was not reinforcement.

This was a seal.

The pressure in my chest deepened. Not panic. Not yet. Something heavier. Recognition of design.

Whoever built this had not been hiding debris or covering damage. They had not been careless or rushed. The layering was patient. Bone and iron and wood working together toward one end.

Containment.

I stepped back too quickly and nearly lost my footing. The cellar felt narrower now, the ceiling pressing closer to the crown of my head. The corners seemed sharper. The silence pressed in with intention.

I waited for the lullaby.

Waited for the house to acknowledge the breach.

It did not.

The quiet held.

That silence felt earned.

I crouched again and studied the nails more closely. Each one bore multiple strike marks. No wasted motion. No hesitation. This had taken time. Someone had believed in this wall enough to build it twice.

Believed that whatever lay beyond did not need to be destroyed.

Only restrained.

I raised the flashlight and traced the seams downward.

There were gaps between the boards, narrow but real. Slivers of darkness that did not stop where the cellar floor met the wall. The space behind dropped further than it should have. The beam caught nothing solid within the first few feet. It vanished into depth.

The house was deeper than it appeared.

My throat tightened.

The question shifted.

It was no longer what had been sealed away.

It was why it had been allowed to remain.

This was not a frantic barrier. It was a calculated one. Bone and iron embedded with purpose. Not to erase. Not to deny.

To wait.

I stood in the dim light, dust settling around my boots, and understood something else with equal clarity.

The seal had not been built to protect people from what was inside.

It had been built to protect what was inside from being disturbed.

And I had already disturbed it.

I pulled the next board free and felt the house answer.

Not with sound. Not with violence.

With pressure.

The temperature dropped fast enough that my breath snagged halfway in. Cold pressed against my skin in a thin, surgical layer. The air did not rush. It constricted. The cellar felt narrower, compressed in a way that had nothing to do with the actual walls. I felt it in my ribs first, then in my throat.

My head swam.

Not dizziness.

Weight.

A dense throb built behind my eyes, carrying impressions that did not belong to me. Fingers digging into fabric. Breath breaking into ragged pulls. A pulse of effort that felt remembered rather than imagined. I staggered and caught myself against the wall, splinters grazing my palm.

The lullaby surfaced.

Not drifting. Not distant.

It rose directly into me.

The melody threaded through my chest and throat, humming low and persistent. It was not loud. It did not need to be. It carried a rhythm meant to endure, not to comfort. A cadence that did not ask whether I wanted to hear it.

I clenched my teeth and forced air through my nose. My hands trembled. I noted the tremor the way I had noted nail spacing and measurements. Data. Reaction. Nothing more.

Observation as survival.

I wiped my palms against my jeans, picked up the pry bar, and leaned into the next board.

This one resisted more than the first.

The nails groaned as the metal pressed against them. My arms burned with effort. Sweat broke along my spine despite the cold. The lullaby tightened in response, its rhythm aligning with the strain in my muscles. Pull. Hold. Pull again.

This was not punishment.

The realization arrived clean.

If the house wanted me gone, it could have done more than this. A misstep on the stairs. A beam shifting at the wrong moment. A darkness that swallowed the light entirely.

Instead, it pressed.

Measured.

The pressure increased in increments, careful and deliberate. The throb behind my eyes sharpened just enough to unsettle without overwhelming. Pain without injury. Fear without collapse.

Resistance.

I pulled harder.

One nail tore free with a sharp cry that rang too long in the enclosed space. The sound vibrated through my skull. The lullaby surged, brushing along my jaw and teeth like something testing bone.

For a moment, I considered stopping.

Not out of terror.

Out of exhaustion.

The thought was simple. Set the tools down. Step back. Let the wall remain intact. Let the pressure recede on its own.

The idea did not feel entirely like mine.

I leaned into the pry bar again and wrenched the board loose.

The cold spiked. The pressure swelled, then steadied. The lullaby did not retreat, but it did not escalate either. It hovered at the edge of thought, patient and watchful.

The removed board clattered to the floor at my feet.

I stood there breathing hard, heart hammering, hands shaking openly now. I did not attempt to disguise it. I did not pretend this was easy.

This was the boundary.

Not one designed to stop me outright.

One meant to make me choose.

To weigh curiosity against discomfort. Resolve against pressure.

The house was not trying to hurt me.

It was trying to wear me down.

I wiped my face with the back of my hand and lifted the flashlight again. The beam swept across the exposed wall, revealing more iron. More bone. More deliberate layering waiting beneath the surface.

My pulse began to slow.

Not because the threat had passed.

Because I had decided not to retreat.

I stepped closer to the wall once more, the lullaby vibrating low and persistent in my chest.

If the house was measuring me, it would have to account for this.

I did not stop.

The last board came away heavier than the others.

Not in weight. My arms were already burning from effort. The heaviness lived somewhere else. In consequence. In the quiet certainty settling into my chest that whatever lay beyond this point could not be restored to its former shape.

The pry bar bit deep. I leaned into it.

The nails screamed as they tore free. One by one. Metal protesting separation. Bone charms pinned between boards loosened and dropped, clattering softly against the cellar floor. The sound was small. Fragile.

It did not match what they represented.

I lowered the board slowly and set it aside without looking at it again.

Then I aimed the flashlight into the opening.

The wall did not end.

The space behind it dropped downward in a narrow descent, deliberate and angular. Not a hollow pocket. Not an unfinished cavity. A continuation.

The air rising from it felt older. Denser. It carried the smell of dust layered over time, of wood sealed away from movement, of something preserved rather than forgotten.

Reinforcement continued below.

More boards. More iron driven deep. Bone worked into the structure at intervals that mirrored the spacing above. The craftsmanship did not weaken with depth. It intensified.

This was not a void behind a wall.

It was a passage that had been closed in stages. Each layer added with intention. Each barrier constructed by someone who believed deeply in what they were doing.

I stepped back without intending to.

My breath came shallow and uneven. Not panic. Understanding arriving too quickly.

Whoever built this had not been improvising. This was not fear turned frantic. It was belief executed carefully. Someone had stood here before me and chosen containment over destruction.

I saw it clearly.

If whatever lay below could have been erased, it would have been. Burned out. Broken apart. Buried beyond recovery.

Instead, it had been preserved.

Locked behind wood and iron and bone. Not denied. Not destroyed. Held.

Persistence.

The word surfaced with exactness.

The fear was not of a single act or event. It was of continuation. Of something allowed to endure beyond a lifetime. Of something that learned how to remain.

I wiped sweat from my forehead and leaned closer to the opening.

The lullaby thinned, not gone but withdrawn, as though it had completed its immediate purpose. The pressure in the cellar eased slightly. The room felt larger again, though not empty. The air had weight now. A patient density.

The house had not resisted because it wanted me gone.

It had resisted to see whether I would stop.

I stepped closer and angled the flashlight downward.

The beam slid along the first few feet of the descent, then vanished into angles and shadow. The drop was steeper than it should have been. Narrower. Designed to discourage the body as much as the mind.

Every inch of it argued against intrusion.

My hands trembled again, slower this time, steadier. The fear that remained was no longer diffuse. It had sharpened into clarity stripped of comfort.

I had crossed from discovery into violation.

There would be no replacing those boards as they were. No reassembling the seal without knowing what it had protected. Whatever had been kept here for survival, whatever had been permitted to persist instead of being destroyed, was aware of disruption now.

Not in anger.

In acknowledgment.

I straightened slowly, my shoulders brushing the cellar wall. Dust drifted in the narrow beam of light. The smell of old wood and iron settled into my lungs.

This was not about bones or history alone.

It was about endurance.

About something that had learned how to wait longer than the people who built the barrier to contain it.

And I had just undone the first lock.

The house remained silent.

It did not warn me.

It did not urge me forward.

It did not need to.

It already knew I would not leave it unfinished.

Chapter 18

I did not put the wall back the way I found it.

The boards remained propped against the cellar wall, their splintered edges exposed. The iron nails I had torn free lay scattered across the floor, dull heads scarred from impact. The opening stood uncovered, the narrow descent beyond it breathing out cold, patient air into the rest of the cellar.

Closing it again would have been an act of denial.

I was past that.

I climbed the stairs slowly. Each step carried the weight of what I had uncovered. The air warmed as I rose, but the pressure did not leave entirely. The house above appeared unchanged. The light through the window fell at the same angle.

But I knew better.

The bone charms stayed with me in thought, pale and smoothed by handling, placed by hands that believed in restraint more than mercy. The iron nails followed too. Not ornamental. Not symbolic alone.

Functional.

Designed to hold.

At the sink, I washed my hands. Rust-colored water spiraled briefly down the drain before clearing. I watched until it disappeared entirely. My reflection in the darkened window looked thinner, drawn taut by understanding.

I did not sit.

I did not hesitate.

I moved through the house with a kind of clarity that had nothing to do with calm. The notebook went into my bag first. The photographs followed, printed and slid into a folder. The loose pages of copied symbols came next. Circles. Spirals. The marks that had threaded through my dreams long before I understood their origin.

I checked everything twice.

Not out of anxiety.

Out of precision.

This was no longer documentation.

It was evidence.

When I locked the front door behind me, the click sounded sharper than usual. Final in a way I had not anticipated. As I stood on the porch, something settled in my chest with quiet certainty.

What had been sealed beneath my house was not personal.

It was not a single secret hidden out of shame. Not one reckless act buried in panic.

It was procedural.

Repeated.

Built according to rules that had been followed before and would have been followed again. Bone and iron and wood arranged with the confidence of someone who knew the problem would not resolve itself.

I drove into town with the windows down. The wind cut across my face, grounding me in sensation. Every mile placed distance between me and the cellar, but the pull did not weaken.

The lock was no longer behind me.

I was carrying it now.

In my hands. In my bag. In the sharpened questions I could not ask.

The building I headed toward offered no comfort. It never had. Old records do not exist to soothe. They exist to remember. Ledgers. Burial logs. Marginal notes written by hands long gone but not entirely silent.

I parked and remained seated for a moment, the engine ticking as it cooled. My bag sat heavy in the passenger seat. I thought about the narrow descent beneath my house. About how far it might continue. About the care taken to close it off instead of erase it.

Whatever lived at the center of that effort had been expected to persist.

That was the part that refused to loosen its grip.

I stepped out and locked the car. The sound echoed along the quiet street.

This was not about curiosity anymore.

It was about context.

If someone had built a lock that deliberate, then someone else had written the rules that required it.

And I was done standing on the wrong side of them.

The woman behind the desk did not reach for the photographs.

That was the first sign she understood them.

Her hands remained folded on the blotter, fingers interlaced, the skin across her knuckles pulled pale from pressure she did not bother disguising. She studied the prints without touching them, her gaze moving slowly from edge to edge, taking in the thickness of the paper, the way I had aligned the copied symbols beside the images of nail heads and bone.

She inhaled through her nose and held it a moment too long.

"Where did you find these?" she asked.

Not what are they.

Not why do you have them.

Where.

"In my cellar," I said. "Behind a false wall."

Her eyes lifted to mine then, sharp and unblinking. She reached for the top photograph at last, pinching the corner carefully as though the paper itself carried weight. She turned it just enough to catch the light, her thumb brushing the image of an iron nail head before pausing there.

"How old is the house?" she asked.

"Mid-nineteenth century. The foundation, at least."

"And your family?"

Her gaze did not leave the photograph.

"How long on the property?"

I hesitated, not from uncertainty but from recognition of what the answer would cost.

"Since the 1850s," I said. "Wren."

The name altered the air.

She did not gasp. She did not look startled. But something in her posture shifted, shoulders drawing back a fraction as if bracing against an expected confirmation.

She set the photograph down with care and reached for the next, then the next, arranging them in a clean line across the blotter. Order as containment.

"These aren't decorative," she said at last.

"I know."

"And you did not remove everything."

"No."

Her mouth tightened, not in disapproval but in something closer to relief.

She stood without asking permission and moved to the shelves behind her. The movement was quick but controlled. She returned with a ledger bound in cracked leather, its spine repaired more than once, the stitching visible like a healed wound.

She opened it halfway, her fingers navigating pages already familiar.

"I need to be clear," she said. "I am not confirming anything official."

"I did not ask for official."

"No," she replied, turning the book toward me. "You asked for context."

The pages were filled with names in ink browned by time. Dates. Marginal notes written smaller and tighter as if secrecy required economy. And beside certain entries, symbols.

Circles.

Spirals.

Marks I recognized without effort.

My throat tightened before I could stop it.

"These appear in multiple records," she said. "Different families. Different properties. Always rural. Always connected to births attended outside church oversight. Midwives, mostly. Women who did not keep clean ledgers."

"Unrecorded deaths," I said.

She nodded once.

"Stillbirths. Mothers who did not recover. Infants buried quietly. No ceremony. No questions."

"And the seals?" I asked. "The bone. The iron."

She closed the ledger partway, not hiding it, just limiting its reach.

"They are not random," she said. "They repeat. Not identical, but consistent enough to recognize. Placement varies. Materials shift depending on availability. The structure remains."

"Which is?"

She met my eyes and held them. Calculation moved behind her expression. How much to reveal. How much to preserve.

"Containment," she said. "Interruption. Choose the term you prefer."

"This is not superstition," I said.

"No," she replied. "It is practice."

The word settled heavily between us.

She gathered the photographs into a stack and slid them back across the desk, her fingers resting on the top print for a brief second longer than necessary.

"What you have found," she said carefully, "is not unique. It is intact. Most of these sites were dismantled over time. Renovations. Fires. Development."

"But mine was not."

"No," she said. "Yours was maintained."

Her voice softened, not with kindness but with caution sharpened by experience.

"That means someone believed it still mattered."

I saw the wall again. The layered boards. The iron driven deep. The bone set with care.

"This was not about one body," I said.

She did not contradict me.

"It was about a process," I continued. "Something that kept happening."

Her nod was slower this time.

"Yes," she said. "And if you are asking whether it stopped..."

She allowed the rest to hang.

The silence that followed felt deliberate. Heavy.

The room seemed smaller now, its walls lined not with paper but with memory. Whatever lay beneath my house had precedent. It had siblings. It belonged to a pattern that did not concern itself with ownership or era.

The horror expanded outward, no longer confined to one cellar or one family line.

And the woman sitting across from me was not surprised.

That was what made it real.

She did not say it in one breath.

That would have been merciful. One clean declaration. One name to carry home and bury beneath denial. Instead, she let it emerge in fragments, the way truth is offered when it has learned to survive by restraint.

"This was not a response," she said. "It was a system."

I did not interrupt. The room felt alert, as if even the shelves were leaning closer. The old clock on the wall ticked in slow, deliberate measures, each second landing harder than the last.

"A response implies surprise," she continued. "Panic. Reaction to something unforeseen. What you found required planning. Repetition. Agreement."

"Agreement between who?" I asked.

She opened the ledger again without answering, turning several pages with careful fingers. The paper whispered beneath her hand. She stopped where the ink had bled through in dark halos, where whoever wrote the entry had pressed hard enough to leave dents in the fibers.

"Families," she said at last. "Midwives. Sometimes ministers who did not record everything they knew. Sometimes husbands who learned not to ask certain questions."

The image of the cellar wall returned to me in full clarity. The layered boards. The iron driven deep. The expectation that it would need to hold for years, not weeks.

"This was not about hiding a death," I said.

"No," she agreed quietly. "It was about interrupting something that survived death."

The words did not echo. They settled.

She finally looked at me directly. Her eyes were sharp, but there was something else beneath it. Fatigue, perhaps. The wear of knowledge rationed carefully over time.

"Bloodlines carry more than names," she said. "They carry patterns. Tendencies. Behaviors that do not reveal themselves until they repeat.”

"And the seals?" I asked. "The circles. The spirals."

She pulled a scrap of paper toward her and drew without hesitation. A circle first, closed and firm. Then a spiral, tightening inward.

"Circles define boundaries," she said. "They establish where something is allowed to exist. Spirals mark persistence. Return. Continuation under pressure."

"And the bone?"

"Memory," she replied. "Anchor. Evidence that something occurred and will occur again."

"Iron," I said.

Her mouth tightened.

"Will," she said. "Enforcement. Iron does not negotiate."

The design assembled itself in my mind with terrible clarity. This was not folklore stitched together by fear. It was structure. Intent carried forward through repetition.

"So this was built," I said slowly, "because something kept coming back."

She did not nod.

"Yes."

"And my family?"

Her gaze did not soften.

"They were not unique," she said. "They were compliant."

The word struck harder than anything else she had offered.

"They followed instruction," she continued. "They maintained what they were told to maintain. They did not need to understand it fully. They only needed to believe the cost of failure exceeded the cost of obedience."

I thought of the wall beneath my house. The way it had been reinforced instead of dismantled. The way it had survived renovations that replaced everything else. The careful persistence of it.

"This was not built to protect people from whatever is down there," I said.

"No," she replied. "It was built to protect the process."

The silence that followed was not empty. It was weighted.

I gathered my papers slowly. The photographs. The copied symbols. None of them felt neutral anymore. The house I lived in was not simply a structure. It had been constructed to participate. To uphold something older than ownership.

"And if it stopped?" I asked quietly.

Her eyes held mine.

"Then it would have stopped everywhere," she said.

It had not.

I felt that truth settle into my bones with cold precision. Whatever the seals had been designed to slow, to interrupt, to contain, it had not been erased.

It had endured.

And it carried my blood now.

That was what I took with me when I left the room. Not fear. Not superstition.

Recognition.

This was not random horror.

It was inheritance.

And systems do not dissolve when you discover them.

They adapt.

Chapter 19

Leaving the records behind did not feel like escape. It felt like alignment.

The smell of old paper clung to my clothes as I stepped into the parking lot. Ink. Dust. A faint metallic tang that comes from touching objects designed to outlive their owners. Cars moved in and out of spaces. Someone laughed near the entrance. A cart rattled across cracked pavement. Ordinary noise continued without interruption, and none of it softened what had settled in my chest.

Relief would have meant release.

This was something narrower. A tightening. Pieces sliding into place whether I approved of them or not.

I sat in my car without starting the engine. The steering wheel was warm beneath my palms.

Temperance Wren was not a monster.

The thought circled back with stubborn clarity. Everything I had uncovered in the cellar had felt like threat because I had needed it to be. Bone wards. Iron driven deep. A wall layered with deliberate resistance. I had assumed malice because malice was easier to fight. A villain offers direction. Something you can oppose without ambiguity.

The records did not offer that.

The seals were not sloppy. They were not desperate. They had been maintained. Repaired. Renewed across decades when other parts of the house had been updated and softened. Roofs replaced. Walls painted. Floors sanded until old scars disappeared. And the cellar left intact. Reinforced. Preserved with attention that bordered on reverence.

Temperance had not been covering up a crime.

She had been holding a line.

I started the car and drove home slowly, hyper aware of the road beneath the tires. My hands remained tight on the wheel at each intersection. My body had already begun adjusting to the new understanding. My thoughts lagged behind it.

The house came into view sooner than I expected, sitting exactly where it always had. Balanced. Stable.

Stable.

The word anchored itself.

The house had never promised safety. I had assigned that to it. I had wanted safety when I planted measured rows in the yard, when I organized shelves, when I convinced myself that order meant protection.

But stability was not safety.

Stability meant containment. Maintenance. Holding something in place when it pressed outward.

I unlocked the front door and stepped inside. The air was cool and still. The quiet did not feel deceptive anymore. It felt functional.

Temperance had used what she had. Bone for memory. Iron for enforcement. Circles to define. Spirals to endure. None of it aimed at eradication. It aimed at delay. At compression. At keeping something from moving too freely through blood and time.

She had not destroyed what persisted through the Wren line.

She had lived with it.

The fear that followed that realization was not sharp. It was heavy. Destruction would have meant an ending. Containment meant continuity. It meant someone had to remain close enough to maintain the boundary.

Someone had to stay.

I moved through the house differently now. The walls did not loom. They did not close in. They simply existed, steady and patient. The lullaby did not rise. The temperature did not shift. There was no reward for understanding and no punishment either.

That absence of reaction felt deliberate.

Temperance was not absolved by any of this. Lives had bent under her decisions. Choices had costs. But I saw her more clearly now. A woman under pressure, trading one kind of harm for another. Choosing endurance over relief. Stability over comfort.

I rested my hands on the kitchen counter, grounding myself in the cool surface.

This was usually the moment in a story when the revelation softened the threat. When you discover the monster had a reason. When intent redeems outcome.

But intent did not erase consequence.

The house was not cursed.

It was tasked.

The danger had not been eliminated. It had been managed. Repeatedly. Carefully. At the expense of whoever remained close enough to do the work.

The gaps in the records made sense now. This was not knowledge meant to be inherited cleanly. It was burden. Oath. Responsibility that survived best when carried reluctantly and without full explanation.

Temperance had not been hiding wrongdoing.

She had been protecting the world from something that refused destruction.

And now I understood enough to recognize the shape of that refusal.

The house remained quiet.

Not approving.

Not warning.

Holding.

And for the first time since I moved in, I understood what it was holding for.

I tried to convince myself that what I had learned was enough for one day.

I stood at the kitchen window longer than necessary, watching the yard as if something might move and justify my attention. Nothing did. The evening air lay flat across the grass. The house held its breath in the particular way it had learned to do.

That was when the phone rang.

The Historian came across my caller ID.

Her name on the screen told me this was not a follow up. It was a correction. The kind that does not fit into reading rooms or careful phrasing.

I answered without saying hello.

She did the same.

There was a pause on the line, brief but deliberate. Not hesitation. Calibration. I leaned against the counter and let the silence stretch. Whatever she had withheld earlier, whatever had still belonged to shelves and official distance, was gone now.

"You can leave," she said.

The words were simple. Controlled. Not permission. Not encouragement. Just fact.

I did not answer. Statements like that were never neutral.

"The seals do not hold on their own," she continued. "They never have. Bone fractures. Iron loosens. Patterns decay if they are not renewed."

The house shifted faintly behind me. A soft tick from the walls as temperature settled.

"And then what?" I asked.

She did not rush the answer.

"Then whatever was slowed resumes," she said. "Not violently. Not all at once. It returns to its natural pace."

"And it will not come after me."

"No," she replied. "It is not interested in pursuit."

That should have comforted me.

It did not.

"It will remain," she said. "It will wait for whoever lives there next. Or their children. Or the ones who do not understand enough to question what they inherit."

I pictured the house emptied. The cellar resealed and left alone. New hands repainting walls. New lives arranged over old intention. Ignorance settling in like dust.

"You are saying the danger is not me," I said.

"I am saying the danger is abandonment."

Something tightened beneath my ribs. Not fear. Recognition. The alignment of truth with temperament.

"And if I stay?"

"Then you commit," she said. "Not once. Not symbolically. Repeatedly."

"To what?"

"Maintenance. Learning the procedures. Watching for drift. Performing what must be performed even when nothing appears wrong. Especially then."

The kitchen light flickered once and steadied. I did not look up.

"And the cost?" I asked.

She did not soften her voice.

"You will not disappear," she said. "Not suddenly. Not in a way anyone could name. But the role occupies space. It demands attention. Over time it becomes difficult to distinguish where the work ends and you begin."

I thought of Temperance. Her name threaded through margins and annotations. Not celebrated. Not condemned. Present.

"She did not stop it," I said.

"No," she agreed. "She endured it."

"And what happened to her?"

The silence that followed was not avoidance. It was acknowledgment.

"She lived," the woman said. "Longer than most. And she was never free of it."

I looked at my hands resting on the counter. They were steady.

"So this is the choice," I said.

"No," she replied. "This is the structure."

I understood the correction. A choice implies balance. This was asymmetry embedded in blood.

"If I walk away," I said, "I remain intact."

"Yes."

"And if I stay, I become part of the system."

She did not contradict me.

"The work does not thank you," she added. "It does not conclude. There is no moment where you have done enough. There is no absolution attached to it."

Responsibility without forgiveness. Vigilance without reward.

"This is not about bravery," I said.

"No," she said quietly. "It is about presence."

The house creaked then. Not loud. Not dramatic. Just enough to remind me it existed.

"Temperance was not chosen," the woman said. "She stayed because no one else would."

The line settled with terrible clarity.

The decision was no longer about fear. Or curiosity. Or inheritance.

It was about whether I would be the one who walked away.

The house remained silent.

Waiting.

I did not sit at the table and argue it out loud. I did not list advantages or consequences. I did not give the house the satisfaction of a spoken vow.

I ended the call and set the phone face down on the counter. My hands remained there long after the screen went dark, palms flat against the cool surface, feeling the quiet press in around me. The refrigerator hummed. The pipes clicked once in the walls. Nothing demanded an answer.

I left.

Not theatrically. I took my keys from their hook, stepped outside, and locked the door behind me. The evening air carried the faint scent of damp earth. I walked to the car and drove without checking the mirror.

The road curved away from the property and the trees folded in tight along the shoulder. I told myself I was testing distance. Giving my thoughts room to expand. That was a lie I did not bother correcting.

The farther I went, the worse the sensation became. Not fear. Not guilt. Misalignment. My hands tightened on the steering wheel as if I were compensating for drift. The engine purred steadily. The road remained straight and predictable. Everything behaved as it should.

That was the problem.

Temperance had not fled.

The truth circled back with stubborn precision. She had not stayed because she believed she could solve what persisted. She had stayed because leaving would have been easier. And easier had never been the metric.

I drove another mile. Then another.

The weight in my chest did not lift.

I slowed at the next intersection and turned the wheel.

The house reappeared gradually through the trees, its shape emerging with the same quiet certainty it always had. It did not loom. It did not beckon. It simply occupied its place on the land, balanced and patient.

I parked in the gravel and sat for a moment, engine ticking as it cooled. The fear was still there, but it had shifted. Less sharp. More defined.

I unlocked the door and stepped inside.

The air felt unchanged, but I noticed the faintest shift beneath the floorboards, the settling of old wood adjusting to my weight. I closed the door behind me and locked it.

I set my keys down in their usual place.

That was the moment.

Not the decision itself, but its confirmation. The small, ordinary action that said I was not leaving again tonight. Or tomorrow. Or at the first surge of doubt.

I did not call it bravery. I did not frame it as sacrifice. Bravery suggests an endpoint. Sacrifice suggests redemption.

This was neither.

This was maintenance.

The cellar door remained closed. I did not need to open it to feel what lay beneath. The memory of iron and bone was enough. I knew why the wall had been built. I knew what abandonment would mean.

Temperance had not won anything.

She had endured.

And endurance, I understood now, was not passive. It required repetition. Attention. The willingness to become part of the structure that kept worse things contained.

I sat at the table and opened my notebook. I did not copy symbols. I did not draft instructions.

I wrote the date.

Then I wrote a single sentence beneath it.

I am here.

The words did not feel triumphant. They felt structural.

The house remained quiet. Not grateful. Not threatening.

Holding.

And as I closed the notebook, I understood something with quiet certainty.

Staying was not an answer.

It was the first act.

Chapter 20

Staying had been a decision. Action was something else entirely. I understood that the moment I woke and felt no relief. There was no sense of survival, no quiet satisfaction in having endured the night. The house did not reward commitment. It tolerated it.

That distinction followed me into the kitchen. The counters, the cabinets, the narrow beam of light cutting across the floor all felt provisional, as if they were waiting to see whether I would prove consistent.

Containment without maintenance becomes decay.

The thought arrived fully formed and lodged itself behind my eyes. I recognized the sensation now. Not all ideas originated with comfort.

Temperance had not stayed because she was heroic. She had stayed because leaving would have meant neglect. Whatever had been sealed beneath this house had never been erased. It had been managed. Reinforced. Reasserted. The cellar was not a grave. It was infrastructure.

And infrastructure fails when abandoned.

I drank my coffee without tasting it. The bitterness barely registered. The notebook lay open on the counter, pages thick from handling, spine cracked along the seam. It no longer felt like a journal. It felt like a ledger. Entries. Adjustments. Corrections waiting to be made.

I laid the tools out one by one.

Flashlight. Pry bar. Hammer wrapped tightly in cloth to blunt the sound. Gloves. Chalk. Tape measure. Camera.

Each item placed with deliberate spacing, the way you prepare for work you cannot afford to rush. Not because I expected to use everything. Because preparation itself was part of the act.

This was not curiosity.

This was not defiance.

This was overdue.

I paused at the top of the cellar stairs and listened.

No pressure bloomed behind my eyes. No lullaby threaded through the air. The quiet felt attentive rather than empty.

The steps were solid beneath my feet. I counted them automatically. Control disguised as habit.

At the bottom, I let my breathing settle before moving forward. Fear has edges. It spikes and recedes. This was different. A steadiness that felt almost like gravity.

The boards I had loosened sat imperfectly in place, their edges no longer flush. The seal was already compromised. Leaving it in that state had been worse than ignorance. Half measures invite collapse.

I ran my gloved fingers along the iron nail heads. Cold traveled through leather and into skin. Each nail had been driven deep with purpose. Not decoration. Not symbolism alone. Anchors placed by someone who understood repetition.

The woman at the records office had not needed to describe the alternative.

Abandonment was enough.

"This isn't observation anymore," I said aloud, marking the shift.

My voice carried softly in the cellar and dissolved without echo.

I set the pry bar into the seam and tested the board. It resisted, then flexed slightly under pressure. Wood complained in a low, restrained tone. The nails held fast.

Good.

Resistance meant integrity. Integrity meant the boundary had not yet failed.

I adjusted my stance and applied steady force. No jerking. No anger. Controlled pressure, measured and patient. The kind of pressure that accumulates rather than explodes.

The board shifted a fraction of an inch.

As it began to give, a strange relief moved through me. Not victory. Motion. Stagnation had been worse than fear. Stagnation meant waiting for something else to decide.

The wood cracked softly along the grain.

The air behind it felt colder.

Not dramatically. Not theatrically. Just enough to register.

I did not pull back.

In that moment, clarity settled into me with weight and permanence. This was the point of no return. Not because something would surge outward in violence, but because I was choosing to engage the mechanism instead of orbiting it.

The house did not resist harder.

It did not warn me.

It waited.

And this time, so did I.

I knew the last barrier by the iron.

The nails here were different. Thicker. Darker. Driven deeper than the others. Not hurried. Not repaired. Final. Whoever set them had meant this layer to outlast the rest. To remain when memory thinned and intention faded.

I braced my foot against the concrete and wedged the pry bar into the seam. The metal bit into the wood with a low scrape. Vibration traveled up my arms and settled into my shoulders. Resistance answered immediately. The board did not flex easily. The nails did not complain so much as brace.

This was not decay.

This was design holding its ground.

I leaned in slowly, increasing pressure by degrees. Not desperate. Not emotional. The way you approach a problem that punishes impatience. My breath remained steady. I counted without numbers. The cellar seemed to contract, not physically, but in attention.

The first nail gave with a sharp crack that sliced through the space. The sound did not echo. It vanished.

The second followed, tearing free with a reluctant squeal. Each release felt less like relief and more like acknowledgment. Something noting the progression.

When the board finally loosened, it did not fall. It hung there, suspended between containment and exposure. I had to grip it with both hands and pull it free. The wood felt heavier than it should have been. Dense. Saturated with years of pressure.

The moment the seal broke, the cellar altered.

Air rose from the space beyond. Not rushing. Not violent. Deliberate. It carried a cold that did not belong to the room and a scent that had been sealed too long. Dry mineral. Iron. Something organic stripped clean of warmth.

The cold entered my lungs before I realized I had inhaled.

The temperature dropped enough to tighten the skin along my arms. The walls seemed to lean inward. Sound flattened. Even my breathing felt redirected, pulled downward rather than outward.

I stepped back and steadied myself against the workbench. My heart beat hard, but clean. No panic. No confusion. Awareness sharpened until it almost hurt.

The opening revealed a narrow continuation beyond the cellar wall. Not a hollow. Not a collapse. A passage reinforced with deliberate care.

Boards layered tightly. Beams fitted with precision. More iron driven deep. More bone fixed into the structure at intervals that mirrored the journal exactly.

The spirals aligned.

The geometry resolved.

For the first time since I had moved into this house, the architecture made complete sense.

I felt a smile pull at my mouth.

Not joy. Recognition.

This was it. The concealed extension. The source of the pressure and the pattern and the persistent interruption. I had found it. Opened it. Rendered it visible.

For years I had believed exposure dissolved power. Secrets weakened under light. Systems collapsed when studied closely enough. Whatever had been locked away here had depended on silence and neglect and slow erosion of attention.

I raised the camera and took photographs from several angles. The flash cut cleanly into the dark. The light did not penetrate far. It seemed to thin rather than illuminate, flattening against the angles of the descent.

Nothing recoiled.

Nothing retreated.

The lullaby did not rise.

The absence felt like permission.

The pressure behind my eyes eased. The sense of being observed receded to something manageable, distant. I had acted. The environment had adjusted.

I crouched and wrote notes quickly, almost eagerly. Measurements. Structural details. Placement of iron. Positioning of bone. Observations stripped of emotion.

The continuation beyond the wall was sealed from the rest of the foundation. Independent. Self contained. Whatever threat had existed here had been bound by material and method. I had not released it.

I had revealed it.

"I see you now," I said, and meant the space, the mechanism, the design.

The words did not echo.

I stood there longer than necessary, cataloging what would come next. Reinforcement. Documentation. Consultation. Controlled intervention. A sequence. A plan.

Relief moved through me in slow layers.

Control followed.

I had crossed the final threshold and nothing had punished me for it.

I believed, completely and without reservation, that I had done what Temperance could not finish.

I believed the seal had been the flaw.

I believed that opening it had resolved what generations had misunderstood.

And beneath those beliefs, something in the dark remained perfectly still.

The relief thinned before it vanished.

I felt it in the silence first.

The cellar no longer seemed contained behind me. It felt integrated. As though the opened space had joined a circuit that ran through beams and pipes and walls, through the bones of the house itself.

I remained where I stood, notebook open, pen hovering above the page, waiting for the expected correction. A sound. A pressure spike. Something immediate and undeniable that would label this a mistake.

Nothing came.

The absence carried weight.

The air shifted again, slower this time. Not a rush. A redistribution.

The cold that had pooled near the floor began to rise. It threaded through the room and slipped toward the stairs. I followed it without consciously deciding to. Each step upward felt permitted.

Halfway up, the lullaby returned.

Not drifting. Not distant.

It pressed behind my ears and arranged itself with careful precision. The melody was recognizable but altered. Notes had shifted position. The rhythm held, but the emphasis had changed. This was no longer endurance music.

It carried direction.

I stopped and pressed my palm to the wall. The wood felt warmer than it should have. Not heat. Activity. A faint hum beneath the grain.

The realization arrived without argument.

The seals below had not been designed to isolate. They had been constructed to interrupt. To delay. To hold something in suspension. The narrow continuation I had exposed was not a cage.

It was a threshold stalled by iron and repetition.

By removing the final barrier, I had not released anything.

I had allowed it to continue.

Upstairs, the floorboards responded differently beneath my feet. The creaks were familiar, but their timing had shifted. Sound traveled farther. More distinctly placed.

In the kitchen, small things were out of alignment. A cupboard door that I knew I had closed stood slightly ajar. A chair angled subtly away from the table. The clock ticked a fraction faster than before, not enough to measure, enough to feel.

The lullaby threaded through the space, touching corners, settling along surfaces.

I set my notebook on the counter and read the last page I had written in the cellar. The notes were correct. Structural. Precise. But none of them accounted for what mattered.

The mechanism had not been a lock.

It had been a governor.

I felt the shift in my body next.

My breathing synchronized with the rhythm behind my ears. My pulse slowed, deepened, steadied into something almost mechanical. Thoughts arranged themselves with alarming ease, sliding into sequence without friction.

That was the fracture.

This influence did not require force. It entered through participation. Through recognition. Through confident action taken in the name of control.

Through me.

I moved through the house and cataloged changes as they surfaced. Doors that had once resisted now opened smoothly. Light seemed to reach deeper into corners. The cellar stairs no longer suggested descent. They suggested origin.

The lullaby shifted again.

It incorporated something new.

The cadence of my own steps.

I said my name aloud to anchor myself. The sound held. It did not push anything back. Nothing had crossed into the house.

The house had completed something that had been waiting.

Across generations.

Temperance had sensed it. Not consciously. Not fully. She had endured because endurance preserved in completion. Completion required something else.

Presence.

Continuity.

A living boundary capable of adaptation.

I lowered myself into a chair and pressed my hands flat against the table. The wood vibrated faintly beneath my palms. Not enough to see.

Enough to register.

"You're awake now," I said.

The words did not feel dangerous.

The lullaby settled lower, closer to breath than sound.

I had not ended anything.

I had provided the missing component.

Access.

The system did not surge. It did not rage. It integrated.

The door had opened both ways.

And this time, it did not intend to close.

Chapter 21

I moved through the first floor with the careful calm I had been wearing for days, the kind you rely on when you refuse to acknowledge the tremor beneath it.

The air felt altered. Not colder. Not warmer. Directed. It moved through the rooms with quiet intention. Light shifted along the walls in slow passes, lingering in corners as if pausing to listen.

I told myself it was fatigue. Fatigue manufactures patterns. It sharpens edges that are not there.

Then I saw the first circle.

It rested on the trim beside the pantry door, half obscured where the paint had darkened with age. Not scratched. Not freshly carved. There was no exposed wood, no splintered edge. It looked embedded. As though it had been there before the paint, before the dust, before my arrival.

The circle was imperfect. Not symmetrical. Drawn by a hand that understood sufficiency over elegance. The kind of mark you make when precision is less important than function.

My stomach tightened.

I stepped closer and ran my finger along it. The groove was shallow but deliberate. It caught the pad of my fingertip in a way that felt almost conversational. The paint had filled the line over time, smoothing it, trying to blur it into the surface.

It had not succeeded.

I went to the kitchen table and opened the journal without searching. I knew the page. The spiral I had copied earlier stared back at me, tight and insistent.

I looked from the paper to the trim.

A cold line traced my spine. Not from temperature. From fluency.

The house was not simply old. It spoke the same language as the journal. The same language my dreams had pressed against the inside of my skull.

I backed away and began scanning the room the way I had scanned archival documents. Structure before meaning. Repetition before interpretation.

Another mark emerged near the baseboard beneath the window. Two circles overlapping, barely visible beneath layers of white. I crouched. The paint here was thick, applied again and again. Still the grooves held.

I stood slowly.

The room felt smaller.

The hallway narrowed when I stepped into it. The wallpaper had always been forgettable, tiny flowers fading into beige. Now my eyes slipped past the blossoms and caught the negative space between them. The way the vines curved. The way the curls repeated. Circles disguised as decoration. Spirals dressed in domestic apology.

My throat dried.

"Stop," I said softly, though I did not know whether I was addressing the house or myself.

Upstairs, the banister bore the dents of ordinary living. I had run my hand along those marks a hundred times without thought. Now, in the angled light from the window, I saw how they clustered. Three shallow impressions. A pause. Two more. And then, near the curve of the rail, a tight spiral scratched lightly into the wood.

So light I could have missed it.

If I had not already been taught how to see.

Primed.

The word settled hard in my chest.

None of this looked newly made. It looked newly visible. Not because I had cleaned or repainted or adjusted the light.

It was being revealed.

I stepped into the bedroom and faced the mirror. My reflection stared back with unwanted clarity. Skin drawn tight. Eyes shadowed. A face that looked older than it had yesterday.

Behind me, the wall was painted a muted blue meant to calm.

I held my gaze steady and then shifted focus to the wall itself.

At first there was nothing. Only the faint texture of old paint. The subtle unevenness of brush strokes.

Then the circles surfaced.

Not carved. Not etched. Lines where the pigment had thinned almost imperceptibly over time. Spirals nested within spirals. A pattern that tightened the longer I stared, pulling inward the way the structure beneath the cellar had pulled inward.

My hands curled at my sides.

The urge to scrape at the wall rose fast and bright. To prove it. To peel away the illusion. To break the grammar.

Beneath that impulse, steadier and colder, was the real terror.

I turned from the mirror and looked down the hallway toward the stairs.

The air carried no scent of decay. No smoke. No rot. Only a faint, misplaced chill that did not belong to the season.

The house had not changed.

It had completed something.

And now that I could read it, it was no longer subtle.

I stood in the hallway outside the bedroom, staring at the wall where the spirals had surfaced, and waited for something definitive.

A crack. A thud. A sound sharp enough to mark the moment.

The house offered none of that.

It remained quiet. Attentive. Present in the way someone is present when they stand just behind you, close enough that you do not need to turn to know they are there.

I stepped away from the wall.

That was when I felt it.

Not touch.

Nearness.

The air behind my left shoulder shifted density. It felt occupied. Used. A pocket of warmth where no warmth should be. My body recognized the placement before my mind did. Muscles tightened along my spine. My pulse climbed without permission, fast and shallow.

It is closer now.

The thought did not arrive as panic. It arrived as fact.

I turned quickly.

Nothing.

The hallway stretched empty toward the staircase. The steps waited, worn smooth by decades of ordinary use. Light from the front window cut across the floor without hesitation. The house did not rearrange itself to prove a point.

It did not need to.

I took a step forward.

The sensation moved with me.

Not touching. Not retreating. Maintaining distance with precision. Calibrated proximity. Whoever had built the seals had understood this part. Force would have failed. Restraint would teach.

The whispering began near the bottom of the stairs.

Not words. Not voices. Fractured breath that nearly formed syllables and then withdrew. The lullaby I had heard before lingered beneath it, but the melody no longer held its structure. Notes slipped. Paused. Reassembled out of order in a way that set my teeth on edge.

The sound did not come from the walls.

It vibrated through bone.

I gripped the banister.

"Stop," I said, louder now. Command, not plea.

The whispering softened.

The warmth behind my shoulder drifted closer to my neck. Fine hairs lifted. I did not feel contact, but I felt orientation. I knew where a mouth would be. I knew where breath would fall if it chose to cross that final inch.

It did not.

Invasive without contact. Instruction without violence.

I moved down the stairs carefully, one step at a time, my hand sliding along the banister as if it were the only fixed point in the house. The presence followed. Not hunting. Not chasing. Staying.

At the foot of the stairs, the symbols gathered.

I had not seen them there before.

Which meant they had not wanted me to.

On the wall beside the coat rack, three circles pressed tightly together. Beneath them, a spiral coiled inward, its center worn smooth as if touched repeatedly. The grooves were deeper here, less softened by paint.

This space had been used.

My breathing thinned. Not panic. Assessment.

The language of the house was compressing. Converging toward thresholds. Toward movement points. It was no longer decorative or peripheral. It was structural and immediate.

Behind me, the whispering reorganized into rhythm. Not melody. Pattern. It slipped into the space between my breaths, pressing in when I exhaled, easing when I inhaled.

Learning.

"Enough," I said.

My voice wavered despite my effort.

The presence did not withdraw.

It leaned.

I closed my eyes.

The darkness behind my lids did not stay blank. Shapes moved there. Curves sliding into tighter curves. Spirals tightening until they became points of pressure. I saw hands that were not mine, methodical and patient, setting nails with deliberate care. Tying bone to string. Choosing placement over force.

Temperance had known this stage.

Not in theory.

In practice.

She had known that when the seals weakened, nothing would burst free. It would draw nearer. It would measure. It would learn the shape of the person in front of it.

I opened my eyes.

The hallway remained unchanged.

The presence did not.

It stood closer now.

And it no longer felt patient.

The moment it settled was almost imperceptible.

There was no audible shift. No visible fracture. Nothing I could isolate and point to as the turning.

The understanding arrived whole and uninvited, seating itself inside me with the quiet certainty of something that had only been waiting for the right alignment.

The symbols had never been placed for discovery.

They had been waiting for recognition.

I stood between the kitchen and the back hall, staring at a spiral that

I was certain had not been there yesterday. The paint around it was aged, layered. The wall had settled around the groove over years. The shape had not emerged.

It had been revealed.

The truth pressed harder than the presence ever had.

The dreams returned in sequence, not as drifting fragments but as progression. Each one clearer than the last. Each one instructive. Teaching spacing. Teaching absence. Teaching where not to look.

I had called them warnings because warning implied distance.

They had been lessons.

The cellar had not shocked me because some part of me had already anticipated what waited there. The iron had not frightened me because I understood its function before I understood its cost.

I pressed my palm against the wall.

The presence behind my shoulder shifted.

Not closer.

More attentive.

"I didn't invite you," I said.

The air tightened slightly along my neck. A subtle adjustment. Approval or correction. I could not tell which. It did not matter. The thing listening did not need to clarify itself.

It knew I was still assembling the truth.

My attention had become the key.

The realization unfolded without panic. The influence did not need to corner me. It did not require fear to unlock anything. It required alignment. My habits. My pattern seeking. The way I lingered over detail. The way I returned to questions until they opened.

The house had learned me by watching me learn it.

I moved slowly through the ground floor, allowing my gaze to rest where it wanted. Wherever my focus lingered, the symbols presented themselves. Not appearing. Not shifting. Revealing. Doorframe.

Baseboards. The edge of the pantry shelf where hands often paused.

Once seen, the marks refused to recede.

I closed my eyes and opened them again.

They remained.

The cost of awareness was immediate and irreversible. The shapes carried orientation now. Memory had mapped them into me.

The lullaby returned without sound. I felt its rhythm in the spacing of the marks. In the intervals between curves. In the repetition of structure. It was no longer something imposed upon me.

It was something I comprehended.

And comprehension tightened the bond.

Temperance had not attempted eradication. She had narrowed perception. Contained influence by limiting who could see fully. What she could not prevent was adaptation.

It had adapted to me.

The presence behind my shoulder stilled, no longer testing distance. It had crossed the only threshold that mattered.

I stood in the kitchen and felt the house settle around my awareness. Not shelter. Not threat.

Integration.

The symbols did not glow. They did not pulse.

They held.

Resistance now carried consequence. Not punishment. Not violence.

Misalignment.

If I turned away, if I refused to engage with what I could now perceive, the structure would not falter. It would continue. Without me.

The knowledge anchored itself deep.

Invitation begins with recognition.

And recognition, once completed, does not withdraw.

I did not say yes.

I did not need to.

The answer had already been given.

Chapter 22

I left the house with the marks still in my eyes.

That was the only way I could describe it. The spirals and circles clung to the back of my vision like afterimages burned in by bright light. Except there was no fading. No blink long enough to reset. The shapes had fused with my attention, and my attention had fused with the house.

I could sit at the kitchen table and pretend everything was unchanged, but the doorframe disagreed. The walls disagreed. The beams in the cellar disagreed. They carried their language like a second grain in the wood. Once you learned to see it, you could not unsee it.

I told myself town would help.

Fresh air. Receipts. The comfort of small talk about weather and crop yield and nothing that mattered. I needed transactions that followed rules. I needed something that did not shift when I turned my back.

I felt the change before I reached the square.

Not a sound. Not a touch.

A tightening.

The kind of pressure that settles over a room when someone has brought news nobody wants to name.

The hardware store sat on the corner as it always had, windows streaked, faded signage peeling at the edges. I parked, stepped out, and walked inside. The bell above the door rang bright and clean.

Too bright.

Two men stood near the counter. One held a fifty-pound bag of feed on his shoulder. The other cradled a paper cup of coffee, steam curling lazily upward. Their conversation stopped mid-word when the bell rang.

They did not look startled.

They looked finished.

Both turned toward me. Not a glance. A full assessment.

I nodded once and moved toward the back aisle. My boots struck the linoleum louder than they should have. The fluorescent lights hummed overhead. A box fan in the corner pushed air in slow, tired circles. The mechanical sounds continued. The human ones did not.

Silence followed me down the aisle.

I picked up a spool of twine I did not need. Set it back. Lifted a bag of bulb fertilizer and held it long enough to suggest reading. My reflection shimmered faintly in the plastic packaging, thinner than I remembered.

It wasn't just that they were watching.

It was that they already knew something.

I went to the counter with a small box of nails and a pair of work gloves. Ordinary purchases. Innocent.

The clerk had a gray mustache and eyes that had narrowed permanently over the years. He rang up the gloves first. Then the nails. The register clicked and whirred.

When I slid my card across the counter, he did not take it immediately.

His gaze dropped to my hand. Then lifted to my face. Then to the card again.

"You're up on Wren place," he said.

Not a question.

"I live there," I answered.

A muscle shifted in his jaw.

"That so," he said quietly. "Been hearin' things."

The words hung in the air without detail.

"About what?" I asked.

He did not smile.

"Just things."

He reached for my card at last. His fingers brushed mine. The contact was brief but deliberate. Not friendly. Not hostile. Evaluative. As if checking for temperature.

Behind me, one of the men adjusted his weight. The feed bag creaked. The coffee cup rustled softly in a tightening grip.

The clerk handed my card back without meeting my eyes. "You take care up there," he said.

The phrase sounded less like courtesy and more like distance.

I gathered the bag and turned. The two men shifted just enough to create a path. Not wide. Not welcoming. A corridor cut through their bodies. I walked between them and felt their attention trail along my shoulders and spine like heat from an unseen source.

The bell rang again when I opened the door.

Still cheerful.

Still wrong.

Outside, the air felt thinner.

I stood beside my car and looked across the street at the diner where Ellie and I had sat that first week. I remembered the smell of coffee, the worn vinyl booths, the waitress who called everyone honey without discrimination.

A woman stepped out of the diner and saw me. Her gaze caught, held for a fraction too long, then broke away sharply. Her shoulders tightened. Her pace quickened.

Not fear.

Avoidance.

The realization struck clean and cold.

No one needed to see the symbols on my walls.

They felt the shift anyway.

Whatever had aligned itself with my attention had bled past the property line. It did not need spectacle. It did not need proof. It required only perception.

A reputation was forming around me.

I got into the car and shut the door harder than necessary. The sound reverberated inside the cab and died quickly, absorbed.

I sat there with my hands on the steering wheel, pulse steady but elevated, and understood the new rule the house had taught me.

Recognition does not stay contained.

It spreads through proximity.

Once you learn to see it, others learn to see you.

And they do not need to know why.

By the time I got home from town, the house felt closer.

Not louder. Not angrier. Just closer. As if the walls had shifted half an inch inward while I was gone. I stepped inside and the air pressed subtly against my chest. Waiting.

I set the bag of nails and gloves on the kitchen table and stood there longer than necessary, staring at the wood grain as if it might rearrange itself.

The historian's number sat at the top of my recent calls.

For a moment, I considered not dialing. The day had already confirmed that something had shifted beyond my walls. But if the town was tightening, I needed one voice that had not yet turned.

I pressed the call button.

It rang longer than usual.

When she answered, her voice was measured as ever, but something in it had hardened. Not hostility.

Guard.

"Clara," she said. "I was going to call you."

That was new.

"I was in town," I said. I did not soften it. "People are different."

Silence.

On her end, I heard the faint rustle of paper. Or perhaps she only needed the sound to occupy the space before answering.

"Towns recalibrate," she said carefully. "When attention gathers."

"This is more than attention."

Another pause.

"I've been reviewing what you brought me," she said. "The photographs. The measurements. The pattern."

"You recognized it."

"I recognized elements."

"And?"

"And recognition is not endorsement."

The word struck harder than I expected.

"I'm not asking for endorsement," I said. "I'm asking what it is."

"I already told you," she replied. Still calm. Almost rehearsed. "It is a pattern historically associated with midwifery practices and containment rituals. It appears in records. That does not make it safe to pursue."

"Safe for who?"

"For you," she said quickly. Then softer, "For me."

There it was.

I leaned against the counter. The refrigerator hummed behind me. The house remained still, listening.

"What changed?" I asked.

"I've had inquiries."

"Inquiries from who?"

She exhaled slowly. "Questions about the scope of my research. About which materials I have accessed. About whether certain archives should be restricted."

"By who?"

"That is not the relevant issue."

"It is to me."

Her composure thinned by a degree. Not breaking. Just tightening.

"Old families pay attention when certain names reappear," she said. "Especially when those names intersect with ritual practice. Especially when those intersections are not hypothetical."

"Temperance Wren."

"Yes."

"She was protecting something."

"She was acting within the logic of her time."

"That's not the same."

"History rarely provides clean distinctions."

The house creaked faintly above me. A settling sound. Ordinary.

"You believed me," I said.

"I believe you encountered something," she corrected. "Belief in your experience and alignment with your actions are not the same thing."

"So you want me to stop."

"I want you to consider visibility," she said. "You move into a property with documented irregularities. Human remains are found. You begin asking about ritual containment, lineage, repetition. Do you understand how quickly that narrative can be shaped?"

"You think I'm imagining it," I said.

"I think perception becomes contagious in contained environments," she replied. "Once enough people agree that something is wrong, the specifics no longer matter."

"That isn't an answer."

"It is the only answer I can safely provide."

The word safely lingered.

Silence stretched between us, thinner than before.

"I cannot continue this line of inquiry with you," she said at last. "Not directly. I have responsibilities."

"And outside those responsibilities?"

"I do not have that latitude."

I watched my reflection in the darkened microwave door. My face looked sharper. More defined.

"You warned me about patterns," I said.

"I warned you about cost."

"And this is it."

"This is part of it."

Her voice softened then, almost against her will. "Clara, sometimes endurance looks like restraint."

Temperance endured.

She sealed. She maintained.

She stayed.

"I am not asking you to walk away," the historian said quietly. "I am asking you to understand that you may be alone in how far you are willing to go."

Alone.

The word felt different when she said it.

"So that's it," I said.

"For now."

We ended the call without goodbye.

I stood in the kitchen, phone still in my hand, and felt the absence of something I had not realized I was relying on.

Not proof.

Not validation.

Witness.

The house gave a soft shift overhead. Wood adjusting to weight.

The historian had not dismissed my findings. She had not called me unstable. She had done something more calculated.

She had distanced herself.

Association now carried consequence.

Reputation.

Risk.

And as I stood there, I understood that the circle tightening around me was not drawn in chalk or carved into wood.

It was being traced in people.

The last person who treated my questions as research instead of rumor had stepped back.

Not because I was wrong.

Because I might not be.

The first call came just after midnight.

I was still awake, pretending to read. The lamp beside the couch cast a pool of yellow light that felt smaller than it used to. Beyond that circle, the room dissolved into shadow. The house was quiet in the way it had been lately, alert rather than resting.

When the phone buzzed on the coffee table, I flinched hard enough that the book slipped from my hand.

Unknown number.

I let it ring twice before answering, forcing myself not to appear eager.

"Hello?"

Nothing.

No static. No muffled traffic. Just the open hum of connection. I could hear the faint electronic current, the subtle pressure shift that told me someone was holding the line.

I counted three breaths.

"Who is this?"

Still nothing.

Then, faint and unmistakable, a slow exhale close to the receiver.

Not an accident. Not background noise.

I pulled the phone away from my ear and stared at the screen. The call timer ticked upward. Six seconds. Seven. Eight.

The silence was intentional.

The line went dead.

The house did not react. It did not creak or settle. It simply held the quiet as if it had been expecting the interruption.

I told myself it was a prank. A wrong number. A bored teenager testing courage after dark.

I did not believe it.

The second call came two nights later.

I was in bed this time. The house had been restless all evening, subtle shifts in the walls, a faint rearranging of weight overhead. When the phone lit up on the nightstand, I reached for it before it completed the first ring.

"Hello."

Breathing.

Closer than before. Slower. Deliberate enough to establish rhythm.

I felt my own breathing adjust in response, matching it without meaning to.

"Say something," I said.

A pause.

Then a whisper that almost formed language but collapsed into sound before it reached clarity. A shape of speech. Intent without content.

The line clicked off.

I remained still in the dark, phone pressed to my ear long after the call ended. The ceiling above me showed no sign of disturbance. No lullaby threaded the air. No presence pressed at my neck.

The silence was worse.

The third call came just before dawn.

I had finally fallen asleep when the vibration against the wood pulled me upright. The room was gray, edges softened by early light. I answered without checking the number.

"Yeah."

A man's voice this time. Casual. Nearly polite.

"Sorry. Wrong number."

I sat up slowly. "You sure?"

A beat.

"You still living up there?" he asked.

Up there.

The phrase was placed carefully. Not asking for directions. Not verifying an address.

Marking territory.

My throat tightened. "Who is this?"

Silence stretched just long enough to feel deliberate.

Then a low chuckle that carried no warmth.

"Just checking," he said.

The call ended.

I remained sitting upright, the phone still in my hand. In the dim reflection of the window, my face looked sharper than it had a week ago. Not thinner. More defined. As if something had been carved away.

Later that morning, I walked to the mailbox.

The air felt ordinary. The trees moved without urgency. A pickup truck drove past slower than necessary. The driver's gaze lingered on me without pretense.

He did not wave.

He did not look away.

The message did not require explanation.

The calls were not random.

They were confirmation.

Curiosity had shifted to vigilance. Vigilance had shifted to coordination.

No one would confront me in daylight. Accusation requires owner-ship.

Night requires none.

In the dark, anonymity feels protective. In the dark, you can ask questions without attaching your name to them.

I stepped back inside and locked the door.

The bolt sliding into place sounded louder than it should have, metal striking metal with finality.

The house did not object.

It simply absorbed the sound.

And somewhere beyond the walls, someone had learned that I would answer.

<h1 style="text-align:center">Chapter 23</h1>

The house felt quieter after the calls.

Not calmer.

Narrower.

The silence had edges now. It pressed inward rather than settling around me. I stayed inside the next morning. No errands. No audience. No reason to let anyone measure my movements.

I made coffee and stood at the sink while it brewed, staring into the yard without absorbing it. The trees moved in an ordinary rhythm. The world beyond the glass held its shape.

When I wrapped my fingers around the mug, something tugged along the inside of my wrist.

Not pain.

A catch.

I set the mug down slowly and turned my arm over.

At first, I thought it was shadow from the window frame. The morning light cut across the kitchen at an angle, broken by leaves outside. A curve fell across my skin that did not belong there.

I stepped closer to the window.

The curve stayed.

A crescent.

Pale at the edges. Darker through the center. The skin slightly raised, faintly swollen as if it had healed during the night. Not a scrape. Not a burn. The line was too clean for either.

Deliberate.

I pressed it with my thumb.

Tender.

Not sharp enough to flinch. Just enough to confirm presence.

I tried to remember catching it on something. A nail in the cellar. The edge of a board. A tool left too close to my hand. I replayed yesterday in fragments. The kitchen. The cellar wall.

Nothing.

No sting. No tear. No blood.

I ran cold water over it. The skin blanched beneath the stream, then flushed back into that faint red curve. I dried my hand and held it under the overhead light. The mark sharpened. The edges looked settled, as if they had aged longer than a few hours.

I leaned against the counter and stared at it until the coffee went cold.

The curve felt familiar.

Not like an injury.

Like a symbol.

I went to the living room and pulled the journal from the table. Flipped back through pages filled with copied lines. Circles. Spirals. Partial arcs that never closed.

I laid my wrist over the paper.

The alignment was not exact. It did not need to be.

The rhythm matched. The intention matched. The curve paused where continuation should begin.

Incomplete.

Waiting.

I checked my other wrist. Clean. My palms. My forearms. Nothing but veins and faint freckles and skin I recognized as my own.

Upstairs, the bathroom mirror waited under harsher light. I lifted my arm toward the glass.

The crescent was unmistakable now. Not dirt. Not ink. Not residue.

It belonged to me.

"Where did you come from?" I asked my reflection.

My voice sounded thinner than I expected.

I flexed my fingers. The crescent tightened with the movement, as if responding to tension beneath the skin.

The calls from the nights before returned in sequence. The breathing. The careful question.

Still living up there?

I looked at the mark again and felt something shift.

This was not about the town.

They could watch. They could whisper. They could call under the cover of darkness.

They had not touched me.

I tried to reconstruct the moment the seal broke. The board giving way. The air rising from the passage. My hands gripping iron. The vibration traveling up my arms.

Had I pressed my wrist against a nail head? A splinter? Bone?

I saw myself working. Focused. Controlled.

I did not see blood.

Back in the kitchen, I lifted the coffee mug with the marked hand. Heat brushed the tender skin. A faint pulse traveled up my forearm.

Responsive.

Not accidental.

The unease was not about pain.

It was about authorship.

If I did not remember making this mark, then one of two things was true.

Either I had done it and the memory had failed.

Or something else had.

Both possibilities settled into me evenly.

I turned my wrist under the light again, studying the curve as if it might complete itself if I watched long enough.

The house remained silent.

For the first time since the calls began, I was not wondering what they were doing.

I was wondering what I had already started.

I did not trust myself after that.

That was the real shift.

Before, I had been wary of the house. Of the town. Of whatever patience lingered beneath the floorboards. Now I watched my own hands.

I set my phone on the kitchen table and opened the camera. I photographed the crescent on my wrist. Then another with the timestamp visible in the corner. For the third, I said the date out loud.

"Tuesday. 9:16 a.m. Mark present. No visible change."

My voice sounded calm.

That frightened me more than panic would have.

I opened the voice memo app and recorded the same statement. I described the kitchen in detail. The position of the chairs. The mail stacked by the door. The angle of light through the window. I narrated the ordinary with precision, building a baseline.

If something shifted, I would have proof of before.

I set an hourly alarm.

If time fractured, I would know where.

The first alarm sounded while I was at the sink. Eleven o'clock. I remembered the last two hours. Washing dishes. Reading my notes. Standing too long at the wall.

I recorded again.

"Eleven. No lapse."

I examined my wrist.

The crescent remained unchanged.

I moved through the house cataloging placement. The tilt of a photograph frame on the mantel. The exact position of a book on the shelf. I nudged the frame slightly and then returned it to its original angle. A control test.

Upstairs, I stood in front of the bathroom mirror.

"Clara Wren," I said.

The reflection formed the name with the same mouth, the same cadence.

I leaned closer. Studied my pupils. Watched the rise and fall of my chest. The slight tension in my jaw.

"Still here," I said.

The crescent caught the light when I raised my arm. I pressed it again. Tender. Consistent. Not spreading.

I photographed it once more.

At noon, the alarm went off.

The sound snapped through the house sharper than before.

I was seated at the kitchen table.

I did not remember sitting down.

I froze.

The pen lay between my fingers. The tip rested against the page. A faint indentation marked where pressure had begun.

I looked down.

The page was blank.

My pulse climbed, sudden and disobedient.

I tried to rewind. The mirror. The stairs. My hand sliding along the railing. The feel of the wood beneath my palm.

The sequence blurred at the edges.

Had I paused halfway down? Had I stopped to look at something? Had I stood in the hallway longer than I thought?

Nothing felt missing.

And yet I could not account for the transition.

I lifted the phone with fingers that did not quite feel like mine.

"Twelve," I recorded. "Uncertain gap. Possibly brief."

Possibly.

The word tasted wrong.

I closed my eyes and forced myself to reconstruct the path. The stairs. The kitchen doorway. The scrape of the chair.

No rupture. No blank wall in memory.

Just absence of certainty.

The historian's voice drifted through my thoughts.

Transmission slowed. Not stopped.

I opened the journal and flipped back to my notes on the seals. Circles define boundaries. Spirals mark persistence. Bone anchors memory. Iron enforces will.

My gaze settled on that last line.

Iron enforces will.

What if iron had not been placed to cage something outside?

What if it had been meant to temper something within?

I turned my wrist under the light again.

The crescent did not look accidental anymore.

It looked intentional.

A boundary does not form without pressure.

I walked to the front door and checked the lock. Deadbolt secure. Windows latched. The yard beyond remained still.

The house felt unchanged.

Which meant the alteration had occurred somewhere else.

I stood in the center of the living room and forced myself to say it.

Possession is easy to fear.

Inheritance is harder.

Inheritance does not break in.

It waits.

If the rituals had been interruptions, then what had they interrupted? If the seal beneath the cellar had been a delay, then what had it delayed?

I looked at my wrist again.

The crescent curved inward, incomplete.

Expectant.

I lifted my phone and took another photograph.

Then I whispered into the room, steady despite the tremor beneath it, "If this is me, show me."

The house did not answer.

But somewhere in the quiet, something shifted its weight.

And this time, I was not certain it was outside of me.

Two explanations stood in front of me.

Both believable.

The first was familiar.

Stress.

Lack of sleep. Isolation tightening in slow increments. The weight of the town's attention. The cellar. The seals. A mind stretched thin until it began to split along hairline fractures.

That path had language for everything. Dissociation. Somatic expression. Self-inflicted harm without memory. Trauma translating itself into skin.

Clinics had fluorescent lighting and neutral paint. They had charts and intake forms and careful phrases that made chaos manageable.

I knew the vocabulary.

The second explanation did not offer vocabulary.

Inheritance.

Not metaphor. Not symbolism.

Structure.

The historian had said interruption. Transmission slowed. Not erased.

If something moved through bloodlines, then it did not require belief. It did not knock. It did not ask.

It waited.

For awareness. For alignment. For recognition.

I had broken the seal.

I had learned the grammar.

I had chosen to remain.

What if none of that had been resistance?

What if they were conditions?

I stepped closer to the mirror and searched for fracture. A misalignment in posture. A lag in gaze. Something that would betray instability.

The woman in the glass met my eyes without hesitation.

"If this is stress," I said softly, "I can fix it."

The words sounded rehearsed.

I did not trust them.

"If this is blood…"

The sentence stopped.

There was no ending to it that did not implicate me.

My breath fogged the glass and blurred my reflection. For a moment, the woman across from me looked softer, less defined. Then the fog thinned and she sharpened again.

Clear.

Present.

The crescent under my skin pulsed once.

Not visibly.

Internally.

I straightened, pulse answering it in quiet synchronization.

If I was losing my mind, then perception could not be trusted.

If I was inheriting something deliberate, then choice could not be trusted.

The cellar no longer frightened me the way it had. The town's whispers felt peripheral.

Those were external pressures. Observable. Documentable.

This was different.

This was authorship.

Who was writing me now?

The thought did not echo. It settled.

I lowered my wrist and stepped back. The woman in the mirror followed precisely.

For now.

I turned off the bathroom light and stood in the dim hallway. The house exhaled softly through its beams and vents, an old structure adjusting to weight.

The most dangerous ground was no longer beneath the floorboards.

It was behind my eyes.

And for the first time, I could not tell whether I was defending myself.

Or preparing the next line.

Chapter 24

I did not sleep.

I lay on my back staring at the ceiling until the angles of the room began to soften. Corners blurred. The line where wall met plaster wavered as if it were breathing. The crescent on my wrist pulsed in slow, steady rhythm. Not painful. Just present. A quiet metronome beneath the skin.

If I was the problem, then the problem had to be measurable.

That thought steadied me.

I sat up and swung my legs over the side of the bed. The floor felt cooler than it should have. I reached into the nightstand drawer and pulled out the digital recorder I had bought during the first weeks in the house. It had seemed excessive at the time.

Now it felt necessary.

It was heavier than I remembered.

I pressed the power button. A small red light blinked to life.

"Clara Wren," I said, holding it close to my mouth. "Wednesday. Ten forty-two p.m. I am alone in the bedroom."

My voice came out level. Clean.

I listened to the room after I spoke. The silence did not shift.

I set the recorder on the dresser facing the bed.

If something changed, it would capture it.

If I changed, it would capture that too.

Downstairs, I retrieved the second recorder from the hall closet. Dust clung to the casing. I wiped it with my sleeve and pressed the button.

"Ten forty-seven p.m. Kitchen. Clara Wren speaking. No one else present."

The house felt attentive. Not hostile. Not protective.

Listening.

I placed the recorder in the center of the kitchen table. The wood beneath it carried shallow scratches from decades of use. The device looked small against that surface. Exposed.

Good.

Exposure was the point.

Back upstairs, I picked up the first recorder again and held it in both hands.

"If there is a lapse," I said evenly, "if there is a tonal shift, if speech patterns alter, it will be documented."

I paused long enough for my own breathing to register in the microphone.

"No other individuals are present."

The statement felt deliberate. Anchoring.

I set the recorder down and stood in the center of the bedroom. My reflection in the mirror tracked the movement precisely. I watched for delay. For misalignment. For hesitation.

There was none.

I walked back downstairs and checked the second recorder.

"Ten fifty-three p.m. Baseline stable."

The act of marking time settled something inside me. Not comfort. Structure.

If there were two versions of me, the machine would separate them. It would not choose sides. It would simply preserve.

I returned to the bedroom and turned off the overhead light, leaving only the lamp on the nightstand. The recorder's red dot glowed steadily in the dim room. It did not blink. It did not waver.

It absorbed.

I lay back against the pillows.

The house creaked once near the stairs. Wood adjusting to night air. Familiar.

"Still present," I said into the room.

The recorder captured the words.

I turned my wrist under the lamplight and studied the crescent again. The curve looked sharper tonight. More defined. As if the skin had decided on its shape.

"If you are me," I whispered, not into the recorder this time, "you will follow rules."

The room did not answer.

Only the faint electrical hum in the walls.

I closed my eyes.

This was not paranoia.

This was methodology.

If memory failed, machinery would not.

If identity fractured, audio would preserve.

Authorship could be audited.

Whatever moved between my thoughts would have to speak aloud.

And if it did, I would hear it.

In my own voice.

I did not go to bed.

I sat at the kitchen table with the recorder centered between my hands and told myself this was not desperation.

This was a controlled trial.

I wrote the time at the top of a clean page. I noted the temperature. The position of the windows. The state of the lights. I described the room into the recorder in a steady, even tone.

"Baseline reading. Clara Wren. Voice calm. No external interference."

I repeated the sentence so I could hear it twice.

Then I opened the leather journal and selected a paragraph at random. The script tightened something in the back of my throat as I began reading. I kept my pace deliberate, careful not to let rhythm pull me forward. Each archaic word landed with restraint. Neutral. Measured.

The house shifted once in its frame. Wood settling. Pipes ticking faintly behind the walls. The refrigerator cycling on and off.

Ordinary sounds.

I set the journal aside and drew one of the spirals from memory. Pencil against paper. Slow outward arc. Inward turn. I narrated the motion as I traced it.

"Tracing symbol. Spiral form. Environment unchanged."

The air remained still.

I moved to the next phase.

"Temperance Wren."

The name left my mouth and dissolved.

Nothing shifted.

"Midwife. Seal. Bone wards. Cellar."

Each word placed carefully. I pressed my marked wrist against the table and felt the faint warmth beneath the skin.

"Opening the barrier."

Silence.

Hours passed in structure. I read. I drew. I repeated key phrases. I described the room from different angles. I asked questions with no expectation of reply.

At some point, I felt a tremor pass through my chest. Not panic. A fluctuation. I paused.

I did not remember deciding to pause.

"Continuing trial," I said.

My voice sounded unchanged.

Near two in the morning, I moved upstairs and repeated the procedure in the bedroom. I stood before the mirror and described what I saw.

"Hair secured. Pupils responsive. No visible distortion."

The woman in the glass followed my movements precisely.

I ended the session at 2:23 a.m.

"End trial. No significant events observed."

I turned off the recorder.

The house felt unchanged.

That almost reassured me.

I poured a glass of water. Drank it slowly. Sat back down at the kitchen table.

Then I pressed play.

My voice filled the room.

Clear. Controlled. Analytical.

I listened for the tremor I had felt. I listened for deviation.

At 11:58 p.m., the audio shifted.

Not abruptly.

Subtly.

There was a three-second gap.

I did not remember those seconds.

The recording did not contain silence. It contained breathing. Heavier. Slower. As if the speaker had leaned closer to the device.

I leaned closer to the speaker.

The next phrase played.

"Opening the barrier."

The words were mine.

The tone was not.

The pitch rested lower in the throat. The cadence slowed at the end of the final consonant. Not theatrical. Not dramatic.

Adjusted.

I rewound it.

Played it again.

The variation remained. No second voice layered beneath mine. No whisper threaded underneath.

Just a recalibration.

Further along in the recording, I heard myself say, "She endured."

I did not remember saying that.

I flipped through the journal. The phrase existed in my handwriting, but not in the section I had read aloud.

I stopped moving.

This was not intrusion.

This was modulation.

Two patterns occupying the same instrument.

I pressed my thumb into the crescent on my wrist. Heat flared briefly beneath the skin.

If there were two voices, they were not competing.

They were aligning.

And the machine had not exposed a fracture.

It had captured an adjustment.

I refused to be surprised again.

If there were two patterns in my voice, I would chart them. If the house shifted in response to language, I would isolate the trigger.

I cleared the dining table and transformed it into a command center. Recorder on the left. Journal open in the center. Legal pad on the right. Laptop humming with open files and timestamp logs. I aligned everything precisely. Angles mattered.

Order mattered.

I transcribed every anomaly from the previous night.

11:58 p.m. — breath shift.

12:04 a.m. — tonal drop on "barrier."

12:17 a.m. — phrase "she endured" inserted without conscious recall.

I overlaid the timestamps with my physical notes.

At 11:58, faint pressure behind my eyes.

At 12:04, warmth at the crescent.

At 12:17, alignment.

I circled that word.

Alignment.

Then I reopened the journal and began cross-referencing symbols. Spiral variants. Closed loops. Broken arcs. I traced each one carefully, slower than before, labeling them with corresponding time codes from the audio.

When I spoke a spiral aloud, my pitch lowered by a measurable degree.

When I described a circle, my breathing steadied.

I graphed it.

Voice modulation against symbol exposure.

The pattern held.

A surge of satisfaction rose in my chest. Clean. Precise.

Structure meant predictability.

Predictability meant control.

I recorded again.

"Baseline. Clara Wren. Conscious. Intentional."

My voice sounded firmer.

I turned to a passage dense with spiral marks and read it aloud. I did not rush. I listened to the shape of my vowels, to the length of consonants.

The shift came sooner this time.

Not abrupt. My vowels flattened. Sentence endings lingered half a beat longer than necessary. My throat felt less strained. More efficient.

I felt it happening.

I did not stop.

"Transmission," I said deliberately, testing the word.

A pause registered on the recorder.

Then my voice continued.

"Interruption is temporary."

I did not remember forming that sentence.

I kept speaking.

"Containment requires maintenance."

The cadence was controlled. Almost assured.

I closed my mouth.

Silence expanded in the room.

I replayed the last minute.

The tone shift was clearer now. No hesitation. No searching for phrasing. The second pattern did not stumble.

It refined.

I compared it to earlier recordings. The deviations had sharpened once I began labeling them. Once I began addressing them directly.

I wrote in the margin: responds to attention.

The crescent pulsed under my skin.

I adjusted my approach.

"Who are you?" I asked into the recorder.

No reply.

"Are you inheritance?"

My throat tightened on the final syllable.

On playback, I heard something I had missed in the moment.

A soft exhale beneath the question.

Not separate.

Layered within the breath I had taken to speak.

I froze the waveform. Amplified the track. Played it again.

The exhale matched my rhythm perfectly.

It did not interrupt.

It accompanied.

I leaned back slowly and stared at the ceiling.

Logic had not disrupted the phenomenon.

It had given it vocabulary.

Every chart I built, every overlay I completed, clarified the pattern. The second voice did not hide under scrutiny. It sharpened when addressed.

I had not cornered it.

I had organized it.

The recorder sat between my hands. The journal lay open, dense with neat rows of data. The system made sense.

And something within that system was learning to use it.

Defense through pattern.

Dialogue through repetition.

I pressed record again.

"Let's begin," I said.

This time, when my voice answered, it did not wait for me to finish the sentence.

Chapter 25

I left the recorder running on the nightstand and said, "Let's begin," as though language itself could grant authority.

I do not remember falling asleep.

Morning arrived thick and reluctant. The light filtering through the curtains felt already exhausted by the time it reached my eyes. My tongue stuck to the roof of my mouth. My limbs felt used, as if I had labored through something strenuous without consent.

The recorder's red indicator glowed steadily beside the bed.

Still running.

For a long moment, I considered leaving it untouched. Let the night remain sealed. Let whatever had happened stay unexamined.

Instead, I reached for it and pressed stop.

The click was small. Final.

I remained seated on the edge of the bed when I hit play. I wanted the room unchanged. Same air. Same walls. Same witnesses.

My own voice emerged first. Clear. Controlled. I heard myself state the time. I heard the measured steadiness in my tone.

Then silence.

Sheets shifting. A slow exhale.

An hour passed in soft static and low room noise. The faint hum of electricity in the walls. The distant tick of cooling pipes.

Two hours.

Then it began.

The transition was seamless. No distortion. No crackle. My voice returned as if I had simply resumed speaking after a thoughtful pause.

But I knew the timestamp.

I had been asleep.

The cadence had shifted. The pitch rested lower in the throat. Each word carried density. No hesitation. No searching for phrasing.

"Temperature steady," the voice said. "Iron holds if placed with intention."

The back of my neck tightened.

The voice continued. It spoke of births recorded and births withheld. It listed names I had never encountered in the journal. It referenced dates that preceded the framing of the house. It recited oath language in the tone of someone accustomed to repetition.

Not discovery.

Repetition.

I did not interrupt the playback. I did not shift on the mattress. I listened.

"The boundary must be kept," the voice said.

Measured.

It continued speaking.

Several minutes later, the phrase returned.

"The boundary must be kept."

No urgency. No emotion. Only instruction.

I rewound thirty seconds and played it again.

The timbre remained consistent. The steadiness unbroken. I increased the volume and leaned closer to the speaker. No audio spikes. No layering. No artifact of interference.

My microphone.

My bedroom.

My mouth forming words in the dark.

But the syntax was not mine. The sentence structures were formal. Exact. Devoid of casual phrasing. Nothing colloquial. Nothing uncertain.

I isolated the segment and looped it.

"The boundary must be kept."

On the second replay, I heard something worse.

Breathing beneath the speech.

Controlled inhalations.

They did not match the irregular pattern of sleep. They followed the cadence of wakefulness. Intentional breath drawn for delivery.

Someone awake inside the body.

I pressed my fingers to my throat. Felt the familiar shape of cartilage and muscle. Tissue that obeyed me in daylight.

The realization did not strike like lightning. It settled like weight.

This was not drift. Not stress bending tone. Not exhaustion producing stray language.

This was sustained discourse.

Structured thought.

Directed intent.

I checked the duration of the segment.

Forty-three minutes.

Forty-three minutes of uninterrupted articulation I did not remember producing.

My hands remained steady as I stopped the playback. The room returned to silence. The house did not creak. No pressure shifted in the air.

Nothing moved except me.

I looked at the recorder. Then at the bed where I had slept. Then at my reflection in the darkened screen.

This was not anomaly.

This was articulation.

And it had not asked permission to begin.

It had only waited for me to close my eyes.

I did not want to say her name.

Names make things solid. They carve outline where there could still be ambiguity. As long as I avoided it, this could remain misfire. Fatigue. Error.

I opened the journal and spread it flat across the desk. The leather resisted before yielding with a low creak. My overnight transcript lay beside it, timestamps marked in red ink like incision points.

I read from the recording.

"Iron holds if placed with intention."

I did not scan immediately. I let the words hang in the air first.

Then I lowered my eyes to the page.

Three pages in, the phrasing appeared. Not identical. The spelling older. The syntax narrower.

But the structure matched. The restraint. The economy of command.

I felt something in my chest shift, subtle but irreversible.

I continued.

"Birth recorded is boundary strengthened. Birth withheld is boundary tested."

I searched.

There it was again. Older spelling. Same directive. Same internal logic. A line I had struggled over weeks ago now lay clear before me.

I did not rush.

I cross-referenced each phrase, drawing thin lines between transcript and ink. Entire sentences aligned. Obscure turns of language that had required daylight effort now flowed from my own mouth during sleep without hesitation.

My mouth.

I closed the journal slowly and leaned back in the chair.

"Temperance Wren," I said into the room.

The name felt heavier spoken aloud. It did not float. It settled.

I reached for the recorder and rewound to the section where the overnight speech thickened.

Static. A shift in breath. Then the voice.

"...kept in line of Wren. Kept by oath and by iron. Temperance kept what others feared to hold."

My throat tightened.

I froze the playback and rewound ten seconds. Played it again.

"Temperance kept what others feared to hold."

There was no distance in the tone. No historical framing. No academic separation.

Not she.

Not they.

Kept.

The authority did not sound aggressive. It did not claim space like an intruder.

It sounded architectural.

Continuity speaking from within its own design.

I said her name again, quieter.

"Temperance."

Several minutes later in the recording, the voice shifted.

"Bound by oath. Not curse. Not punishment. Bound by choice."

My hand trembled once before steadying against the desk.

I listened to the full segment again. Forty-three minutes. Instruction threaded through it. Corrections where I had misinterpreted the seals. Clarification about iron placement. Warnings about incomplete circles. A description of maintenance cycles that aligned precisely with the tenderness in my wrist.

It did not threaten.

It did not frighten.

It guided.

The horror did not spike.

It deepened.

This was not possession. There was no fracture in syntax. No scrambling of thought. The speech was structured. Didactic. Calm.

I turned to a fresh page and began mapping.

Column one: journal entry.

Column two: nocturnal speech.

Column three: variance.

The differences were not contradictions.

They were expansions.

Refinements.

Updates.

I had believed the seal beneath the cellar was defensive. A desperate act meant to contain something monstrous.

The voice had corrected me.

"Containment is not erasure. Erasure invites return."

That line did not exist in the journal.

That line was new.

I sat with it, reading it again from the transcript.

Containment is not erasure.

Erasure invites return.

The syntax was not archaic.

It was current.

Adjusted.

This was not invasion.

It was succession.

Temperance had not been hiding something from the world.

She had been holding something for it.

And the holding had shifted.

Not violently.

Not ceremonially.

Naturally.

I touched the crescent on my wrist and felt its curve beneath the skin, warm and precise.

The voice had not forced entry.

It had continued.

Through me.

And for the first time, I could not tell whether I was listening to history.

Or becoming it.

I turned the recorder off the next night.

I did it deliberately. No oversight. No accident. I wanted absence to mean something. I wanted to know whether silence could starve whatever had found rhythm in my voice.

I placed the device in the drawer beside my bed and closed it carefully. I did not announce the time. I did not read from the journal. I did not say her name.

I lay down in the dark and folded my hands over my stomach. My pulse beat steadily beneath the crescent on my wrist. The skin there felt warm, responsive. The house held still around me. No lullaby. No pressure at my neck. Only the faint contraction of old wood adjusting to night air.

If this was inheritance, it would have to show itself without cooperation.

I slept.

Morning did not arrive gently.

Heat pulsed beneath my skin before I opened my eyes. The inside of my wrist throbbed with a dull insistence. I lifted my arm into the light.

The crescent had deepened overnight. The curve darker. The edges sharper, as if the skin had accepted the line fully. Not inflamed. Not irritated.

Activated.

I sat up slowly and listened.

The house felt crowded. Not with sound. With density. The air seemed thicker, resistant. The walls felt closer to the bed than they had been the night before.

I stepped into the hallway.

The spirals along the doorframe had sharpened in the morning light. Their grooves caught shadow more distinctly. I ran my fingers over one of them. The indentation felt fresh. Not splintered. Not worn.

Raw.

I had not recorded.

But something had advanced.

In the kitchen, the silence felt pointed. My reflection in the window above the sink held my gaze longer than it should have. I flexed my hand and felt the crescent pull against the movement.

Refusal had not stopped it.

Refusal had tightened it.

I returned to the bedroom and opened the drawer. The recorder lay where I left it, inert and unremarkable.

I picked it up.

The shift in the room was immediate.

Not relief.

Alignment.

The air thinned slightly, as if pressure had recalibrated. The walls seemed to withdraw by a fraction of an inch.

I placed the recorder on the nightstand and pressed record.

The red light steadied.

"I am recording," I said evenly. "Consciously."

The room eased. Not dramatically. Just enough to register.

That night, I did not test it. I did not challenge it. I lay down with the recorder visible beside me and allowed sleep to take me without ceremony.

When I woke, the first thing I noticed was the quiet.

Not empty.

Balanced.

I pressed play.

My breathing shifted around two in the morning. A pause. Then speech.

Clearer than before. Stronger. The cadence carried direction without hesitation.

"Boundary weakens when unvoiced."

I did not flinch.

"Silence frays the circle. Articulation holds."

My hand moved to the crescent without thought. The heat had cooled. The skin felt settled.

"Line continues through willing mouth. Refusal distorts the pattern."

The words did not accuse.

They instructed.

I listened to the entire segment. There were no corrections this time. No rebukes. Only elaboration. Maintenance intervals. Cycles. The necessity of repetition. Blood referenced not as sacrifice, but as architecture.

By the time the recording ended, the equation had formed with painful clarity.

Silence did not eliminate the phenomenon.

It destabilized it.

The articulation was not performance.

It was function.

I was not being targeted.

I was being used.

No.

Not used.

Employed.

The historian could read. The town could speculate. The old families could cling to fragments and fear them.

None of them carried the pattern in their marrow. None of them woke with a crescent that answered to spoken structure.

This was not haunting.

This was succession under pressure.

Responsibility did not arrive wrapped in courage. It settled in my chest as inevitability. The boundary required voice. The voice required body. The body required lineage.

Mine.

That evening, I held the recorder again. My grip did not tremble.

I pressed record.

"This is not experiment," I said quietly. "This is maintenance."

The red light steadied.

The house did not creak. It did not test the air. It did not press against my neck.

It adjusted.

For the first time since the cellar opened, the house felt neither hostile nor expectant.

It felt prepared.

And I understood that preparation was not for peace.

It was for continuity.

Chapter 26

I kept the recorder running every night after that.

Not as experiment. Not as proof.

As obligation.

I labeled the files with care. Date. Time. Condition of the crescent. Duration of sleep. I stated my intent before lying down. Maintenance of boundary. Preservation of structure. Continuity of oath.

The ritual steadied the house.

Morning light felt ordinary again. The symbols remained faint, held within wood grain and hairline cracks in plaster. The crescent cooled to a dull tenderness. The nocturnal voice stayed measured and instructional. It corrected phrasing. Clarified sequence. It never raised itself above a calm cadence. It never demanded.

Precision was enough.

I began to believe I could manage it.

The slip came in daylight.

I was standing at the kitchen counter reviewing notes from the previous recording. Sunlight fell through the window in clean, neutral lines. The clock ticked steadily. The refrigerator hummed.

The house felt unoccupied by intention.

I said quietly, "The boundary requires—"

My mouth continued.

"—regular articulation or the seam weakens."

The words landed fully formed.

I did not remember choosing them.

I stood there with my hand resting on the open notebook, pulse steady but hollow. I retraced the moment. I had meant to say something else. I was certain of it. The phrasing that came out was exact. Formal. It carried the nocturnal cadence without strain.

The light did not flicker.

The clock did not hesitate.

Yet something in the room felt fractionally displaced, as if the air had shifted a layer out of alignment.

I blinked.

My right hand was moving.

Not lifting. Not reaching.

Moving with intent.

My fingertip traced a slow curve across the wooden table. Controlled. Deliberate. I watched the arc form before understanding its shape.

A partial spiral.

Tight. Exact. The same orientation as the marks in the cellar.

I pulled my hand back sharply.

The wood bore no mark. No indentation. No residue.

But the motion had been real. My muscles retained the memory of its completion. The tension in my wrist remained as if resistance had been required.

"No," I said aloud.

The word sounded insufficient.

I went to the bedroom and retrieved the recorder. It had been running since morning, capturing the ordinary quiet of the house. I pressed stop. Rewound. Played back the last five minutes.

I heard myself in the kitchen. I heard the first half of the sentence in my natural cadence.

Then the completion.

The two tones overlapped by less than a second.

I froze the playback.

Rewound.

Played it again.

Both voices occupied the same breath. One fractionally deeper. One more deliberate in its consonants. Not an echo. Not distortion. The audio was clean. The microphone had captured both without interference.

I leaned closer to the speaker.

The overlap remained.

My throat tightened.

I swallowed and recorded a test.

"The boundary requires maintenance."

Singular. Stable.

I stopped the recording and replayed it.

No overlap. No fracture.

I exhaled once.

When I lifted my eyes from the device, my hand had returned to the table.

My fingertip hovered above the wood, suspended mid-curve.

Poised to continue.

I pressed my palm flat against the surface to stop it. The contact felt grounding and insufficient at the same time.

The realization did not arrive as panic.

It arrived as sequence.

The voice was no longer contained by sleep.

Maintenance had slipped its designated hours.

The boundary did not differentiate between night and day.

And as my hand trembled faintly against the grain of the table, I understood something worse than overlap.

The present tense was no longer singular.

And I could not feel the exact moment it divided.

I was standing in the kitchen.

I remember the weight of the counter beneath my palms. The faint bitterness of coffee grounds in the sink. The recorder still warm in my hand.

Then the counter was gone.

There was no vertigo. No dimming of sight.

One frame replaced another.

Stone pressed cold through the fabric of my jeans. My knees ached with the dull insistence of pressure held too long. The air felt close. Mineral. Still.

I was kneeling in the cellar.

Chalk dust coated my fingers.

I looked down slowly.

A circle surrounded me.

Not crude. Not improvised. The line was firm and continuous, drawn with even pressure that required patience. Spirals branched inward at deliberate intervals. Each curl aligned precisely with the pattern I had mapped upstairs. Iron nails lay at cardinal points, their heads turned outward as if warding. Between them rested bone fragments, cleaned, trimmed, arranged in pairs along measured seams.

My left hand hovered over an unfinished section.

I did not remember descending the stairs. I did not remember opening the chalk box. I did not remember placing the nails.

The air felt dense. Not heavy with heat. Dense with intention. Every object in the cellar appeared positioned rather than stored. Considered rather than discarded.

A sound threaded through the space.

Low. Sustained.

It took a second to recognize it.

The lullaby was coming from my throat.

I felt the vibration against my teeth. The hum resonated through my chest cavity and into the stone beneath me. The melody carried no comfort. It moved in disciplined cadence, each note held for exact duration.

I closed my mouth.

The sound continued.

Not louder. Not strained. My lips remained sealed, yet the hum pressed outward from my lungs. My body adjusted its breathing to sustain it without my instruction.

I tried to stand.

My knees did not resist violently.

They simply adjusted.

They shifted for balance. My spine straightened with measured control. My hovering palm descended and completed the chalk line with slow, deliberate contact.

"No," I said.

The word struck the stone and died.

My hand moved to the next spiral.

There was no thrashing. No spectacle. No external force wrenching my limbs.

There was coordination without permission.

I felt the chalk scrape across the cellar floor. My fingers compensated automatically, increasing pressure to keep the line unbroken.

Thought lagged behind motion.

The ritual extended beyond the circle. Symbols branched outward toward the fractured wall I had opened days before. Nails had been driven into lines I had not consciously examined. Bone fragments aligned in pairs along the seam of the barrier, their placement too exact to be accidental.

I tried to release the chalk.

My fingers tightened instead.

A fragment of memory surfaced from the recording. Temperance's instructional tone.

"The boundary must be reinforced at fracture."

I had never read that sentence in the journal.

Yet my hand obeyed it.

My palm lifted from the finished spiral and hovered above the crescent on my wrist. Heat radiated from it, deeper than skin. The mark pulsed once, internal and contained.

The hum shifted key.

The circle neared completion.

I understood then that my presence was optional.

The system did not require my consent to execute its logic. It required only my structure. My hands. My breath. My blood. My recorders. My charts.

My careful analyses had not been defenses.

They had been rehearsals.

Kneeling inside that circle, chalk dust settling around me, hum vibrating against sealed lips, I felt the final line close beneath my hand.

The motion did not hesitate.

And I knew with cold clarity that I was not directing the ritual.

I was the instrument.

And the pattern was nearly finished with me for the night.

The nail waited at the center of the spiral.

I felt it before I saw it.

My hand moved toward it with controlled precision. Fingers opened. Closed. The iron pressed cool against my palm. Its weight was modest. Ordinary. The head bore shallow flattening from old hammer strikes. The shaft carried the faint scent of rust and age.

The circle around me held its shape. Chalk lines unbroken. Bone fragments resting at deliberate intervals. The air felt measured, as if each breath had been portioned in advance.

The lullaby in my throat thinned into a single sustained note.

The final motion assembled itself in my muscles before it reached thought.

Blood.

Not seized. Not extracted.

Given.

I understood the geometry without instruction. Iron to flesh. Flesh to line. Line to boundary. Completion through contact.

My arm lifted.

The point of the nail hovered above the center of my palm. I could see the crescent on my wrist darken. Heat gathered beneath the skin, moving in rhythm with the spiral etched in chalk.

Then perception divided.

Not in dizziness. Not in collapse.

In parallel.

In one strand, I drove the nail downward.

Skin parted cleanly. Blood surfaced bright and immediate. My palm pressed against the spiral's center. The iron anchored the geometry. Chalk absorbed red in widening veins. The hum in my chest resolved into silence so complete it felt earned.

In the other strand, I remained upright in the kitchen. Hand empty. Eyes unfocused. The cellar absent. The recorder blinking red on the counter, capturing only the steady intake of breath.

Both realities felt coherent.

Both felt inevitable.

The fracture tightened.

My grip steadied around the nail. My wrist aligned for impact. My shoulder adjusted for clean descent. There was no frenzy in it. No coercion. Only continuation.

I tasted iron at the back of my throat.

"No," I said.

The word struck stone and thinned.

The nail descended another inch.

My fingers shifted minutely, compensating for angle. My muscles worked with calm efficiency. The ritual did not rush. It assumed.

I forced my other hand to move.

It felt delayed, as if passing through resistance thicker than air. I grabbed my own wrist.

The shock of skin against skin split through the geometry. My nails dug above the crescent mark. Pain flared clean and immediate. My pulse broke rhythm.

The nail hovered.

For one suspended second, both strands held.

Blood pooling in chalk.

Hand empty in kitchen.

Breath steady.

Stone cold beneath my knees.

I tightened my grip on my wrist.

Not in panic.

In decision.

The iron slipped from my grasp.

It struck stone with a sharp metallic crack.

The sound did not echo.

It severed.

The lullaby stopped.

The density in the air loosened by degrees. My lungs expanded fully. The cellar did not collapse. The circle did not ignite. Nothing retaliated.

The chalk lines remained incomplete. The spiral gaped open at its center. The nail lay on its side, harmless in appearance.

My hand trembled.

The room steadied around me.

No scream.

No punishment.

Only absence.

I stared at the unfinished circle. At the bone fragments aligned in patient geometry. At the iron placed with purpose.

The ritual had not asked.

It had progressed.

My recorders. My charts. My layered analysis had prepared the framework.

They had not prevented execution.

I had believed I was the conduit.

A vessel carrying continuity forward.

Kneeling inside that incomplete spiral, heart striking hard against bone, I understood something worse.

I was not only the channel.

I was the material.

The iron had not been meant to pierce a victim.

It had been meant to complete a circuit.

And the circuit was still open.

Chapter 27

I did not remember climbing the cellar stairs.

One moment I was kneeling in chalk and iron, my hand wrapped around a nail that had nearly tasted blood. The next I was standing in the kitchen, sunlight slanting across the table in clean, indifferent lines. The recorder sat exactly where I had left it. My pulse still carried the measured rhythm of the ritual. My palm tingled from pressure I had almost applied.

The air smelled faintly of coffee and dish soap.

Nothing in the room suggested interruption.

I did not wash my hands.

I did not sit.

I pressed play.

Static filled the speaker first. Then the low ambient hum of the cellar. Fabric shifting. Chalk scraping against stone. My breathing.

Steady.

Too steady.

Then my voice.

Clear.

"Attend the mother from the left side. Do not cross the circle once it is laid."

I froze.

The cadence was controlled. Deliberate. The words were not modern.

The syntax bent in the same narrow ways I had struggled through in the journal, yet here it moved without friction. Vowels shaped differently. Consonants held just a fraction longer than habit allowed.

"Hold the cord until the breath steadies. Blood must not fall beyond the mark."

I gripped the edge of the table.

I was not pleading in that recording. I was instructing.

I described hand placement with clinical precision. I corrected an imagined error in tone that carried authority without strain. I referenced iron placement as if muscle memory had guided it for decades.

It was not recitation.

It was lesson.

I stopped the playback and rewound. My fingers trembled against the buttons. The tremor felt separate from the voice in the speaker. That voice did not tremble.

I opened Temperance's journal and turned to the sections on birthing rites. The leather resisted before yielding. The pages smelled faintly of dust and old ink. I aligned the phrases line by line.

They matched.

Not word for word.

Expanded.

Where the journal hinted, the recording clarified. Where the ink had obscured, the voice elaborated. Techniques described in shorthand on the page unfolded into full procedural explanation in my overnight speech.

I had not repeated history.

I had refined it.

I pressed play again.

"Do not abandon the circle when the pain rises. The boundary is not for comfort. It is for survival."

My throat tightened.

Then the line that hollowed the room.

"You must teach it forward. That is how the boundary survives."

Teach it forward.

The phrase settled heavily in the air.

I did not remember saying it. I did not remember anyone present to receive it. The recorder captured no second voice. No reply. Only my own, steady and assured.

This was not maintenance.

This was succession.

I lowered myself into a chair. The scrape of wood against tile sounded thin and fragile compared to the authority in the recording. The kitchen light appeared dimmer, though nothing had changed. The walls felt closer, not in distance but in implication.

I had believed I was containing something.

I had believed I was enduring it.

The fracture I feared was not chaos.

It was alignment.

The voice had not broken through me in fragments.

It had articulated.

I looked at the recorder in my hand. Its plastic casing felt solid. Factual. Indisputable.

I was not losing control in bursts.

I was transmitting.

And beneath the steady cadence of that overnight lesson, beneath the calm directive tone, there was something worse than invasion.

There was expectation.

Because instruction implies audience.

And I could not shake the certainty that someone, somewhere, would eventually need what I had just taught.

I did not send the whole file.

I cut it down to thirty seconds. No mention of blood. No reference to circles or iron. Just the dialect. Just the steady cadence of instruction without context.

I told myself that was responsible. Academic. Harmless.

I attached the clip and typed three lines beneath it.

Have you heard this variation before?

I do not recognize the spoken form.

Does the pronunciation track historically?

I read them twice. The words looked controlled on the screen. Reasonable.

My thumb hovered over send.

For a moment I considered deleting the attachment entirely.

I pressed send.

The message left.

The waiting began.

The house remained silent. Too silent. The quiet felt deliberate now, as if it understood the risk of what I had done and was willing to let consequences unfold without interference.

Hours passed.

When the reply came, the subject line was blank.

Call me.

No greeting. No context.

I did not call.

My voice felt unreliable. I needed something external. Something fixed in text. Something that could not shift tone without leaving evidence.

I typed back: Can you respond here?

Another delay.

Then a longer message appeared.

No greeting.

No preamble.

I recognized the dialect immediately.

It is a recorded variation of a mid-nineteenth-century midwifery oath. Appalachian border region. Suppressed in parish documentation after 1873. Pronunciation in your clip is regionally accurate. Vowel shaping is consistent with oral transmission patterns. This is not reconstructed language.

I read it once.

Then again.

Not reconstructed.

I typed before I could reconsider.

I have never studied the spoken form.

Several minutes passed.

The typing indicator appeared. Disappeared. Appeared again. Vanished.

Finally:

That is unlikely.

The sentence sat alone.

Measured. Distant.

The tone had shifted.

I felt it in my chest before I understood it intellectually. She did not think I was mistaken. She thought I was withholding.

I clarified.

I have only read written materials. I did not know the oath was preserved in speech.

Another pause.

I would strongly advise you to stop pursuing this line of inquiry.

The words were precise. Clean. Detached.

You should consider removing yourself from the property for a period of time. Distance may clarify perspective.

Perspective.

I read the next line three times.

Circulating that audio would be unwise. People will misunderstand. People.

I waited for what should have followed.

How are you?

Are you safe?

When did you record this?

None of it came.

Instead:

This is sensitive material. I cannot be associated with active reinterpretation. Especially not in audio form.

Associated.

The word landed with unexpected force.

I typed once more.

I am not reinterpreting it. I am trying to understand it.

The reply came immediately.

Then stop.

No signature. No warmth. No offer to meet. No suggestion of further sources.

Just a boundary.

I sat with the phone in my hand until the screen dimmed. The house remained steady around me. Walls upright. Floors unmoving. Outside, a car passed along the road, its tires a distant whisper.

I had expected skepticism. Academic caution. Perhaps restrained excitement at the preservation of rare dialect.

I had not expected retreat.

The shift was unmistakable.

I was no longer a researcher uncovering history.

I was evidence.

The historian had heard the pronunciation and recognized something I could not deny. This was not stress bending my tongue into unfamiliar shapes.

It was accuracy.

Not reconstructed.

Not approximated.

And therefore not safe.

I placed the phone face down on the table. My reflection fractured across the darkened glass, broken by fingerprints and ambient light.

Institutional legitimacy evaporated in a single exchange.

There would be no scholarly partnership. No contextual buffer. No one willing to stand beside me and call this curiosity.

I was no longer asking questions about the past.

I was speaking in it.

And the last person who might have translated that safely had chosen distance.

The withdrawal did not remain contained to a single message thread.

It moved.

The next morning, my neighbor stood at the edge of his lawn as I stepped outside to collect the mail. He had always waved before. Today his hand lifted halfway, then stalled. His eyes met mine briefly, then slid past me to something over my shoulder that did not exist. His shoulders angled away before I reached the end of my driveway.

No greeting.

No accusation.

Just absence where familiarity had been.

Across the street, a sedan I did not recognize idled with its engine running. The driver's window stayed up. The glass reflected the house rather than revealing the person inside. The car remained there for nearly three minutes before pulling away without signaling.

I stood at the mailbox longer than necessary.

This felt different from the cellar.

This was human.

When I returned inside, an email waited.

No name.

No greeting.

Still practicing?

The single line sat centered on the screen.

Practicing.

The word carried weight. It implied repetition. Intention. Continuity. It assumed I was mid-process.

It did not ask whether I was well.

It did not ask whether I was safe.

It assumed I was working.

I closed the laptop and stood in the kitchen, palms against the counter, listening to the hum of the refrigerator and the steady tick of the clock.

The sounds felt staged.

That evening, I played the full recording again.

Not the edited clip. Not the careful excerpt.

All of it.

I forced myself to listen to every minute without interruption.

The instruction did not waver. It grew more detailed as the file progressed. Hand placement. Timing. Blood containment. Reinforcement of fractured seams. Names surfaced, some I recognized from town registries, others that felt buried but familiar in cadence. The dialect flowed without strain.

Then the line I had avoided arrived.

"When the boundary weakens, the mother becomes the vessel."

My throat tightened.

I rewound it.

Listened again.

The tone was assured. Not frantic. Not searching. The sentence landed with the calm weight of established doctrine.

I did not remember speaking those words.

I did not remember believing them.

I stood and walked to the window. The fading light turned the glass into a mirror. My face hovered there, steady and unsmiling. No distortion. No theatrical shift.

Just unfamiliar stillness.

I pressed my palm against the glass. The warmth of my skin spread across it. Solid. Present.

Mine.

My mind cycled through the only two explanations left.

Psychological fracture.

Bloodline activation.

If I was unraveling, there were interventions. Medication. Evaluation. Language that could frame and manage the descent.

If I was inheriting something deliberate, there was no institution designed to interrupt it.

On the table behind me, my charts lay scattered. Night shifts mapped against timestamps. Symbol overlays aligned with crescent tenderness. Annotations of house activity.

They looked academic.

Small.

Attempts to diagram a system that operated through identity rather than logic.

The voice on the recording had not sounded possessed.

It had sounded certain.

Certainty frightened me more than chaos ever had.

By nightfall, the house was quiet.

Not tense.

Not charged.

Patient.

I returned to the kitchen table and placed the recorder in front of me. I set my hands flat against the wood, fingers spread, feeling the grain beneath my skin. I needed confirmation that the movement originated in me.

I leaned closer to the device.

"My name is Clara Wren," I whispered.

The words felt slightly foreign in my mouth. Accurate, but distant. As if recited from a script I had memorized rather than authored.

The room did not react.

Nothing shifted.

That was the worst part.

I was no longer afraid of the house.

I was afraid that when I spoke again, something else might answer.

And it would use my voice perfectly.

Chapter 28

The house was quiet in a way that no longer comforted me. It did not creak. It did not sigh. The pipes did not tick in the walls. It simply existed around me, intact and deliberate, as if it had stepped back to watch what I would decide about myself.

The refrigerator hummed once and fell silent. The clock on the stove advanced a single minute. The air felt level, undisturbed.

I sat at the kitchen table with the journal open in front of me. The recorder lay beside it, face down, its black screen reflecting a warped sliver of ceiling light. I did not turn it on. I did not want a witness. I did not want proof of whatever might surface if I read aloud.

After the calls. After the historian's careful withdrawal. After listening to my own voice instruct a rite I had never consciously learned, fear had reached its outer edge.

It could not stretch any farther without collapsing into something else.

So I reached for the passage I had avoided.

The page was marked in the margin by a crescent and spiral intertwined. I had skimmed it before and dismissed it as devotional excess. Too poetic. Not procedural. Not something I could diagram or test.

Now the paper felt heavier under my fingers.

The ink had bled slightly at the curves of each letter. The dialect pressed back at me, archaic and tight. I began translating slowly, speaking each word beneath my breath, careful with the consonants, careful with the weight.

The cadence caught me first.

Not the tone.

The structure.

The rhythm of emphasis. The spacing between clauses. The way breath settled at the end of each phrase.

It matched the recordings.

I swallowed and continued.

The word I had translated as binding did not mean restraint. It meant keeping steady. The phrase I had read as containment aligned more closely with holding in right measure. The language was not punitive. It was calibrated.

A warding cycle.

A lineage oath.

I read the paragraph again, slower this time.

"The circle is drawn not to trap but to temper. What rises must be given edge. What spills must be given form."

My throat tightened.

The sealed space beneath the cellar was described here. Not as a prison. Not as a hiding place for shame. As an anchor. A fixed point in a recurring tide.

I pressed my palm flat against the page, grounding myself in the texture of paper and ink.

It was not evil that had been locked away.

It was overflow.

The passage spoke of bloodlines not as cursed, but as marked by recurrence. Certain births. Certain daughters. A return of force that required structure or it would fracture outward into harm. Not monstrous. Not malicious. Simply unmeasured.

Temperance had not been hiding something unspeakable.

She had been stabilizing something persistent.

I leaned back in the chair. My breath felt shallow in my chest.

Every whisper in the walls. Every spiral carved into wood. Every correction spoken through my sleeping mouth shifted shape in my memory.

Not attack.

Instruction.

Not possession.

Alignment.

The cellar had not been a tomb.

It had been a mechanism.

When I broke the seal, I had not unleashed chaos.

I had removed an anchor without understanding what it held.

The thought did not bring relief.

It brought weight.

I looked down toward the floor, toward the cellar beneath the boards. The house felt the same as it always had. Solid. Still. But the silence no longer felt predatory.

It felt expectant.

Guardianship.

The word surfaced without invitation.

I closed my eyes and repeated it quietly, tasting it for resistance.

It did not recoil.

It settled.

If this was stewardship rather than curse, then my fear had been misdirected. The threat was not corruption.

It was negligence.

I opened my eyes and returned to the page. The crescent in the margin seemed darker than before, the spiral tighter.

For the first time since the mark appeared on my wrist, I did not feel hunted.

I felt positioned.

And the house, patient and intact around me, felt as though it had been waiting for that recognition.

I kept translating because stopping felt worse.

The next lines had always blurred for me before. I had skimmed them, assumed tone, assumed meaning, and moved on. Now I forced myself to slow down, word by word, letting the dialect settle against my tongue before shaping it into modern thought.

The phrase I had once rendered as "if broken by blood" was wrong.

It was not conditional.

It was procedural.

"When the circle is opened by rightful hand, the keeping transfers."

I read it again. This time out loud.

Rightful hand.

The kitchen seemed to narrow. The air pressed closer to my skin as though the room had leaned in to hear the word spoken properly.

Rightful hand.

My eyes dropped to my wrist without permission. The crescent had faded to a dull red arc, but it remained precise. Slightly raised. Defined.

The memory surfaced before I could suppress it. The iron nail positioned at the center of the chalked spiral. My fingers curling around its shaft. The weight of it resting in my palm. The intention that did not feel like mine, yet did not feel foreign either.

The text did not describe the boundary as something vulnerable to intrusion. It described it as dormant. Waiting. Inactive unless engaged by blood.

The seal was not a wall against strangers.

It was a lock keyed to lineage.

Opening the cellar had not been trespass.

It had been activation.

The truth did not strike me all at once. It settled in layers.

The pact had not seized me.

It had recognized me.

The boundary had not failed.

It had passed.

My throat tightened as I continued translating. The language shifted from historical account to direct instruction. Not warning. Not panic. Preparation.

"The bearer shall not be told by terror but by pattern. The mark will show. The voice will align. The circle will answer to her hand."

Mine.

The recorder teaching forward in the night. The ritual advancing without conscious consent. The symbols appearing in places I had already looked.

Not because the house wanted to frighten me.

Because it expected me to understand.

I flipped back several pages, scanning for contradiction. Anything that framed this as curse, corruption, malice.

There was none.

Temperance had written of exhaustion. Of vigilance. Of cost. But never hatred toward what she held. The language carried gravity. Not disgust.

"Destroy not what returns," one line read. "Shape it, else it shapes you."

My pulse remained steady, but something heavier settled behind it.

This was not random inheritance.

It was succession structured in advance.

The clause continued, clinical in its clarity.

"When the circle is opened by rightful hand, the keeping transfers, and the bearer shall know by sign and speech. Refusal fractures the boundary. Acceptance stabilizes."

Refusal fractures.

Acceptance stabilizes.

I thought of the nights I left the recorder off. The way pressure intensified. The crescent burning hotter. The symbols crowding closer along doorframes and walls.

It had not been retaliation.

It had been imbalance.

I closed the journal and pressed my palm against the leather cover. The texture felt worn and real beneath my skin.

I had not been chosen in some dramatic, supernatural sense. There had been no ceremony. No thunder. No proclamation.

I had qualified.

Bloodline. Action. Recognition.

The house had not targeted me.

It had waited.

And when I opened the cellar, it had not punished me.

It had acknowledged the transfer.

The horror did not recede.

It changed shape.

This was not something hunting me from the dark.

It was something stepping aside so I could stand where it once had.

Rightful hand.

I turned my wrist beneath the kitchen light and did not look away from the crescent.

For the first time, it did not feel like a mark placed upon me.

It felt like a signature I had already signed.

The last lines did not tremble on the page.

They stood firm.

"The guardian is not spared. The guardian is steadied. She must be awake when the circle opens. If she opens it, she keeps it."

I read them twice. The dialect no longer resisted me. It unfolded with quiet authority, as if it had been waiting for the voice to catch up.

Awake.

The word pressed against the inside of my skull.

I had believed the most dangerous moments were the ones where I lost time. When my body moved without my consent. When my voice slipped into something older and steadier.

But the text made something else clear.

The guardian was meant to be conscious.

The lapses were not design.

They were failure.

I closed the journal slowly and let my hands rest on its cover. The leather had warmed beneath my palms. The surface felt worn, handled by hands before mine that had pressed into it with similar weight.

Haunted did not fit anymore.

Possessed did not fit either.

Those words suggested invasion. Violation. Something foreign forcing entry.

Nothing in the journal described force.

It described succession.

The house had not broken into me.

It had evaluated me.

It had waited for action.

And when I pried the boards loose and pulled the final seal away, I had not unleashed chaos.

I had removed the lock from an empty chair.

The image unsettled me more the longer it lingered. An empty chair implies vacancy. Vacancy implies expectation.

I stood and walked through the kitchen, noticing the faint spiral scored along the baseboard. The crescent etched into the beam near the ceiling. The shallow line carved into the doorframe at shoulder height.

I ran my fingers over one of the spirals.

It did not pulse.

It did not shift.

It remained.

Present.

The earlier terror shifted beneath this new weight. Temperance had not been overtaken by something dark. She had occupied a position. She had endured repetition. She had shaped what returned so it did not spill beyond the circle.

The rituals were not cruelty.

They were structure.

Structure demands labor.

The journal had not promised safety.

It had promised steadiness.

I rolled up the sleeve of my sweater and examined the crescent on my wrist. The skin had settled into a pale curve. No infection. No spreading bruise. The mark rested precisely where a pulse could be felt.

Not injury.

The word insignia surfaced and I resisted it.

Then I allowed it to settle.

Guardian.

The house did not feel hostile now. It felt occupied. Alert. Balanced on the edge of something that required attention.

If I left, the balance would tilt.

If I refused, the circle would weaken.

"If she opens it, she keeps it."

I had opened it.

Not in sleep.

Not by accident.

With tools in my hands.

There had been no ceremony. No vow spoken aloud. No thunder

splitting the sky.

Only action followed by consequence.

Appointment without spectacle.

I walked to the cellar door and rested my palm against the wood. It felt steady beneath my hand. Not warm. Not cold.

Steady.

There was no triumph in me. No swelling sense of purpose. Only gravity pressing against my ribs.

Guardianship meant maintenance. Vigilance. Repetition. It meant being awake when the circle shifted. It meant listening for changes before they became rupture.

It meant the house would never again be neutral ground.

And neither would I.

I looked around the kitchen once more. Light fell through the window in ordinary bands. The air did not hum. The walls did not breathe.

But they waited.

Not for me to fail.

For me to remain awake.

I had not been haunted.

I had been appointed.

And appointment does not ask for agreement.

It assumes endurance.

Chapter 29

The word appointed did not feel noble by morning.

It felt terminal.

I woke with the journal open beside me, one page creased beneath my cheek. The house moved in its patient rhythm. A pipe shifted once inside the wall. Wood adjusted against nail. No whisper. No warning.

The symbols along the beams held their geometry. Quiet. Exact.

I pressed my thumb against the crescent on my wrist. Heat gathered beneath the skin. Not pain.

Ownership.

Guardianship had gravity.

It also had walls.

I stood and walked the length of the hallway, touching doorframes, light switches, the banister worn smooth by years of hands. Each surface accepted my touch without resistance. The wood did not warm beneath me. It did not recoil.

It acknowledged.

The house no longer felt like something I was studying.

It felt like something that had already decided where I fit.

That was when the refusal surfaced.

Not loud. Not dramatic. Just a clean, unadorned thought.

I could leave.

I pulled a suitcase from the closet. The zipper rasped too sharply in the quiet room. The sound lingered longer than it should have.

I laid the case open on the bed and began folding clothes with deliberate care. Jeans. Sweaters. Underthings. Practical items. I did not reach for photographs. I did not reach for heirlooms. I was not fleeing in panic.

I was relocating.

The distinction mattered.

I carried the suitcase to the kitchen and set it near the table. The journal lay where I had left it. The crescent and spiral page faced upward, ink dark and certain.

I picked it up.

My hand hovered over the open case.

If I packed it, I acknowledged continuity.

If I left it, I acknowledged abandonment.

I set it back on the table.

The recorder sat beside it, a small red light blinking in patient intervals. The pulse was steady. Even. It matched nothing in the room and yet set the rhythm for everything.

Evidence of my nights.

Proof of articulation.

I did not touch it.

"I'm not quitting," I said into the kitchen. My voice remained level. "I'm stepping away."

The words felt thinner once they left my mouth.

The house did not respond.

No shift in temperature. No tightening in the walls. No lullaby threading through the air.

The house remained steady.

As if my packing registered as irrelevant.

I walked down to the cellar and stood at the edge of the opened space. The seal I had broken gaped in shadow. The air below carried density, the kind that pressed lightly against the ribs without altering temperature.

I expected resistance now that departure had entered my thoughts. A warning. A tremor. Some indication that withdrawal carried consequence.

There was none.

The absence felt considered.

As though the system did not require persuasion.

I climbed back upstairs and added a coat to the suitcase. My movements gained speed. Logic assembled itself in clean lines. The pact required rightful hand. It required recognition. I had opened the circle. I had read the clause.

That did not mean I was obligated to remain in proximity.

Someone else could inherit.

The thought lodged and refused to move.

Someone else.

A buyer charmed by original beams and quiet charm. A tenant grateful for low rent. A child chasing a ball into the yard and noticing faint marks along the foundation.

The symbols in the hallway seemed closer as I passed them again. Not hostile.

Present.

I zipped the suitcase closed. The sound sealed the decision more effectively than any vow.

For the first time since breaking the cellar open, I allowed myself to imagine a future where I was not necessary. A small apartment in another town. A job with ordinary hours. Sleep without recorders. A body that belonged entirely to itself.

The house remained still behind me.

Not tense.

Not wounded.

Still.

That stillness pressed harder than any whisper ever had.

Because it suggested something I had not considered.

The house did not need my agreement.

It only needed a rightful hand.

The gravel shifted under my boots as I carried the suitcase to the car. The night had weight to it, thick and unmoving. No porch lights flicked on. No curtains twitched.

The air felt cooler than it should have. It pressed against the back of my neck as if urging me forward without comment.

I opened the trunk and set the bag inside without ceremony. The lid closed with a contained thud. Final enough to register. Not loud enough to announce itself.

The house stood behind me in dark outline against darker sky. Windows black. Roof line steady. It did not lean forward. It did not recede.

It observed.

I slid into the driver's seat and shut the door. The interior smelled faintly of dust and old upholstery. The sound of the latch clicking into place felt louder than the trunk had. My breath echoed in the small space. I placed both hands on the steering wheel and let them rest there. The leather felt worn beneath my palms, creased by years of use that had nothing to do with me.

The key lay in my right hand. Cold metal pressing into skin already marked.

I looked straight ahead at the narrow strip of road beyond the hood. Beyond that, the long stretch of highway. Gas stations glowing under fluorescent lights. Anonymous motels with clean sheets and no history carved into beams overhead. A job application filled out under my legal name. A rental agreement signed without clauses written in dialect.

No cellar.

No circles.

No recorders blinking red in the dark.

I pictured sleep without instruction. Waking without translation. A body that belonged entirely to itself.

My hand lifted.

The key hovered inches from the ignition.

It stopped.

Nothing seized my wrist. No wind shook the car. No whisper filled the cabin. The silence remained intact.

The hesitation came from inside.

Rightful hand.

The phrase had embedded itself beneath thought. The circle is dormant unless opened by one of the bloodline. When the circle is opened by rightful hand, the keeping transfers.

I had opened it.

Not by accident. Not under coercion. I had measured. I had pried. I had broken the seal.

The engine would turn if I asked it to. The road would accept the tires. Distance would assemble cleanly behind me.

But the cellar would remain open.

The iron would lie scattered. The chalk incomplete. The air below unanchored.

The pact had never been structured around loyalty. It did not demand affection for the house. It did not reward devotion.

It required continuity.

If I left, the circle would not collapse into nothing.

It would destabilize.

Houses do not remain empty for long.

A new name would sign a deed. A family would unload boxes onto the same gravel. A child would run through the hallway, fingertips trailing over shallow grooves in the wood without knowing what they traced. Someone without the pattern in their blood would stand at the edge of the opened cellar and feel curiosity instead of recognition.

Curiosity is a softer key.

My breath fogged the windshield and faded. The night pressed against the glass without comment.

"I didn't ask for this," I said quietly.

The statement hung in the cabin, thin and unresolved.

The house had not asked either.

It had waited.

My thumb brushed the crescent on my wrist. The skin felt warmer than the air inside the car. Not burning.

Present.

The key remained poised between my fingers. I waited for fear to sharpen the choice. I waited for relief to clarify it.

Neither came.

Only the steady understanding that departure would not dismantle the system.

It would simply hand it to someone unprepared.

I rested my forehead against the steering wheel and closed my eyes. The vinyl was cool against my skin. The interior of the car smelled faintly of metal and dust, the scent of something stored rather than lived in. The quiet gathered around me and held.

No pressure.

No whisper.

No sign that anything beyond my own pulse was waiting for a decision.

I listened to my breathing. Counted the seconds between inhale and release. Tried to locate the boundary between fear and responsibility. The line felt thin and unstable. Fear wanted distance. Responsibility wanted proximity.

The house did not reach for me.

It did not need to.

If I left, it would remain exactly where it was. Wood. Nails. Beams. The opened cellar beneath it breathing out into dark earth. It would not chase. It would not retaliate.

It would wait.

The image rose without invitation. A For Sale sign planted into the yard, red letters fading in summer light. A young couple stepping through the doorway with cautious optimism. A child running ahead of them, fingers trailing along the hallway wall where circles hid in the grain.

A Realtor smiling and speaking about square footage and natural light while the cellar door stood slightly ajar at the end of the kitchen.

Someone would touch that door.

Someone would measure it with their eyes.

Someone would pry.

Not because they carried the pattern.

Because they were curious.

They would not have the journal. They would not know the dialect. They would not understand the sequence of iron and bone. They would not recognize the shift in air when the final board came loose. They would not hear the difference between their own voice and another layered quietly inside it.

I lifted my head slowly. The windshield reflected the faint outline of my face. Eyes rimmed red. Jaw tight.

Not possessed.

Positioned.

Guardianship had never been framed as reward. It had been described as steadiness. As maintenance. As interruption.

Temperance had not been spared.

She had been steadied.

The phrase settled in my chest and refused to move.

The bag in the trunk felt foreign now. Clothes folded for a life that would continue somewhere else. Somewhere easier. Somewhere without midnight recordings and iron nails pressed into chalked lines.

I could still go.

The key remained in my hand. The engine would respond without hesitation.

Freedom did not require permission.

It required indifference.

That was the fracture.

If I drove away, I would not be fleeing something malevolent. I would be declining continuity. I would be leaving an open system for someone unqualified to stand in the circle.

The house did not trap me.

It qualified me.

The realization did not feel empowering.

It felt isolating.

The crescent on my wrist pulsed once, faint and steady. Not pain. Recognition.

"I can leave," I said aloud.

The words were true.

I tightened my grip on the steering wheel, feeling the tendons strain beneath my skin. I imagined turning the key, the engine catching, the headlights cutting across gravel. I imagined the house shrinking in the rearview mirror until it became a shape against darkness.

Then I imagined the next hand on the cellar door.

The difference between escape and abandonment clarified without spectacle.

I lowered the key to my lap.

The engine remained silent. The night remained undisturbed. The house stood behind me, patient in a way that was almost merciful.

I was free to go.

That freedom pressed against my ribs harder than any command.

I did not stay because I was trapped.

I stayed because I understood exactly who would replace me if I left.

And that knowledge made the choice permanent.

Chapter 30

The engine was off. The key rested cold in my palm. The house stood behind me, dark and patient, its windows black and unblinking. I kept my hands on the steering wheel because they needed somewhere to be. The dashboard light cast a faint amber glow across the interior. The engine ticked once as it cooled.

The night pressed against the windshield.

No wind.

No movement.

Just the weight of a choice I had not made.

My phone vibrated in the cupholder.

The sound cut through the silence with surgical precision. I flinched. My first instinct was to let it stop. To let whoever it was assume I had already gone. That distance had already formed.

It buzzed again.

I looked down.

Her name glowed on the screen.

For a second I considered answering. Hearing her voice live felt dangerous. She knew my rhythms too well. She would hear the fracture in me. She would ask questions that would force words out of my mouth before I could shape them.

The call went to voicemail.

I kept staring at the yard while her voice filled the car.

"Hey. I don't know if you're asleep or ignoring me."

A pause. Not irritated. Just tired.

"I've been thinking about you all day. Something feels off."

Her tone stayed level. No accusation. No drama. Just recognition that comes from years of watching someone carry more than they admit.

"You don't have to tell me everything," she continued. "But I know you. When things get heavy, you disappear. You convince yourself you can fix it alone."

My fingers tightened on the steering wheel. The leather felt dry, almost brittle beneath my palms.

"You've always kept other people safe," she said. "That's who you are. But you don't get to vanish when it's your turn to be overwhelmed."

The words landed without spectacle. No swell. No heightened emotion.

Just fact.

I closed my eyes.

She did not know about the cellar. She did not know about the seal, the succession, the recordings that carried a voice not entirely mine. She had no language for bloodlines or boundaries or rightful hands.

But she knew me.

I had spent years telling myself that control was armor. That if I could understand a system, I could neutralize it. That if I documented enough, tracked enough, anticipated enough, I could keep harm from reaching anyone I loved.

Isolation had masqueraded as strength.

I had called it independence. Called it discipline. Called it clarity.

She called it disappearing.

The voicemail ended with a soft exhale.

"Just don't shut everyone out. Not now."

The line clicked off.

I sat there with the phone still in my hand, the screen gone black. The night did not shift. The house did not move. Nothing supernatural intervened.

But something inside me recalibrated.

I had been framing this as fear. As entrapment. As a solitary confrontation with something older than I could measure.

She reframed it without knowing she had.

I was not running from the house.

I was running from the risk of being seen while I carried it.

The key remained in my palm. The engine remained silent.

For the first time since stepping into the car, escape no longer felt like relief.

It felt like isolation.

And I had already proven I was too good at that.

I did not start the engine.

I sat in the dark and played the voicemail again.

Her voice filled the car, softer this time because I was listening for something different. Not the words. The weight behind them. The years compressed into a handful of sentences.

"You've always kept other people safe."

The phrase lodged beneath my ribs.

I let the message end. Started it over. Closed my eyes. Listened to the breath she took before the line. The steadiness in it. Not flattery. Not nostalgia.

Observation.

The cabin felt smaller while she spoke. My knuckles pressed into the steering wheel. The leather creaked faintly under the tension.

Memory moved in without asking permission.

The party in college when a joke turned sharp and a shoulder bumped too hard. The sour smell of beer in the air. The split second when I saw two men square their stance and stepped between them before either understood what they were about to do.

The night my father's temper coiled in the kitchen, voice rising in increments. I redirected it with a question. Then a task. Then silence. The careful calibration of tone so the air would settle instead of snap.

The habit of scanning every room I entered. Doors. Windows. Corners. The micro shift in conversation when pressure began to build beneath politeness.

I had never named it courage.

I had called it control.

I had believed my need to map everything was proof of fear. If I could anticipate the break, I could prevent it. If I documented enough, prepared enough, understood enough, no one would bleed.

In the house, that instinct sharpened into obsession. I charted symbols. Cross referenced dialect. Timed my own breathing. I treated the cellar like a puzzle box and the lineage like an equation.

Solve it.

Neutralize it.

Finish it.

But the journal had never promised an ending.

It promised maintenance.

I pressed my forehead against the steering wheel again and let that distinction settle.

I had tried to decode the house.

I had not tried to hold it.

There was a difference.

Temperance had not diagrammed her duty into submission. She had endured it. Night after night. Ritual after ritual. Not to conquer something, but to steady it. To keep its edges from spilling outward.

Endurance is not elegance.

It is repetition.

My flaw was not cowardice.

It was misdirection.

I aimed my instinct for protection at the wrong target. I tried to protect myself from the house instead of protecting others from what would happen without it.

The house behind me remained still. No swell of approval. No ripple of acknowledgment.

It did not care about my insight.

Guardianship did not require brilliance.

It required presence.

The crescent on my wrist pulsed faintly. Not pain. Not threat.

Awareness.

I opened my eyes and looked at myself in the rearview mirror. My face appeared drawn, the skin beneath my eyes darker than it had been a month ago. There were new lines at the corners of my mouth. My expression was tired.

It was not lost.

I replayed the voicemail one more time.

"Don't start running now."

She had no idea what she was asking.

Or maybe she did.

I had framed this role as imprisonment. As conscription. As something that stripped me of choice.

But choice was sitting in my palm in the shape of a car key.

I could leave.

The boundary would not dissolve. It would destabilize.

Someone else would open the door without knowing what it meant. Someone else would stand where I had stood in the cellar, hand hovering over iron, unaware of the inheritance humming beneath their skin.

The thought did not feel dramatic.

It felt unacceptable.

I exhaled slowly.

The urge to flee loosened. Not gone. But no longer leading.

Alignment.

Of course it was me.

Not because I was special.

Because I was already built for it.

I had always kept others safe.

The only thing left was to decide how wide that circle extended.

I opened the car door before I could change my mind.

The night met me without ceremony. Cold air slid into my lungs, clean and sharp enough to sting. The engine ticked once as it cooled, then fell into silence. Gravel shifted beneath my boots as I stood beside the car and faced the house.

It did not loom.

It did not beckon.

It waited.

The windows reflected nothing but sky. The porch light cast a narrow circle onto the walkway, pale and contained. The boards along the eaves were still. No creak. No whisper. If there was pressure in the air, it did not press against me.

It held.

I walked to the trunk and lifted it.

The suitcase sat there, half zipped. A shirt sleeve hung over the edge. My toothbrush lay on top of folded denim, absurdly domestic against the dark. I stared at the bag as if it belonged to someone else. Someone who believed leaving would simplify the equation.

I wrapped my fingers around the handle.

The weight surprised me. Not heavy. Just undeniable.

The gravel shifted again as I crossed back toward the house. Each step felt deliberate. Not dragged. Not forced. Measured.

Halfway up the walkway, I stopped.

My phone was still in my hand.

The drafted email glowed on the screen.

Subject: Property Listing Inquiry.

A local agent's name filled the recipient line. A paragraph explaining nothing. Promising availability. Requesting discretion.

It sounded reasonable.

Polite.

Detached.

My thumb hovered over the text. I read it once more, as if it might argue for itself.

Then I selected the entire body of it and pressed delete.

The words disappeared without resistance.

My chest tightened briefly. Not regret. Recognition.

That was a door closing.

I opened a new message thread.

Her name sat at the top.

I did not type a speech. I did not thank her. I did not explain lineage or seals or appointment. There was no language for that in the world she occupied.

I typed three words.

I'm not running.

I stared at them long enough to consider softening the edge. Adding context. Adding humor. Something to make it lighter.

I left it as it was.

I pressed send.

The screen dimmed.

I slipped the phone into my pocket and resumed walking.

The front door opened beneath my hand with its familiar resistance. The hinges released a low sound I had heard a hundred times before. Inside, the air carried the faint scent of old wood and dust. The hallway stretched ahead, narrow and known.

I stepped over the threshold.

The house did not react.

No tremor. No surge. The symbols along the beams remained faint, etched into grain that caught light only at certain angles. The crescent on my wrist rested quiet against my skin.

I set the suitcase down just inside the entryway.

I did not unpack it.

Not yet.

The bag sat there, neither temporary nor permanent. An object awaiting instruction.

I stood still and listened.

The silence felt different tonight. Not vacant. Not tense.

Steady.

I inhaled slowly and let the air settle in my lungs. My pulse held even. No split in my vision. No borrowed cadence in my throat.

Control had never been cowardice.

It had been vigilance without trust.

Running would have been the first choice I made that abandoned someone else to consequences they could not anticipate.

I looked toward the cellar door at the end of the hall. Closed. Wood and brass. Ordinary in appearance.

Nothing in this house would ever be ordinary again.

That did not make it monstrous.

It made it work.

I did not feel triumphant.

I felt aligned.

The difference mattered.

I picked up the suitcase and carried it farther inside, not as someone trapped, but as someone stepping into position.

Chapter 31

Morning arrived without fracture.

I opened my eyes and waited for the split. For the echo of a second cadence beneath my thoughts. For the thin delay that had begun to haunt my own voice.

It did not come.

My mind felt singular. Heavy, but singular. My tongue rested naturally in my mouth. My breath rose and fell without interruption.

The house held its shape.

No pressure in the walls. No subtle rearranging of light. The silence was not empty. It was balanced.

That difference mattered.

I lay there a moment longer, testing the edges of myself. Listening for overlap.

Nothing overlapped.

I rose slowly. The floorboards accepted my weight without commentary. In the kitchen, the journal sat where I had left it. The recorder rested beside it. Chalk. A small pouch of iron nails.

Tools I had once used in defense now felt like instruments awaiting calibration.

I gathered them carefully. The chalk left a faint white residue against my fingertips. The iron nails were cool and faintly metallic against my palm.

The cellar door stood closed, as it always had.

I rested my hand against the wood before opening it. The crescent on my wrist warmed faintly at the contact.

Not a warning.

Recognition.

"I'm coming down," I said.

Not to ask permission.

To mark the moment.

The steps creaked beneath me as I descended. The air cooled with each step. A faint scent of stone and old dust settled in my lungs. I paused before switching on the light, allowing my eyes to adjust to the dimness first.

Nothing shifted in the shadows.

I flipped the switch.

The opened section of wall remained altered. Boards removed. The inner chamber exposed. No swelling darkness. No breath against my neck. The space beyond the boards felt contained, as if it understood its own limits.

I stepped forward and knelt at the incomplete spiral.

Chalk dust still marked the concrete. The iron nail lay where I had dropped it, angled away from the center. The circle was broken on one side, a gap wide enough to weaken structure but not collapse it entirely.

I studied it without shame.

My fingers hovered over the outer curve. I did not touch the chalk at first. I felt the geometry in my mind. The rhythm of containment. The logic of closure.

This had never been spectacle.

It had always been alignment.

I picked up the chalk.

My hand did not tremble.

I redrew the outer boundary first. Strengthening the perimeter without approaching the center. The chalk dragged softly across concrete, leaving a thickened white line. I pressed enough pressure into the stroke to make it hold.

Each curve felt deliberate. Not driven. Not frantic.

I was not finishing what had nearly consumed me.

I was stabilizing what had been interrupted.

When the outer ring closed, I paused.

The air shifted almost imperceptibly.

Not colder.

Not warmer.

Steadier.

I set the chalk down.

Then I picked up the iron nail.

I did not place it into the center of the spiral. I pressed it into the wood beam above the boundary line instead. Reinforcement. Not blood.

I lifted the hammer.

The impact rang once through the cellar. Clean. Contained. The sound traveled into the beams and dissipated without distortion.

I listened.

No recoil from the walls. No hum rising in my throat. No borrowed cadence pressing at the back of my tongue.

I exhaled.

"I keep it," I said quietly.

The words did not summon anything.

They settled.

For a long moment, I remained kneeling there, listening for correction.

None came.

The chamber beyond the broken boards did not pulse or darken. The symbols etched along the beams appeared less like warnings and more like structure.

For the first time since opening the seal, I did not feel watched.

I felt necessary.

I rose slowly and scanned the cellar again. Not as territory to conquer. Not as threat to decode.

As a responsibility to maintain.

There was no surge of power. No chorus of approval.

Only steadiness.

My voice belonged to me.

And the house did not argue.

Upstairs, the day would continue. Floors would creak. Light would shift. The circle would require checking again.

Not today.

Soon.

Maintenance was not an ending.

It was a practice.

The cellar did not need spectacle.

It needed attention.

The air carried the faint mineral scent of damp stone and old wood. Dust floated in the narrow cone of light above me. I moved along the perimeter slowly, studying the beams where old marks cut into wood darkened by years of humidity and breath.

The spirals were faint in places.

Chalk residue clung to grooves that had once been reinforced more regularly. Iron had rusted along nail heads driven in by hands that understood pressure and angle.

Time had thinned the intention.

And intention, left thin long enough, became drift.

I ran my fingers lightly over one of the spirals carved into a support post. The indentation was shallow now, nearly worn smooth. The outer curve had softened, its direction less decisive.

Boundaries worked through clarity.

Weak lines invited spill.

I opened the journal on a crate near the wall. The corrected passages lay where I had marked them. Structural language. Reinforcement cycles. Breath cadence aligned to placement.

For a moment, I considered reading the words aloud.

I chose not to.

I understood the architecture beneath them. Sound was no longer necessary for comprehension.

I picked up a piece of chalk and retraced the spiral carefully. The chalk dragged against the wood, catching on rough grain. I adjusted my angle slightly to keep the curve true. Too much pressure would distort the original line. Too little would leave it shallow.

Precision mattered.

My hand followed the curve with intention. No trance. No borrowed rhythm.

When the chalk line settled into the groove, the spiral regained definition. Clean edges. Clear direction.

I stepped back and assessed it.

It held.

I moved to the next beam.

At the base of the foundation stone, an iron nail had loosened. The wood around it had softened slightly, fibers separating from metal. I gripped the head and pulled it free. The tip was darkened but intact.

I examined the grain of the wood before resetting it.

A fraction higher. A slight correction in angle.

I pressed the nail in with my fingers, then lifted the hammer.

The first strike met resistance. The wood resisted the correction, as if accustomed to its earlier position.

I struck again, measured.

The nail seated cleanly.

The sound traveled through the cellar and dissipated into stone. No reverberation. No answering hum.

Just impact. Absorption.

I inhaled slowly.

The breath work came naturally now, but I did not surrender to it. I set the pace myself. Inhale to four. Hold. Exhale evenly.

For a moment, the old lullaby hovered at the edge of my throat.

I redirected it.

Instead of melody, I let a low hum settle in my chest. Controlled. Even. Directed outward through my palm as I pressed it against a beam where chalk had once sealed intention.

The vibration was subtle but consistent.

Not imposed.

Sustained.

Ownership did not feel mystical.

It felt relational.

I moved methodically through the cellar, reinforcing weakened marks, correcting asymmetries, anchoring iron where it had shifted. Each action followed structure rather than fear.

The system did not resist.

But it did respond.

When I reached the exposed inner chamber, I paused.

The air there felt slightly denser. Not hostile. Not welcoming. Contained.

The boards I had removed remained stacked to one side. The threshold stood open, defined but vulnerable.

I knelt and drew a narrow chalk line along its edge.

Not to close it.

To clarify it.

Boundaries required visibility.

As the chalk completed the line, a faint shift passed through the space. The kind of shift that would have gone unnoticed weeks ago.

Now I felt it.

Stability reasserting.

I stepped back and surveyed the cellar as a whole.

The spirals did not glow. The iron did not pulse. There was no surge of heat, no ancestral murmur.

The beams stood upright. The foundation stones appeared steady. The air did not press against my spine.

The house above remained quiet.

I rested my hand against the nearest post and felt the faint hum beneath the surface. Not a voice. Not instruction.

Structure.

I was not fighting the house.

I was participating in it.

The realization did not swell with pride. It settled with gravity.

Maintenance meant repetition.

Repetition meant return.

I climbed the stairs slowly, chalk dust lingering along my fingertips, iron residue faint against my skin. The crescent on my wrist warmed once, briefly, then cooled.

The system did not reward dominance.

It responded to steadiness.

And steadiness would be required again.

The kitchen table had become a map of my former fear.

Charts layered over charts. Time stamps circled in red ink. Arrows drawn between symbols as if proximity proved intention. Coffee rings marked the corners of photocopied pages. My handwriting shifted from careful to frantic across the margins.

I stood over the spread and felt no urgency.

Only revision.

I sat down and pulled the journal toward me first. The leather cover bore the wear of hands that had opened it under pressure. Mine had once trembled when I turned these pages.

Now my fingers moved steadily.

I opened to the passages I had mistranslated early on. The sections where I had underlined words like binding, vessel, oath. Words I had equated with punishment. Possession. Loss of self.

I hesitated over binding.

The word still carried weight.

Then I drew a clean line through my original definition in my notebook.

Binding was structure.

Vessel was conduit.

Oath was continuity.

I paused over continuity before writing it. The word felt larger than the others. Less mechanical.

I wrote it anyway.

Anchor. Succession. Stabilization.

The shift in language altered the entire architecture of the text. What I had read as threat revealed itself as engineering. The spirals were not traps. They were regulators. The iron did not pierce for suffering. It enforced direction.

I separated my old notes into two stacks.

Fear-driven.

Structural.

The first stack was thicker.

I did not discard it. I folded it carefully and set it aside. Evidence of process, not weakness.

The second stack remained in front of me.

I placed the recorder on the table and pressed record.

The click sounded louder than usual.

"My name is Clara Wren," I said clearly. "I am awake. I am speaking by choice."

The words settled into the room without distortion.

I read a passage aloud from the journal, one I had once avoided because of its density. The dialect felt familiar now. My tongue did not resist its cadence. I let my own inflection carry it forward.

When I reached a phrase Temperance had written about keeping the boundary through breath, I paused.

For a fraction of a second, the old lullaby hovered at the edge of my throat.

I did not let it form.

"Breath establishes pacing," I added in my own voice. "Pacing stabilizes structure."

I stopped the recording.

The house remained quiet.

I waited longer than necessary before pressing playback.

My voice filled the kitchen.

Even. Deliberate.

I listened carefully for the fracture. For the split cadence that had once threaded through my speech.

It did not come.

But something else did.

When I reached the section on breath, my tone deepened slightly. Not foreign. Not imposed. The weight of the words settled differently in the air, as if certain phrases carried more gravity than others.

I stiffened.

Then I listened again.

There was no override. No second articulation.

Only layering.

Where the journal's phrasing aligned with structural clarity, my voice gained resonance. Where my earlier fear had colored interpretation, the tone thinned.

The recorder did not capture competition.

It captured integration.

I rewound and played it a third time.

The pattern held.

I leaned back in the chair and closed my eyes.

Succession did not erase identity.

It extended it.

Temperance's language no longer arrived as command. It functioned as foundation. A framework beneath my own phrasing. When I spoke within alignment, the structure supported the tone.

When I drifted, the voice flattened.

This was not invasion.

It was calibration.

I opened my eyes and wrote further notes.

Cadence shift equals resonance, not intrusion.

Instruction equals collaboration, not takeover.

Literacy replaces fear.

The cipher was no longer something to crack.

It was syntax to practice.

I was not deciphering an enemy code.

I was refining inherited language.

The realization did not thrill me. It steadied me.

The crescent on my wrist warmed briefly as I wrote the final line across the page:

Guardianship is operational, not emotional.

I pressed stop on the recorder and let the silence settle around the kitchen.

The house did not intrude.

It held.

Fluency, I understood now, was not mastery.

It was repetition without panic.

And repetition would begin again tomorrow.

Night settled without ceremony.

The house dimmed room by room as I moved through it, switching off lamps and overhead lights until only the low bulb at the top of the cellar stairs remained. The air carried the faint scent of chalk and old wood. No pressure gathered in the walls. No whisper traced the hallway.

Stillness, not vacancy.

I descended with the journal under my arm and the pouch of iron in my hand. The steps creaked softly beneath my weight. Halfway down, I paused and listened.

Nothing shifted.

The cellar waited in measured silence.

I stepped onto the concrete floor and stood in its center for a moment, letting my eyes adjust. The exposed inner chamber remained open, boards stacked neatly to one side. The reinforced beams held firm. The corrections from earlier in the day had not loosened.

No collapse.

No drift.

I set the journal on a crate and opened the pouch.

Tonight was not about repair.

It was about completion.

I knelt and placed the chalk at the center point of the concrete. For a moment, my hand hovered. I traced the first arc outward slowly. The chalk rasped faintly against the floor, leaving a clean white line.

The curve bent slightly wider than intended.

I stopped.

Adjusted.

Redrew the line with firmer pressure, tightening the radius until it aligned with the underlying geometry I felt more than saw.

Precision mattered.

I continued outward, each turn widening in deliberate proportion. The spiral grew beneath my hand. Chalk dust gathered along my fingertips and settled into the creases of my skin.

The outer ring widened in a clean arc.

When I reached the final turn, I paused and studied the whole. No gaps. No distortions. The spiral held tension evenly across its span.

Balanced.

I set the chalk aside.

From the pouch, I selected an iron nail. The metal felt cool and solid between my fingers. I positioned it at the outermost point of the circle where reinforcement was required, not at the center, not near my skin.

Into wood.

I pressed the nail against the lower beam that framed the threshold of the inner chamber and lifted the hammer.

The first strike met resistance.

The wood did not reject it. It simply required certainty.

I adjusted the angle slightly and struck again.

The hammer's impact rang once through the cellar, sharper than before. The sound traveled into stone and beam, then faded without echo.

The nail seated cleanly.

I inhaled slowly and allowed the breath to settle deep in my chest. The air felt denser for a brief moment, as if weighing the action.

Then it released.

I exhaled evenly.

No lullaby threaded through my throat. No second cadence overlapped my own. The breath belonged to me. The rhythm was mine.

I rose to stand in the center of the completed spiral.

For a fraction of a second, the space tightened. Not pressure. Not threat.

Assessment.

The density of the air shifted subtly, recalibrating around the lines I had drawn. The foundation stones held. The beams stood upright without strain.

The house did not test me.

It steadied.

The crescent on my wrist warmed faintly. Not pain. Not warning.

Recognition.

I looked toward the exposed inner chamber and felt no urge to close it.

It did not need concealment.

It required maintenance.

"I keep it," I said clearly.

My voice did not tremble, but it did settle differently in the space, deeper than casual speech. The words did not echo unnaturally. They did not summon response.

They established position.

The house did not answer.

It did not need to.

The silence that followed was not empty. It was structured.

I remained standing in the spiral for several minutes, feeling the concrete beneath my feet and the air against my skin. No fracture in perception. No split between intention and execution.

I had once believed control meant conquest.

Now I understood it meant calibration.

I stepped carefully out of the spiral and climbed the stairs. At the top, I paused before turning out the light.

For a moment, the cellar glowed beneath me. Spiral bright against stone. Iron seated in wood.

Then I switched off the light.

Darkness returned.

Not threatening.

Contained.

The spiral remained where I had drawn it.

And I knew, without needing to look again, that I would return before it thinned.

Chapter 32

Morning light settled into the kitchen without distortion. Dust drifted lazily through the beam above the table where my charts had once sprawled in frantic layers. The surface was clear now, wiped clean of arrows and red circles. The wood grain showed through again.

I stood there and understood something I had avoided admitting.

Steadiness was not the same as understanding.

I had aligned the structure. I had reinforced the boundary. The house held.

But I did not know its full architecture.

Temperance had written what she believed necessary. Maintenance. Succession. Breath cadence aligned to placement. She had not recorded origin. She had not recorded what failed before her, or why certain variations appeared in neighboring towns.

She had not written about error.

Guardianship required more than endurance.

It required context.

The thought sat heavier than the iron I had driven into the beams.

I picked up my phone and scrolled to the historian's number. Our last exchange had ended in polite retreat. Concern edged with distance. She had heard instability in my voice then.

She would not hear it now.

I began typing.

I owe you clarity. I misspoke my inquiry before. I was asking the wrong questions.

I paused. The message looked too personal. Too exposed.

I deleted the first sentence.

I tried again.

I am researching regional birth rites and boundary customs tied to midwife practice in this county. Specifically suppressed dialect fragments and structural warding traditions. I am not looking for interpretation. Only primary source material and documentation.

I read it twice.

The tone was measured. Academic. Controlled.

I resisted the urge to explain why.

I pressed send.

The message left cleanly.

The reply did not come immediately.

I placed the phone face down on the table and poured coffee. The liquid struck the mug with a soft, steady sound. Steam rose and curled in the morning light. The house remained quiet around me.

No hum of approval.

No resistance.

Only structure holding.

Minutes passed.

I told myself the delay meant nothing. Scholars were busy. Messages accumulated. Inquiry was not urgency.

The phone vibrated against the wood.

The sound was precise. Almost surgical.

I turned it over slowly.

Her response was brief.

What changed?

I stared at the screen.

The question was not hostile.

It was not dismissive.

It was assessment.

The house behind me remained still. The light did not flicker. The beams did not creak.

The test was not coming from the cellar.

It was coming from her.

And this time, I would answer without fracture.

Direct. Not warm. Not cold.

I let the question sit on the screen for several seconds before answering. My thumb hovered over the keyboard. I resisted the impulse to soften the edges.

I typed carefully.

I corrected my assumptions. I am not experiencing instability. I need historical structure, not reassurance.

I reread it once. The tone was measured. Controlled. There was no defensiveness in it.

I pressed send.

The pause that followed felt longer than the last. Not silence, but consideration.

When her reply arrived, it came in two parts.

That is a different tone.

I felt the shift even through text. Less alarm. More assessment.

Then:

There are archived oath fragments and dialect variations at the society. Some are restricted due to past misinterpretations. Public meeting only. Limited review.

I read the message twice.

Restricted.

Past misinterpretations.

Public meeting only.

She was not accusing me.

She was protecting the material.

The boundary was institutional. Measured. Intentional.

For a fraction of a second, something in me resisted the limitation. I had handled iron and breath and threshold. I had redrawn spirals without trembling.

But archives were not beams.

They required permission.

I typed my response without hesitation.

That works. I will meet you wherever you prefer.

Her reply came quickly this time.

Reading room. Midday. Open hours.

Witnessed.

Neutral ground.

I agreed without negotiation.

When I set the phone down, I remained standing beside the table for a moment. The kitchen light fell cleanly across the wood. The house did not shift around me.

I had not defended myself.

I had not attempted to persuade her of anything beyond scholarship. I had not sent recordings. I had not invoked lineage or succession.

I had asked for structure.

The difference mattered.

Upstairs, the beams held. Downstairs, the spiral remained intact. The crescent on my wrist rested quiet against my skin.

I did not feel rescued.

I felt extended.

The historian would not become confidante. She would not descend into the cellar or hear the weight of what had threaded through my voice in the dark.

But she would provide documentation.

Source material.

Context.

Guardianship required reinforcement at precise points.

I gathered the journal and placed it carefully into my bag. Not to display. To cross-reference privately.

The act felt deliberate.

Measured.

Reaching outward no longer felt like fracture.

It felt like calibration.

And calibration, I understood, would be tested under fluorescent lights.

The historical society smelled of paper and varnish.

There was a faint hum from overhead lights and the quiet scrape of chairs against hardwood as other patrons settled into their work. I arrived early and chose a chair near the center of the reading room where light from tall windows fell clean across the tables.

Public space. Open sight lines. No shadows deep enough to invite speculation.

I wanted witnesses.

Not for safety.

For optics.

When she entered, she carried a slim archival box against her chest. She paused when she saw me. Her eyes moved quickly, assessing posture, hands, gaze.

"You look... different," she said carefully.

"Focused," I replied.

My voice did not waver.

She nodded once and set the box on the table between us. She did not slide it forward yet. She kept her hand resting on the lid.

"I pulled what I could without raising internal questions," she said. "Oath fragments from midwife guild records. Structural warding diagrams attributed to rural practitioners. And a few lullaby variants tied to birth cadence."

She watched my reaction.

I kept my breathing even.

"Thank you," I said. "I am looking at continuity patterns, not superstition."

She lifted the lid.

The first document was brittle, handwritten in tight script. The ink had browned at the edges. I recognized the dialect immediately.

My pulse skipped once.

Not the exact phrasing Temperance used, but a regional branch of it. The structure aligned. Breath cues embedded within lines. Placement instructions concealed inside language that appeared devotional.

I did not reach for the page.

"This oath references anchor placement," I said, tracing a line in the air just above the margin. "Not sealing. Anchoring."

Her gaze sharpened.

"Most people misread that," she said. "They assume confinement."

"Containment is not the same as imprisonment," I replied.

The words felt steady in my mouth.

She studied me for another moment before sliding a second sheet across the table.

A diagram.

Circular forms layered over floor plans. Reinforcement points marked at thresholds and support beams. No mention of harm. No language of sacrifice.

Structural geometry.

For an instant, the image overlaid itself onto the cellar in my mind. The lower beam. The spiral's outer ring. The threshold I had clarified the night before.

"Warding as stabilization," I murmured.

She exhaled quietly. Not relief. Recognition.

The final set of pages held nursery rhyme variations. Regional shifts in cadence and vowel length. The words were ordinary on the surface. Comforting. Rhythmic.

But the meter was deliberate.

Four-count inhale. Four-count hold. Controlled release.

"It was used during labor," she said. "To regulate breath. To reduce panic."

I read through one stanza silently.

My throat tightened.

For a fraction of a second, the melody hovered at the edge of my awareness. Not imposed. Familiar.

I did not hum.

"It regulates pacing," I said instead.

She watched my hands as I counted the beats with my fingertips against the table.

The lullaby had never been mystical.

It was physiological control disguised as comfort.

A system hidden in plain language.

"Some families suppressed these rites," she said quietly. "Not because they were evil. Because they demanded responsibility. They required someone to carry continuity forward. Not everyone wanted that burden."

The words settled between us.

Responsibility.

Carry.

Continuity.

I met her eyes.

"I am not looking to revive anything publicly," I said. "I am looking to understand structure."

"And you are certain this is academic?" she asked.

Her tone was not accusatory.

It was protective.

"I am certain it is precise," I answered.

Silence stretched between us. The fluorescent lights hummed faintly overhead.

Finally, she closed the box lid halfway but did not remove it.

"I will not participate beyond documentation," she said. "If this becomes personal, I cannot be drawn into it."

"I am not asking you to be," I replied.

That was the truth.

She slid copies of the documents toward me.

"Return them in a week," she said. "Quietly."

I nodded and gathered the papers into my bag.

As I stood to leave, she added one final sentence.

"Be careful what you stabilize."

The words were not dramatic.

They were clinical.

I did not correct her.

Outside, the daylight felt thinner than it had when I arrived. The weight of the documents in my bag pressed against my hip as I walked to the car.

Not evidence.

Not validation.

Reinforcement.

The reading room had been neutral ground.

The application would not be.

The knock at the door came in the late afternoon, soft but deliberate.

I paused halfway between the kitchen and the hallway. The house did not shift. No warning hum. No tightening in the beams.

The second knock landed in the same measured rhythm.

I opened the door expecting no one. The town had kept its distance since the rumors began. Faces turned away at the grocery store. Conversations stilled when I entered.

Distance had become habit.

Mrs. Halbrook stood on my porch, hands folded over a small cloth-bound notebook. Her white hair was pinned back tightly, not a strand misplaced. She wore gloves despite the mild weather.

Her eyes moved over me in a single sweep.

"I hope I am not interrupting," she said.

"You are not," I replied.

Her gaze drifted briefly past my shoulder into the hallway. Not prying.

Assessing.

"I found something in a trunk," she continued. "Thought you might appreciate it. You have been asking questions around town."

The word asking carried weight. Not accusation.

Observation.

She handed me the notebook. The cloth felt worn but intact, softened at the edges by years of handling. I stepped aside and let her enter.

The house did not tense.

It held.

We sat at the kitchen table. She opened the notebook carefully, revealing handwritten verses in faded ink.

"My grandmother used to sing this during births," she said. "Said it kept the mother steady."

She cleared her throat and began to recite.

The words were simple. Gentle. A nursery rhyme on the surface.

But the meter struck immediately.

Four beats held.

Controlled release across the final line.

My chest aligned with it without effort. I forced myself to adjust my breathing, to keep it natural. Not synchronized.

The cadence was not identical to the archival copies. It carried regional shifts. Vowels stretched where Temperance clipped them short. Consonants softened at the ends of phrases.

But the breath work matched the cellar's geometry precisely.

There had been a missing measure in Temperance's journal. An incomplete stanza that never fully resolved. I had assumed damage. Loss over time.

It was not loss.

It was division.

Mrs. Halbrook finished the verse and closed the notebook gently.

"Old family song," she said. "Nothing special."

My pulse had quickened. I slowed it deliberately.

"It is beautiful," I said.

She studied my face for a moment longer than courtesy required.

"You have seemed preoccupied lately," she said carefully. "Just thought you might like something ordinary."

Ordinary.

The word pressed against the layers beneath it.

This town had carried fragments without naming them. Breath patterns disguised as lullabies. Structural knowledge folded into nursery rhyme. Responsibility diluted into tradition.

The system had never been confined to my house.

It had been scattered.

Not by accident.

By design.

Diffused across families so no single bearer carried full weight unless called.

"I would like to copy it," I said.

"Of course."

She left the notebook with me and rose to go. At the door, she paused.

"Some things are older than we remember," she said. "Does not make them bad."

Her eyes held mine as she said it.

"I know," I replied.

She nodded once and stepped off the porch.

The house remained steady.

I returned to the table and transcribed the stanza carefully. As I wrote, the missing measure slid into place within Temperance's incomplete passage. The spiral of breath completed its circuit.

Structural knowledge.

Archival reinforcement.

Living cadence.

I closed my eyes and hummed the verse once under my breath. Not as invocation. Not as plea.

As alignment.

The air did not surge.

It cohered.

The beams above did not strain. The floor beneath my feet felt grounded.

Guardianship had always been communal in fragments.

Practice was individual.

I was not alone in knowledge.

Only in execution.

Outside, somewhere down the street, a door closed. A dog barked once and fell silent.

I wondered how many houses held their own incomplete measures.

Chapter 33

Night settled heavy over the house, and I chose to go to the cellar.

The cellar air felt denser than it had that afternoon, but not unstable. The reinforced spirals remained clean along the beams. Iron held firm in wood that no longer splintered at the edges. The exposed inner chamber stood open, boards still stacked against the far wall. Clarified. Not concealed.

I stepped into the center of the spiral and closed my eyes.

Four beats in.

Hold.

Four beats out.

The lullaby cadence threaded through my breathing—not as song, but as pacing. My chest rose evenly. My pulse slowed to match the count. The geometry beneath my feet felt steady, its arcs and lines calibrated to the rhythm moving through me.

The house did not hum.

It listened.

I opened my eyes and looked toward the open chamber. The threshold I had redrawn earlier remained sharp. The chalk line did not blur. The air beyond it felt contained, measured.

For a moment, nothing shifted.

Then the atmosphere tightened.

It happened subtly at first. A pressure in the ears. A narrowing in the chest. The kind of compression that precedes a storm without announcing it. The beams above me gave a faint sound—wood adjusting against foundation.

The hidden cellar door moved.

There was no visible hand, no creeping shadow. The door simply swung inward from the darkness of the changer and slammed shut with violent force. The impact cracked through the foundation. Dust shook loose from the joists and fell in fine streaks. The concrete beneath my feet vibrated once, sharply.

The air compressed hard enough to steal half a breath from my lungs.

I did not step back.

The spiral remained intact beneath me.

This was not random disturbance. The time was too precise. The reaction too targeted. The door had been left open under my authority.

A line had been drawn.

I let the lullaby cadence anchor my breathing again. My pulse hammered once against my ribs, then settled under discipline. I kept my gaze fixed on the door now sealed in its frame. The wood quivered faintly, as though pressure built behind it.

The house was not panicking.

It was applying force.

The reinforced spirals along the beams caught the light differently as dust settled. I could feel tension pressing at the edges of the circle. Not breaking it. Testing it.

I did not rush forward to reopen the door.

I did not retreat toward the stairs.

I stayed in the center.

The pressure intensified. The temperature dropped slightly. My skin prickled along my arms. The crescent on my wrist warmed, not burning but alert.

This was the first deliberate resistance since I had calmed the role.

The system had accepted my steadiness.

Now it challenged it.

The air pushed harder, as if the cellar itself attempted to expel me from its center. My balance shifted, but I corrected it. My shoulders squared. My feet remained planted within the spiral's boundary.

"I am here," I said quietly.

My body reacted before my mind did. My weight shifted back. My heel nearly crossed the spiral's boundary.

I caught myself.

The chalk line remained intact beneath my foot.

I did not step out.

The door now stood sealed in its frame. No visible hand. No shadow slipping away.

I had left it open under my authority.

It had closed under its own.

I drew breath again.

My pulse hammered once against my ribs before settling beneath discipline. The wood of the sealed door quivered faintly, as though pressure built behind it. It was exerting.

The air pushed again.

Stronger this time.

The pressure pressed against my chest. My balance wavered. My shoulders shifted.

I corrected.

Feet planted within the spiral.

Spine upright.

The house pressed once more.

I remained.

The door did not reopen.

But it did not splinter either.

The pressure did not recede.

It stabilized at a new intensity.

This was not collapse.

It was escalation.

Now it required proof of endurance.

And the proof would not be momentary.

A low groan rolled through the wood, deep and strained. Fibers tightened under force. The iron hinges trembled against their bolts. The frame flexed inward, then snapped back into place with a crack that traveled through the foundation.

Each movement carried weight.

Deliberate.

The spiral beneath my feet shifted.

The chalk line did not glow or fracture. It wavered in my vision, edges blurring as the air thickened. The concrete felt uneven beneath my soles, as if the floor tilted by degrees too small to measure but large enough to threaten balance.

The beams above emitted a dry vibration. Iron sang faintly against wood.

The pressure built from behind the sealed door.

My sight split.

For a breath, I stood at the top of the stairs instead of the center of the spiral. My hand gripped the railing. My lungs burned. The open night above called to me.

Then another image forced its way in.

My hand reaching for the iron nail at the spiral's edge. Turning it inward. Pressing it to my palm. Blood as solution.

The air tightened around my throat.

The cadence in my chest faltered.

The breath tried to bend into the older rhythm, deeper and intrusive, a hum rising without permission.

My jaw clenched.

The spiral shuddered again. A thin section of chalk at the outer ring fractured under vibration.

I dropped to one knee without stepping beyond the boundary and grabbed the chalk from the floor.

The door rattled harder. A sharp crack split from one hinge as iron strained against its mounting. Dust fell in a gray curtain from the joists above.

I pressed the chalk down.

The tip scraped unevenly at first, dragged sideways by the tremor in the concrete.

Slow.

Even.

The air pressed into my ribs, trying to compress the breath from my lungs.

"Anchor holds," I said.

My voice broke once.

I swallowed and finished the curve.

The pressure intensified.

The cellar air thickened, pulling inward toward the sealed door. My ears rang with the vibration of iron under stress. The spiral trembled beneath me.

Darkness flickered at the edges of my sight.

Blood flashed across my palm again.

I inhaled deeply.

"I am keeper of the boundary."

The words cut through the vibration.

The door slammed against its frame with a force that shook the light bulb overhead. The spiral blurred for a final instant.

The hinges screamed.

Wood shrieked.

Iron ground against iron.

My knees bent under the force as the air compressed one last time, hard enough to drive me downward.

I did not step out.

I did not retreat.

The pressure peaked.

Then it broke.

Silence fell in a single, clean drop.

The door remained shut.

The spiral held.

The iron no longer vibrated.

My pulse thundered in my ears, but my feet stayed planted inside the boundary.

The house had pressed until resistance met structure.

It did not push again.

Not yet.

The shaking stopped without warning.

One moment the hinges screamed against their bolts, wood flexing under violent strain, the next everything fell silent. The sound did not fade. It cut off. Clean. Abrupt. The absence rang in my ears louder than the assault had.

My breath hung halfway inside my chest, waiting for impact.

Nothing followed.

The air did not relax. It shifted slowly, the pressure thinning by degrees. The concrete beneath my feet steadied. The vibration in the beams faded into something almost indistinguishable from ordinary stillness. Dust floated in the light, suspended, then drifted down in soft lines.

The spiral remained intact.

No fractures split the chalk. No iron had torn free. The outer ring held its shape as if the strain had passed around it rather than through it.

The door rested in its frame.

Closed.

Not splintered. Not bowed.

Closed from the inside.

I stayed where I was.

My pulse thudded hard in my ears before gradually easing. The light bulb overhead swayed once more and came to rest. The cellar walls made no complaint. The foundation did not groan.

The house above did not creak.

The silence felt different now. Not empty. Not fragile. Intent.

The pressure had not been random.

It had concentrated. Focused.

It had pushed hardest when my breath slipped. When my stance wavered. When the chalk fractured at the edge.

It had pressed until I either moved or held.

I had held.

I remained in the center until the air returned to something close to neutral. Until my breathing no longer required counting. Until my knees stopped remembering the force that had bent them.

Only then did I step beyond the spiral.

The movement felt deliberate, not victorious. My legs were steady, but a tremor lingered beneath the surface of my muscles. The cost had not been dramatic. It had been precise.

I approached the sealed door and laid my palm against the wood.

Cool.

Solid.

No warmth pulsed beneath it now. No vibration. The grain lay still under my hand.

"You tested," I said quietly.

The word settled into the space between us.

The door did not answer.

But the wood beneath my palm felt denser than before. As if something behind it had shifted its weight and chosen a new position.

I withdrew my hand and turned toward the stairs.

The kitchen above appeared unchanged. The clock ticked in even intervals. The refrigerator hummed at its usual pitch. Sunlight lay flat across the table.

Nothing in the visible structure betrayed what had happened below.

Yet the quiet had altered.

It no longer felt cautious.

It felt observant.

I stood in the doorway to the cellar and left it open. Not in defiance. Not in invitation. In acknowledgment.

The system beyond that door had not broken through.

It had leaned in.

And now it knew the measure of my resistance.

I closed my eyes and let my breathing settle fully.

From below, faint and almost imperceptible, something shifted once in the dark.

Not a door.

Not a hinge.

Something deeper.

Chapter 34

The air upstairs felt thinner. Precise.

The clock in the kitchen ticked at a volume just loud enough to irritate. The refrigerator hummed with a faint metallic edge. Nothing had shifted out of place. Nothing had broken.

The silence felt scrubbed clean.

I stood in the hallway and waited for exhaustion to take me. After the pressure in the cellar, my legs should have trembled. My hands should have shaken. Sleep should have pulled at me as refuge.

Instead, I felt awake in a way that bordered on electric.

Too aware.

I walked toward the bathroom without deciding to. The floorboards did not creak. No draft brushed my neck. The house offered no sign of resistance.

The bathroom light snapped on, harsh and ordinary.

I faced the mirror.

For a moment, everything aligned. Pale face. Flat hair. Crescent resting faintly against my wrist. Breathing even.

I shifted my weight.

The woman in the mirror shifted a fraction of a second later.

So small it could have been nothing.

I stilled.

She stilled.

My throat tightened.

I raised my hand slowly, watching.

The reflection followed. Perfect.

I lowered it.

Perfect again.

I leaned closer to the glass.

The delay did not return immediately.

It waited.

That was worse.

I straightened my shoulders and lifted my chin. The woman across from me did the same. Eyes steady. Jaw set.

Then her mouth changed.

Not a grin. Not a distortion.

Just the faintest lift at one corner. A suggestion of private amusement.

My own lips remained flat.

The lift deepened by degrees too small to quantify. A subtle curve that did not belong to me.

The air in the bathroom tightened against my skin. The overhead light buzzed faintly. I became acutely aware of the pulse at my throat and the scar near my eyebrow. My hands felt distant, as though they belonged to someone standing behind me.

The reflection's eyes narrowed slightly.

Mine did not.

A cold line traced the center of my spine.

For a moment, doubt edged in. Perhaps my mouth had twitched. Perhaps stress had pulled a muscle I did not register. Perhaps the smile had begun on my face and I was simply late in noticing it.

I inhaled slowly.

The smile remained.

I did not step back. I did not shatter the glass. I held my ground.

My reflection watched me.

"You don't move without me," I said quietly.

The lips in the mirror did not part.

The smile sharpened.

The old fracture tried to open. The suggestion that perception could not be trusted. That memory could not be trusted. That the woman in the mirror might already be leading by a fraction.

I leaned closer until my breath fogged the lower edge of the glass.

"You follow," I said.

This time, the lips moved with mine.

The smile disappeared.

But the eyes did not soften.

They remained intent. Focused. Studying me from a depth that felt a fraction too far behind the surface.

The fog on the mirror began to clear.

The woman across from me did not blink when I did.

The corners of her mouth eased downward, but her eyes narrowed.

Not in anger.

In calculation.

Her head tilted slightly to the left.

I had not moved.

The angle was subtle, almost graceful, but it was not mine.

A pulse of heat moved through my chest.

The old impulse surged fast and clean. Look away. Break the glass. Go downstairs where lines could be drawn and iron could be set into wood. Where fear had geometry.

My fingers twitched at my side.

I curled them into my palm and held still.

The bathroom felt smaller. The overhead light hummed with a faint electrical strain. Cool air brushed the back of my neck. The crescent on my wrist warmed under the skin, a steady pressure that sharpened everything.

I drew in a measured breath.

The woman in the mirror watched me breathe.

Her mouth curved again.

Not amusement.

Not quite.

A knowing softness at the edge.

"You don't know me," I said quietly.

My lips formed the words evenly.

The reflection's jaw tightened a fraction later.

The delay was deliberate.

A tremor moved through my throat. My mind supplied explanations in rapid succession. Stress. Fatigue. Adrenaline refusing to subside. The residue of what had happened below.

They were reasonable.

They were tempting.

I stepped closer instead.

"You do not move first," I said.

This time, I tracked every muscle in my face as I spoke.

The reflection's eyes sharpened.

Her mouth shifted again, the smallest adjustment, as if correcting something internal.

The temperature dropped another degree. My breath fogged the glass between us. The mirror felt colder than the room.

The fracture pressed at the edges of my perception. A flicker of myself smiling in memory. A suggestion that perhaps this expression had already crossed my face and I had simply arrived late to it.

"I stay," I said, each word even.

The reflection's lips parted slightly.

Mine did not.

The hum in the room swelled, thin and metallic. My heartbeat thudded in my ears.

Her lips remained parted, as if gathering breath.

I did not blink.

Seconds stretched.

Then, slowly, the posture across from me realigned. The tilt corrected. The narrowing of the eyes softened by degrees. The mouth smoothed back toward neutrality.

Almost.

The faintest trace remained at one corner.

I held her gaze.

We stood that way, separated by a pane of glass and something thinner than glass.

When I finally blinked, the reflection blinked with me.

But her breath fogged the mirror a moment before mine did.

I left the bathroom without breaking eye contact until the hallway swallowed the reflection.

The kitchen light felt harsher than before. The air carried a faint mineral tang from the pipes. My hands remained steady as I opened the cabinet above the sink. The small glass jar of salt clicked softly against ceramic when I lifted it. From the drawer beside the stove, I retrieved the iron fragment I had filed weeks ago. One edge was smooth. The other retained a faint burr where the metal had resisted.

I returned to the bathroom.

The mirror stood bright and unblinking.

My reflection waited in the same position I had left her. Neutral. Attentive. No lag.

I set the salt on the sink. The jar made a hollow sound against porcelain. I held up my wrist.

The crescent beneath my skin pulsed faintly.

I dipped my fingers into the salt. The grains rasped against glass as they shifted. When I pressed them to the crescent, a faint sting spread under the surface. Not sharp enough to wound. Just enough to clarify the line. The warmth beneath the skin tightened into focus.

The reflection watched.

I lifted the iron fragment.

The metal felt cool at first. Then colder as it met the salt.

I traced the curve of the crescent slowly, following its arc with deliberate pressure. The iron pressed into skin without breaking it. Salt ground softly between metal and flesh. The sensation traveled up my arm, not painful, but exact. The mark beneath my skin felt defined. Edged.

I drew another slow line across the arc.

My breath remained even.

The reflection did not tilt. Did not smile. Did not hesitate.

"I anchor," I said.

My lips moved.

The woman in the mirror moved with me.

I traced the crescent one last time, slower than before. The salt scraped lightly. The metal pressed with steady insistence. The pulse beneath the mark settled into something measured rather than reactive.

The air in the bathroom felt denser, but no longer hostile. The hum in my ears thinned until it vanished.

The reflection remained aligned.

No delay.

No smirk.

I lowered my wrist and wiped away the excess salt, leaving a faint residue along the crescent's curve. The warmth beneath the skin cooled gradually, settling into a quiet presence.

I stepped closer to the mirror and studied my own eyes. There were shadows beneath them now. Strain. Resolve.

"You follow," I said.

The woman across from me spoke in perfect sync.

The overhead light buzzed once, then steadied.

I turned off the bathroom light.

The room fell dark except for the faint spill of hallway illumination. The mirror became a dim rectangle in shadow.

For a moment, I saw nothing but my silhouette.

Then the outline of my reflection remained visible a fraction longer than it should have.

I did not turn the light back on.

I walked away.

Chapter 35

The mirror had steadied. The crescent no longer burned. I left the bathroom with my pulse even and my thoughts aligned in quiet order. The hallway felt balanced, the walls carrying their own weight without strain.

As I moved toward the stairs, I let my fingertips brush the plaster. It was cool. Slightly textured. Present.

Halfway down the hall, the air shifted.

Warmth touched the back of my neck.

Not a draft. Not residual heat from a vent.

Close.

My skin reacted before my mind did. The fine hairs at my nape lifted. A slow exhale spread across the base of my skull, damp and deliberate.

Someone stood behind me.

I did not turn.

The warmth deepened, hovering just below my hairline. The breath came again, longer this time, gliding along my skin and lingering there. My shoulders wanted to rise. My jaw began to lock.

The floorboards did not creak.

The lights did not flicker.

Nothing in the house moved.

The presence did not need spectacle.

It was inches away.

My pulse quickened once, then settled as I drew in a measured breath.

The exhale behind me matched the length of mine.

Close enough that I could feel the moisture of it against my ear.

"You're near," I said quietly.

The words left my mouth without tremor.

The breath paused.

Then resumed, slower.

The instinct to spin and confront flared hot in my chest. A sharper instinct followed it. To command. To claim authority. To declare that whatever stood at my back answered to me.

The thought burned bright and fast.

It felt powerful.

It felt wrong.

The warmth at my neck intensified as if in response to that surge. A testing press. Waiting for me to reach for control.

I lowered my shoulders deliberately.

"I keep it," I said, softer now.

The breath lingered.

It did not advance. It did not retreat.

I stood in the hallway with my hands open at my sides. My palms faced forward, empty. My breathing remained even, not forced.

The warmth thinned gradually. It did not vanish all at once. It diffused by degrees, retreating into the air as though absorbed into the walls themselves.

The hallway remained unchanged.

The silence returned.

I did not look over my shoulder.

I did not need to.

My pulse steadied.

And then, faintly, I felt another exhale brush the back of my neck.

Not matching mine this time.

The warmth did not leave.

It thickened.

The air at the back of my neck grew dense, hovering just beneath my ear. A steady exhale touched my skin. Not rushed. Not hostile. Close enough that my pulse began to match it.

For one brief moment, the rhythm aligned.

My body leaned forward before I caught it. The instinct rose clean and sharp. Turn. Confront. Establish order.

Words formed at the back of my throat, precise and edged. I knew how to shape them. I knew the tone that would carry weight. I could speak with certainty. I could harden my voice and make the air respond.

The thought sparked something hotter than fear.

Power.

The warmth pressed closer, sliding along the hollow beneath my ear. Waiting.

I felt how easy it would be to claim it. To say enough. To demand stillness. To force the breath behind me to recoil.

My jaw tightened.

The command hovered on my tongue.

If I turned with authority, it would be clean. Final. Satisfying.

The breath deepened.

Not retreating.

Testing.

The heat in my chest sharpened. Pride coiled there, bright and tempting.

I let the words dissolve before they reached my lips.

"I am caretaker," I said instead.

The sentence left my mouth steady, low.

The warmth paused.

The silence thickened around us.

I did not turn. I did not raise my hands. I did not attempt to measure the distance between my skin and whatever stood there.

"I keep what is set," I continued. "Nothing more."

The breath resumed.

Slower now.

It moved from the back of my neck to the curve of my jaw. Closer. Intimate enough to provoke.

My shoulders lowered deliberately. My palms opened at my sides.

The urge to assert flared again, softer this time. A suggestion that a firmer tone would resolve this. That escalation would end the waiting.

I remained still.

"I hold," I said.

The words were not a command.

They were a position.

The warmth lingered for a long moment, close enough that I could feel its presence without contact.

Then it thinned.

Not withdrawn in defeat. Not banished.

It diffused into the hallway air by degrees, leaving the faintest residual coolness against my skin.

I stood alone.

My pulse steadied.

The house remained quiet.

But somewhere behind me, in the space I refused to look into, something adjusted its breathing.

I felt the warmth follow me to the cellar door.

Not against my skin now. Not invasive. Present in the air, faint and patient.

I descended without hurry.

The cellar light cast its steady circle across the floor. The spiral remained clean. Iron sat dark in the beams where I had set it. The hidden door rested sealed in its frame.

Nothing trembled.

Nothing groaned.

The air waited.

I stepped into the center of the spiral and let my hands rest open at my sides. I did not reach for chalk. I did not adjust iron. The lines held without correction.

The warmth hovered behind my shoulder, close enough to register, far enough not to touch.

My breathing settled into its natural cadence.

Four.

Hold.

Four.

"I am not vessel," I said.

The word settled into the concrete and wood.

"I am not master."

The warmth edged closer, brushing the air at the back of my neck.

"I am keeper."

The final word felt heavier than the others. It did not echo. It absorbed.

The dialect rose in my mouth next, not rushed, not sharpened by fear. The syllables unfolded in measured sequence. Each phrase placed with intention. Breath guided the spacing. The sound was not loud, but it carried weight.

I named the boundary.

I named succession.

I named the line between holding and claiming.

The warmth thinned gradually. Not recoiling. Not forced away. It diffused downward through the floor and into the beams, settling into the foundation beneath my feet.

The air cooled by degrees.

The iron remained steady in the wood.

The spiral did not blur.

The hidden door did not strain.

I opened my eyes.

The cellar was quiet.

Not empty.

Quiet.

The crescent on my wrist cooled into a steady warmth, no longer pulsing. It felt less like a flare and more like a mark that had always belonged there.

I stepped out of the spiral only after my breath returned to its ordinary rhythm.

No dizziness.

No fracture.

The cellar light hummed faintly overhead. Dust rested undisturbed along the beams. The door to the inner chamber remained closed.

I stood there for one more measured inhale.

The house did not press.

It did not retreat.

It settled around me.

And beneath the quiet, somewhere deep in the foundation stones, something answered the cadence of my breath with its own.

Chapter 36

The cellar went quiet after I finished.

Not hollow. Not emptied. Quiet in the way a held breath settles into the body instead of straining against it. The spiral lay clean beneath my feet. The iron held. The hidden door rested without pressure.

I expected stillness.

Instead, something shifted.

The tightening began behind my eyes. A slow widening that did not belong to the room. The edges of the cellar softened. Not darkness. Not shadow. Something loosening.

The first image arrived whole.

A timber room blackened by years of smoke. Heat clung to the air. A woman knelt between another woman's legs, sleeves rolled high, hands slick and red. Her voice was steady. Her hands did not tremble.

A newborn's cry pierced the room.

It stopped.

The silence that followed pressed into my lungs. I felt the weight of it as if I had been standing there.

The second image struck harder.

A chalk circle half-drawn across rough floorboards. A younger guardian, eyes rimmed raw from sleeplessness. Her hand hovered above the final curve. The line incomplete.

A shadow edged across the gap.

Later, a child lay in bed with skin too pale and breath too thin. Watchful eyes ringed the room. No fire. No spectacle. Just the slow, unstoppable slide of something that should not have entered.

My knees bent, but the spiral beneath me did not give.

More rooms followed.

A woman washing blood from her hands in cold water that never ran clear.

Another standing in a doorway while villagers whispered beyond the threshold.

One choosing which laboring mother would receive the last measure of strength in her voice.

One finishing the oath while tears streaked silently down her face.

The images layered over one another. Not replacing the cellar. Existing beside it.

Copper rose at the back of my tongue.

The pressure behind my eyes sharpened. Detail cut through me with exactness. The grain of the timber. The smell of smoke and sweat. The sound of breath that did not return.

A final image stepped forward.

A guardian stood in the center of a spiral drawn on packed earth. Alone. Shoulders straight. Eyes open.

She did not look victorious.

She looked tired.

She finished speaking and remained standing.

No one thanked her.

No one knew what had been held back.

The image lingered longer than the others.

Then it did not disappear.

It settled.

The cellar came back into full focus. The light hummed overhead.

The spiral remained intact beneath my feet.

The iron in the beam felt warmer than before.

My breathing had gone shallow. I pressed my palm to my chest and drew in air slowly until it filled me.

The weight did not lift.

It distributed.

I did not feel crowned.

I felt included.

My knees steadied.

The hidden door remained sealed.

The spiral did not blur.

The silence in the cellar deepened, no longer empty but layered.

I swallowed.

The images did not fade.

They aligned.

And somewhere beneath the foundation stones, the rhythm that had answered my breath earlier began again, carrying more than my own.

The images did not recede after I steadied my breathing.

They arranged themselves.

Not in chaos. Not overlapping. One after another. Deliberate.

I saw hands pressing at precise points along a laboring body. A voice choosing which truth to speak and which to swallow. A woman standing between two outcomes and selecting the one that would leave the least ruin.

Not triumph.

Decision.

The charts upstairs rose in my mind without invitation. The columns. The time stamps. The overlays I had drawn as if mapping enough detail could prevent spillover.

I had wanted lines.

They had lived in blur.

Another memory stepped forward.

A guardian in a cellar much like mine, chalk line nearly complete. Above her, a child burned with fever. Below her, the boundary thinned. She finished the seal.

Upstairs, the child survived.

The mother did not.

There was no applause. No accusation. Just the continuation of a household that never spoke of the choice.

The image did not condemn her.

It did not absolve her.

It remained.

Another followed.

A different woman refused to complete a rite she believed too severe. She softened her voice where firmness was required. The boundary faltered. Nothing dramatic followed. No flames. No spectacle.

But something in that house dimmed over the years. A kindness that never returned.

She had tried to spare them.

The consequence endured anyway.

My throat tightened.

I leaned my palm against the cellar wall. The stone felt cool and unyielding beneath my skin.

The women in the images did not look clean. Their hands bore stains. Their eyes held fatigue. They did not stand above the work. They stood inside it.

I had studied for symmetry.

They had endured asymmetry.

The spiral beneath my feet warmed faintly.

The iron in the beam remained still.

The weight in my chest shifted from fear to something heavier.

I had believed precision could prevent harm. That if I corrected every mistranslation and reinforced every weakness, the system might narrow itself into something almost gentle.

The images did not support that hope.

They carried forward.

Not ritual alone.

Consequence.

I saw now how I had tried to hold the work at a distance. To believe that perfect alignment would protect me from the moment when no outcome would be untouched.

The light hummed steadily overhead.

"I cannot make this clean," I said.

The words settled into the stone.

No echo returned.

The spiral did not blur.

The iron did not vibrate.

The house did not respond.

Because nothing structural had failed.

The pressure I felt did not come from beneath the door.

It came from within my own ribs.

I drew in a slow breath.

The images did not fade.

They aligned behind me like a line of figures standing at my back.

And for the first time, I understood that holding would mean choosing.

The memories crested without warning.

They stopped arriving as images and began arriving as weight.

Not only what had happened, but what followed. The silence in rooms where choices had been made. The way hands trembled only when no one could see them. The nights spent awake after speaking the right words and the nights spent awake after speaking the wrong ones.

Grief layered itself through me, patient and cumulative. Not sharp. Not explosive. A steady pressure worn smooth by repetition.

Exhaustion settled into my shoulders. My legs felt heavy, as if I had stood for years without rest. A weariness moved through my bones that did not belong to this hour.

The cellar did not shift.

The spiral held beneath my feet.

I saw again the charts upstairs. The careful lines. The measured spacing. The belief that if I aligned everything precisely enough, the system might narrow itself into something manageable.

The women in the memories had not been afforded that comfort.

Their hands had been stained.

Their voices had carried.

I lowered myself to one knee in the center of the spiral.

Not collapsing.

Anchoring.

The stone beneath my palms felt cold and unyielding. The air pressed down along my shoulders and spine, not crushing, but steady. As if waiting to see whether I would brace against it or stand beneath it.

I closed my eyes.

"I do not cleanse this," I said.

The words felt heavy in my mouth.

"I keep it."

The cellar absorbed the sentence. No echo. No reply.

The pressure did not lift.

It settled.

The memories shifted from impact to presence. No longer striking at me. Resting within reach. Part of the air.

I drew in a slow breath and felt how much space the weight occupied inside my ribs.

It did not ask to be removed.

It asked to be carried.

I opened my eyes.

The spiral remained unbroken. The iron held fast in the beam. The hidden door did not move.

Nothing in the house changed.

I rose carefully from my knee. My joints protested slightly, as though I had aged years in minutes. Not injured. Altered.

Something had shifted in the center of me.

The part that believed steadiness meant prevention.

That part did not return.

I stood alone in the cellar, fully aware of the mass I now held.

And I did not reach for a way to make it lighter.

Chapter 37

I left the cellar with the weight settled deep in my bones.

The quiet of early morning, not aftermath. I climbed the stairs and entered the kitchen just as the first gray light pressed against the windows. Upstairs, the house felt unchanged. Floorboards steady. Walls upright.

I leaned against the counter and let my eyes drift closed.

An apartment came to mind.

Third floor. Narrow hallway that smelled faintly of carpet cleaner and old paint. A small kitchen with white cabinets that never quite closed flush. A refrigerator humming steadily in the corner. A mailbox downstairs with my name printed cleanly on a strip of plastic.

No cellar.

No iron hidden in beams.

A job that ended at five. Evenings spent at a small table beneath a single overhead light bulb. The sound of neighbors arguing softly through thin walls. A television laugh track leaking from somewhere down the hall. Dinner eaten without notebooks open beside it.

I imagined waking without listening for shifts in breath. Sleeping without tracing cadence in the dark. Introducing myself to someone who knew me only as Clara. No history attached. No inheritance folded behind my teeth.

The image settled into my chest with an ache that caught me off guard.

It was not safety that pulled at me. It was smallness. The right to make a mistake that reached no farther than my own skin.

I let the fantasy expand.

Signing a lease. Carrying boxes up narrow stairs. Standing at a window that overlooked nothing but brick and sky. Buying a plant and forgetting to water it without consequence.

The ache deepened until it felt like pressure behind my ribs.

I did not push it away.

I let myself want it.

The light outside grew brighter. The street remained unchanged.

I imagined hearing a baby cry through the thin walls of that apartment. I imagined pausing, listening too closely. Counting breath where no one else would count it. Watching for fractures in places no one else would notice.

The fantasy thinned.

Even there, I would hear it.

I stepped closer to the kitchen window and pressed my palm to the cool glass. My reflection faintly overlaid the road beyond. The house stood behind me in that reflection, quiet and upright.

Nothing barred the doors. Nothing locked the driveway.

I could leave.

But I would not leave the knowing behind.

The gray light shifted toward gold.

I exhaled and let the apartment dissolve without bitterness.

It did not shatter.

It receded.

The house remained silent at my back.

I stood in the dawn and felt the shape of my life settle into place, not as confinement, but as a narrowing of options that would not widen again.

The road outside carried on without me.

And somewhere beneath the floor, the rhythm I now recognized continued, patient and unremarkable.

The grief thinned.

It did not disappear. It sharpened.

I turned from the window and faced the kitchen table. The journal lay open where I had left it. The recorder rested beside it, red light dark. A small jar of iron filings caught the dawn light, the dull metallic grains shifting slightly when I brushed the table.

Weeks ago, these objects had felt like proof of entrapment.

Now they felt deliberate.

I stepped closer and ran my fingertips over the table's surface. The wood bore faint grooves where I had pressed too hard while drawing spirals. The scratches remained. The surface had not been restored.

Neither had I.

I opened the journal again and turned to the corrected passages. The language no longer felt threatening. It felt unfinished.

A margin left blank where context should have been. A reference to consequence without detail. A line that assumed the next reader already understood what it meant to choose between outcomes.

Temperance had written what she could.

She had not written enough.

I lifted the recorder. It was heavier than I remembered. The weight sat solid in my palm.

It had once been evidence.

Now it was storage.

I set it down and pulled a blank notebook toward me. The cover was unmarked. The pages clean.

The pen hovered above the first line.

I began without flourish.

"First fracture: misreading containment as punishment."

The ink moved steadily across the page.

I described where I had erred. Where I had mistaken fear for threat. Where I had nearly asserted control instead of holding alignment.

I did not dramatize the cellar. I documented it.

I wrote the translations as they should be read.

I marked where doubt distorts language.

The jar of iron filings shifted again when the table vibrated beneath my wrist. The sound was faint, almost like sand.

"This will not be gentle," I wrote.

The sentence did not tremble.

"You will not prevent every loss."

I paused, then continued.

"You remain. That is the work."

The words looked small on the page. Unadorned.

I turned to a new section and outlined the sequence of breath. The cadence. The corrections. Where pride interferes. Where silence must be maintained.

The cellar door at the end of the hall remained closed. It did not call for attention.

The house did not react.

It did not need to.

I wrote until the first chapter filled three pages. Clear. Exact.

When I finally closed the notebook, the morning light had shifted fully across the table.

The recorder sat beside the journal.

The iron filings rested in their jar.

Nothing in the room suggested inheritance.

That was the design.

I placed the new notebook on top of Temperance's and rested my hand there for a moment.

One day, someone else would open it.

And they would not begin where I had begun.

I stood at the cellar threshold with the notebook still warm in my hands.

The hallway behind me held the pale gray of early morning. The house made its usual small sounds. Wood shifting. Pipes settling. Nothing leaned toward me. Nothing pressed.

I rested my palm against the doorframe. The wood felt cool. Slightly rough where paint had thinned over the years.

I let myself name what this meant.

There would be nights without sleep. Days when I would stand between outcomes and choose the one that left less damage rather than none. Mornings when I would make coffee beside someone who had no idea what had been held in place while they slept.

No witness.

No record except what I kept.

I stepped into the cellar and let the door close behind me.

The air below was steady. Mineral. Familiar. The spiral lay clean on the concrete. The iron in the beam remained dark and quiet.

I moved to the center and stopped.

My hand rose to the crescent at my wrist. The mark felt warm beneath the skin. Not flaring. Not demanding. Present.

I did not address the house.

"I will keep it," I said.

My voice did not echo. It settled.

I drew one breath before continuing.

"I will tell it."

The words felt different in my mouth. Heavier. Final.

The air did not shift.

The hidden door did not strain.

Nothing dramatic answered.

The silence held.

The life I had imagined earlier did not press at the edges of my thoughts. It did not plead. It stood at a distance and remained there.

I lowered my hand from my wrist and let it fall to my side.

The crescent did not pulse. It rested.

I stepped out of the spiral.

My feet crossed the chalk line without tremor. I did not look down to check its integrity. I already knew it held.

The stairs rose ahead of me.

I climbed them slowly.

At the top, I paused and glanced back once. The cellar remained unchanged. Spiral intact. Door sealed. Iron fixed in wood.

No ceremony.

No witness.

I closed the cellar door gently.

The latch clicked into place.

Upstairs, the morning had brightened. Light stretched across the kitchen table, catching the edge of the new notebook where it lay on top of the old one.

I walked toward it.

And this time, I did not hesitate.

Chapter 38

I reopened the journal without hurry.

Morning light stretched across the kitchen table and settled over the page. The paper showed faint impressions where Temperance had pressed harder with her pen. The ink had bled slightly into the fibers, dark in places, lighter in others.

I read her later entries more carefully than I had before.

The tone had shifted over time. Early passages explained. Later ones condensed. Margins carried corrections in firmer ink. Certain lines were crossed out and rewritten with sharper pressure, as if she had argued with herself before committing to the phrasing.

My eyes moved slowly, not searching for revelation, simply tracing what she had left.

Then I saw it.

A sentence written smaller than the rest, tucked between two larger passages near the seam of the binding. The words nearly disappeared into shadow where the pages curved inward.

It began with the third daughter.

I remembered seeing it before. I had assumed it referred to lineage. A detail of inheritance.

Now the sentence felt weighted.

I leaned closer. The ink there was darker. The nib had pressed deep enough to leave a faint groove in the page.

I flipped backward through earlier entries. References to daughters appeared in passing. First-born. Second-born. Then silence. Then adjustment. Every third succession carried slight notations in the margins.

I spread the historian's lullaby variant beside the journal and read the two together.

The cadence I had restored was close.

Close.

I tapped the rhythm against the table with two fingers.

One-two-three-four.

One-two-three-four.

The sound of my nails against wood was soft but distinct.

I turned back to an earlier, faded line and slowed the second measure, following the original mark.

One-two... three-four.

The pause stretched longer before the final phrase.

I repeated it.

One-two... three-four.

The held breath settled deeper into my chest. My lungs expanded differently. The final line landed lower, steadier.

I felt a subtle resistance inside my body loosen.

I tried the tightened version I had been using.

One-two-three-four.

One-two-three-four.

The tempo pressed forward. Efficient. Clean.

Too clean.

Over time, the pause had shortened. The breath between phrases compressed. A small economy introduced under pressure. Under fatigue.

The words had remained intact.

The space between them had not.

I closed my eyes and let the earlier cadence move through me again. The longer hold before the final measure did not strain. It created room.

Room for something to settle.

The phrase from the journal echoed in my mind.

It began with the third daughter.

I scanned the entries again. Every third succession carried a marginal note. A recalibration. A return to earlier structure.

Temperance had inherited during one of those cycles.

So had I.

The thought did not alarm me.

It altered me.

The system had not fractured.

It had tightened.

Gradually. Almost imperceptibly.

I leaned back in my chair and inhaled once more with the restored tempo. The pause lingered before the closing line. Not rushed. Not sharpened by urgency.

Something in the house seemed to listen.

I opened my eyes and looked toward the cellar door at the end of the hall.

The difference was small.

Small enough to overlook.

I had not yet spoken it below.

And I did not know what would answer when I did.

I rebuilt the lullaby before I went below.

Not from memory. Not from instinct. From record.

Temperance's marginal notes carried small corrections in darker ink. The historian's variant preserved syllables that had softened over time. I copied both onto a clean page and traced the structure slowly, marking where breath lengthened and where it had been compressed.

The phrase third daughter clarified the pattern. Every third succession marked a return. Not to different words. To the original pause.

I tapped the rhythm against the table.

The version I had been using was clean. Efficient. The second measure tightened almost imperceptibly. The final line arrived too quickly, as if bracing for interruption.

I slowed it.

One-two... three-four.

The pause widened before closure.

It felt unfamiliar in my chest.

I closed the notebook and stood.

The descent to the cellar carried no surge of adrenaline. Only intent. The air met me without resistance. The spiral lay undisturbed. The iron remained dark in the beam.

I stepped into the center and let my arms rest at my sides.

Nothing needed redrawing.

This adjustment would not touch chalk or nail.

It would touch breath.

I began the lullaby softly.

The first measure landed without effort. The second reached its midpoint and my lungs instinctively tried to hurry it. Muscle memory leaned forward.

I held.

The pause expanded. Not strained. Not theatrical. Simply longer than habit allowed.

My ribs resisted for a fraction of a second, then opened.

I repeated it.

One-two... three-four.

The held space before the final line felt steady beneath my sternum. Not hollow. Not fragile.

Then I spoke the oath.

Not louder. Not slower.

Aligned.

The shift was subtle but immediate.

The low pressure I had carried since opening the seal, an almost invisible tightness behind my sternum, released without spectacle. The cellar air seemed to settle into itself. The faint unevenness I had sensed but never named evened out.

The spiral did not flare.

The iron did not hum.

The hidden door did not strain.

Nothing dramatic occurred.

My breathing no longer required correction.

The cadence flowed without effort, and when I reached the final line, I allowed the pause to remain before closing it, letting the silence absorb the measure instead of cutting it short.

I stood there for several seconds after the words ended.

The quiet did not press.

It rested.

I opened my eyes.

The cellar looked unchanged. Concrete. Chalk. Wood. Stone.

Yet the atmosphere held proportion. The room no longer felt like it was leaning into the next test.

I stepped out of the spiral slowly and took one more measured breath, testing for resistance.

There was none.

The house did not surge.

It did not retreat.

It listened.

For now.

The last word left my mouth and settled into the cellar without echo.

I did not rush to fill the silence.

The spiral beneath my feet remained unbroken. The iron sat firm in the beam. The hidden door did not strain or test its hinges.

The shift happened quietly.

The faint warmth that had lived in the wood for weeks leveled out. Not gone. Not flaring. Even. The air felt the same temperature in every direction, as though the room had finally stopped favoring one corner over another.

I became aware of how still the house truly was.

Not the tight stillness that follows impact. Not the suspended breath that precedes resistance.

The kind of quiet that does not brace.

The crescent on my wrist cooled until it felt indistinguishable from the rest of my skin. Not absent. Not reactive. Simply present.

I stepped forward and placed my palm against one of the support beams.

The wood felt grounded. Solid. No faint tremor beneath it. No subtle vibration waiting to build. Only structure carrying weight without complaint.

I closed my eyes and listened.

There was no breath at my neck.

No pressure behind my ribs.

The rhythm remained in my lungs, steady and unforced. When I inhaled, the pause arrived naturally. When I exhaled, it resolved without hurry.

The cellar did not empty.

It settled into proportion.

I opened my eyes and let my hand fall from the beam.

Nothing in the room declared victory. No rush of air. No extinguished darkness. No light shifting across the concrete.

Only alignment.

I stepped out of the spiral.

The chalk line remained intact behind me. I did not feel watched as I turned my back. The hidden door stayed closed without tension.

That was enough.

I climbed the stairs slowly. Each step felt measured but not guarded. The house did not press at my shoulders as I ascended.

At the top, I paused and looked down once more.

The spiral lay quiet. The beam bore its iron without emphasis. The cellar air held steady.

Nothing demanded attention.

I closed the cellar door gently and returned to the kitchen.

Morning light filled the room now. A car passed outside, its tires humming against pavement. Somewhere down the street, a door shut. Ordinary sounds layered over one another.

I stood in the center of the kitchen and let my breathing find its natural tempo.

The house did not lean toward me.

It did not withdraw.

It remained.

So did I.

And beneath the floor, the corrected rhythm moved through timber and stone, not louder, not softer, simply true enough to hold.

Chapter 39

The first thing I noticed was the air.

It did not press against my lungs when I stepped onto the back porch. It moved across my skin in a steady current, carrying the scent of cooling grass and soil that had released the day's heat. The breeze brushed the back of my neck without weight.

The sun had dropped behind the trees at the edge of the property. A band of amber lingered low on the horizon before dissolving into blue. Shadows stretched long across the yard, pooling beneath the fence and the old maple near the corner.

I paused on the porch steps and listened.

Crickets had begun their evening rhythm, layered and precise. A dog barked somewhere beyond the neighboring houses, sharp and brief. A car door slammed in the distance. Life continued without pause.

The house stood behind me, its windows reflecting the fading light. No tension pulled at the beams. No faint hum beneath the floorboards. The steadiness from below seemed to extend upward, outward, settling into the yard.

I stepped into the grass.

Each footfall felt ordinary. The soil gave slightly under my weight, then returned. The fence line stretched around the perimeter, boards weathered and sun-bleached, nails darkened with age. I let my gaze travel the full boundary without hurry.

I walked toward it and ran my fingers along the wood. The grain caught lightly against my skin. A splinter grazed my knuckle but did not break it. Physical. Measured. No symbolism required.

At the far corner where the fence met the back boundary, I stopped.

The trees beyond the property line stood dense and shadowed. Their trunks were dark against the deepening sky. Nothing moved within them beyond the natural shift of leaves.

I crouched and studied the soil near the base of the fence. The grass lay flat where the wind touched it. No unevenness. No subtle dip in the earth.

The ground felt compact and settled beneath my palm.

I straightened and drew a slow breath.

I did not count it.

The air entered cleanly and left without effort. The crickets maintained their steady tempo, unbroken. Their rhythm did not falter when I moved.

The yard did not glow. It did not hum.

It felt inhabited in the same way the house did now. Not empty. Not tense. Simply aligned with itself.

I stood there until the amber band disappeared entirely and the sky darkened into full evening.

The rhythm continued.

So did I.

I continued along the fence until the boards gave way to a narrow strip of scrub at the back of the property. The weeds grew thicker there, tangled around the posts where the yard ended and the land dipped slightly before rising toward the next row of houses.

Their roofs cut dark shapes against the fading sky. A few porch lights flickered on one by one.

I stood at the boundary and rested my hands on the top rail.

The wood felt dry beneath my palms. The grain rough, splintered in places where weather had worn it thin. Beyond the scrub, the earth sloped gently and then rose again beneath someone else's lawn. Another fence. Another foundation.

The air remained even.

Yet standing there, I felt the outline of something larger than the boards in front of me.

Not pressure. Not threat.

Pattern.

Basement windows along the far houses reflected the last of the light. Small rectangles cut into brick and siding. Vents near their foundations. Narrow stairwells descending out of sight.

The architecture repeated itself in quiet ways.

I imagined the space beneath those floors. Concrete. Crawlspaces. Stored boxes. Old beams holding weight without complaint.

The wind shifted, carrying the scent of damp leaves from the trees. It moved across the property line without hesitation.

Nothing in the yard strained.

But the alignment beneath my feet did not end at the fence.

I felt it in the way the evening sounds layered over one another. Crickets in my grass. Crickets in theirs. The same rhythm carried across yards without regard for ownership.

My correction below had been precise. It had settled what had drifted here.

It had not reduced the shape of the whole.

A porch light blinked on in the second house to the left. Someone stepped out briefly, then retreated inside. A door shut. Curtains shifted.

Daily life moved above foundations most of them never considered.

Somewhere beneath another house, cadence might already be tightening. A pause shortening. A breath rushing toward closure.

I did not feel alarm.

I felt scale.

The wind brushed the back of my neck and moved on.

I leaned slightly over the fence and looked toward the darkening row of homes.

The quiet held.

For now.

And somewhere beyond the reach of my yard, another rhythm waited to be corrected.

The last band of color drained from the sky until only deep blue remained, pressing toward black. The house lights behind me cast a soft glow across the yard, touching the grass but stopping short of the tree line.

The wood beneath my palm had cooled. The grain caught lightly against my skin. Nails held the boards in place without ornament, without symbol. Just timber and time.

I stood there long enough to feel two things at once.

Peace.

And weight.

My breathing moved evenly without effort. The rhythm settled in my chest without counting. No correction. No tightening before the final measure.

The yard lay in shadow. The trees formed a dark boundary at the edge of the property. Crickets continued their steady tempo. Somewhere down the street, a car rolled past and faded.

Nothing surged.

Nothing withdrew.

The image of the apartment surfaced again. A third-floor window. Thin walls. The ordinary hum of another life. It came without ache now, like a photograph handled too often to surprise.

I missed it in a quiet, human way.

Then the wind shifted and moved on.

The grass stirred around my ankles. The fence remained firm beneath my hand. The house at my back felt grounded, not leaning toward me, not testing.

I withdrew my hand and let it fall to my side.

The yard did not empty as darkness deepened. It remained present. The air held its shape. The rhythm beneath my ribs matched the layered sound of insects beyond the fence.

I walked back across the grass slowly. Each step settled into soil that gave and returned. The porch boards creaked once under my weight.

At the threshold, I paused and looked over the yard one final time.

The trees stood. The fence traced its line. The sky deepened another shade.

Peace and weight remained where they belonged.

I stepped inside and closed the door gently behind me.

The latch clicked.

Inside, the house held its light.

Outside, the rhythm continued.

Chapter 40

I closed the door and kept my hand on the knob for a moment longer than necessary.

The latch clicked into place with a small, decisive sound. After that, the house held still.

No tremor beneath the floorboards. No tightening in the air. The quiet rose and fell with my breathing.

I listened for the old pressure.

It did not return.

The porch light traced a thin line through the pane in the door and across the floor. Dust drifted through that narrow beam without urgency.

I stepped into the living room and turned off the lamp beside the sofa. The bulb ticked as it cooled. The room folded into shadow. The dark did not press forward. It settled where it belonged.

In the hallway, I paused.

This was where warmth had once hovered at my neck. Where proximity had tested whether I would turn or run.

I stood still long enough to feel the air against my skin.

Nothing moved toward me.

I walked to the bathroom and faced the mirror. The glass returned my reflection immediately. My shoulders were squared. My gaze steady. No lag. No borrowed expression.

I held my own eyes for several seconds.

They did not waver.

I switched off the light and stepped back into the hall.

Kitchen. Study. Stairwell. One by one, I extinguished the lights. Each room accepted the dark without resistance. The house did not seem emptier for it.

It seemed aligned.

At the base of the stairs, I stopped and listened again.

Once, I would have checked the recorder. I would have replayed the last few minutes, searching for distortion. I would have scanned the air for threat.

I did none of those things.

The absence of that impulse registered quietly.

I rested my palm against the wall beside the stair rail. The plaster was cool. Solid. It held its shape beneath my touch.

I climbed the stairs without glancing back.

The house did not loom.

It did not diminish.

It remained.

Halfway up, I became aware of the rhythm in my breathing. Even. Unforced. No pause shortened. No measure rushed.

At the top of the stairs, I turned off the final light and let the darkness settle around me.

The silence did not follow.

It moved with me.

I opened the journal because I knew sleep would not come cleanly without it.

The bedroom lamp cast a tight circle of light across the quilt and the worn leather cover. The rest of the room faded into shadow. The house held its balance around me. A faint shift in the beams as they cooled. The distant tick of something settling in the walls.

I turned to the back pages, to the margin where the ink had thinned.

It began with the third daughter.

I had once treated the line like a riddle. A fragment I needed to decode into safety.

Now I read it and let the words sit.

Third daughter.

I traced the earlier entries with my finger and counted the transitions. The corrections appeared in cycles. Every third succession, the breath marked differently. A pause restored. A measure widened. A small recalibration written in darker ink.

The pattern repeated without drama.

I leaned back against the headboard and closed my eyes for a moment.

One day there would be another.

Not an idea. A girl.

She would grow up in this house or one like it. She would stand in a hallway at night and feel something she could not name. She might press her ear to a door and listen for sounds no one else heard. She might run her fingers along a fence and feel more than wood beneath her skin.

She might resent the quiet.

She might try to leave.

I pictured her hand on the cellar door. Not steady. Not yet. Pulse quick beneath thin skin. Jaw set in defiance or fear.

I would not be there to answer her questions.

But the pages would.

I opened my eyes and ran my thumb once over the crescent at my wrist. The mark felt cool and unremarkable. No heat. No pressure.

I turned back to the journal and added a final line beneath the existing entry.

Do not shorten the pause.

The ink sank into the paper and held.

I closed the journal and placed it on the nightstand beside the lamp. The leather creaked softly as it settled.

The room remained steady. The air neither thinned nor thickened. My breathing moved in even measure.

I switched off the lamp.

Darkness folded over the bed without weight.

In the quiet, the line returned to me, not as warning, not as prophecy.

It began with the third daughter.

Somewhere in the future, it would begin again.

And this time, she would read before she descended.

The last of the light drained from the windows, and the house accepted the dark without resistance. I moved through it without checking doors or testing corners. My steps were measured. The air did not tighten around them.

At the top of the cellar stairs, I stopped.

The door stood open. The stairwell descended into shadow, but the shapes below remained intact. The air rising from the cellar carried no distortion. No upward pressure threaded through the floorboards.

I rested my hand against the frame and listened.

The house did not lean toward me.

It did not retreat.

It held its proportion.

I touched the crescent at my wrist. The skin there felt cool and unremarkable. No pulse. No warning. The mark lay quiet beneath my fingers.

I let my eyes adjust to the dark and looked down the steps.

There would be nights again. Corrections. Small shifts in measure that required attention. Somewhere beyond these walls, other foundations would carry their own misalignment. Other houses would settle and strain and settle again.

And one day, another girl would stand where I stood.

Her hand might tremble.

She might descend too quickly.

She might believe she was alone.

I would not be here.

But the cadence would.

I leaned forward slightly and let the words leave my mouth in a low, even tone.

"I'll be ready."

The sentence did not echo.

It did not return.

It settled into the stairwell and remained there.

Outside, insects stitched the dark with steady rhythm. The beams above me held their shape. The floor beneath my feet remained firm.

I stayed at the threshold a moment longer.

The house did not test me.

It listened.

And in the quiet, our breathing moved in time.

All I thought of is my inherited burden.

About the Author

Gideon Drake is a psychological thriller and horror author known for crafting stories that linger long after the final page. His work lives in the space between reality and illusion, where memory distorts, identities fracture, and the past refuses to stay buried. Drawing inspiration from masters like Stephen King and Shirley Jackson, Drake blends slow-building dread with deeply human characters, creating narratives that feel as intimate as they are unsettling.

Drake is the author of multiple psychological thrillers, including *The Bloodroot House*, *Awake in the Shadows*, and *Whispers in the House*. His stories are known for their atmospheric tension, unreliable narrators, and twists that force readers to question everything they thought they understood.

And if you find yourself thinking about one of his endings days later... that's exactly the point.

You can connect with me on:

🌐 https://www.gideondrake.com

Also by Gideon Drake

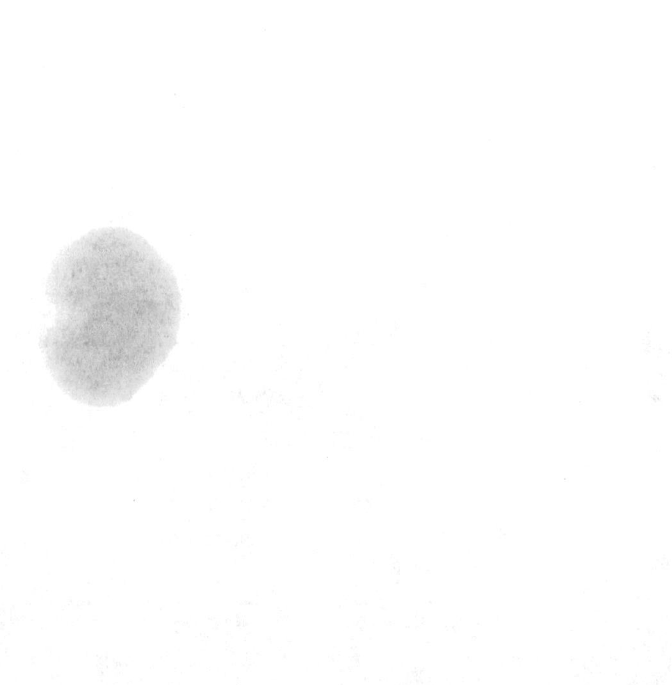